Ray of Hope

JAN 2011

CH

Also by Vanessa Davis Griggs

The Truth Is the Light

Goodness and Mercy

Practicing What You Preach

If Memory Serves

Strongholds

Blessed Trinity

Published by Kensington Publishing Corp.

Ray of Hope

VANESSA DAVIS GRIGGS

KENSINGTON PUBLISHING CORP.
www.kensingtonbooks.com

DAFINA BOOKS are published by

Kensington Publishing Corp.
119 West 40th Street
New York, NY 10018

All Kensington titles, imprints, and distributed lines are available at special quantity discounts for bulk purchases for sales promotion, premiums, fund-raising, educational, or institutional use.

Special book excerpts or customized printings can also be created to fit specific needs. For details, write or phone the office of the Kensington Special Sales Manager: Kensington Publishing Corp., 119 West 40th Street, New York, NY 10018, Attn. Special Sales Department. Phone: 1-800-221-2647.

Dafina and the Dafina logo Reg. U.S. Pat. & TM Off.

ISBN-13: 978-0-7582-5960-8
ISBN-10: 0-7582-5960-3

First Printing: January 2011
10 9 8 7 6 5 4 3 2 1

Printed in the United States of America

*To those grandmothers who hold things down
when necessary—refusing to allow the next
generation to be taken away or lost*

Acknowledgments

I would like to begin here the way I begin every single day of my life: acknowledging the one true and living God who holds every aspect of my life in His hands.

This book is a departure from the characters of my previous novels. For those of you who find yourself a little nostalgic hearing this, let me assure you that everything is going to be all right. A great many people who've read *The Truth Is the Light* have expressed a desire and hope for a follow-up book. Well, for now, that book has been put on hold. I've always set myself to give you my best. Whatever I write, my desire is to do that and that God will always be glorified. You'll find the same commitment with this newest saga, entitled *Ray of Hope*.

To the wonderful folks at Kensington / Dafina, starting from the very top all the way down, I give my heartfelt thanks for you continuing to believe in me and my gift of stories. It's truly a blessing, not just for me, but for those who are being touched by what God is bringing *through* me. With all of the struggles so many have endured during these difficult economic times, it is an honor that you have tapped me to continue, for now, to do what I do. To my editor, Selena James: thank you for your hard work, dedication, and all that you do to make what we as authors do work wonderfully in the end. Thanks to Adeola Saul for "hooking me up" when you can, in publicizing my books. One such meeting was with the fantastic Go On Girl! Book Club during their eighteenth annual awards' national meeting in 2010. To those at Kensington and beyond (copy editor Amy Maffei and art director Kristine Mills-Noble) who've had anything to do with making this book be one of excellence: my thanks to you!

To my mother, Josephine Davis: Mommy, I love you so much! I always call you Mama, but every now and then, when I want to feel like a little girl again, I'll say Mommy. Mama, you've been with me through the good and the bad, through thick and thin, through my ups and downs. You've cried with me, rejoiced with me, and encouraged me to run on and see what the end will be. I am blessed to call you *my* mother—a true woman of God!

To my father, James Davis Jr.: Daddy, you've been an example of what a real man is, a God-fearing man who loves the Lord, what a husband should be, and how far a father will go to do what needs to be done to take care of his family. Daddy, you haven't just talked the talk, you've walked the walk. Love you, Daddy!

To my son, Jeremy Griggs, and my sister-in-law, Cameron Davis: I love and thank you both for having read every book I've written that's been published. I know how busy everyone is. And to have family to support you by reading the words you've taken so much of your time to write, I appreciate you much for that! To my husband, Jeffery: Thanks for your love and for your continuing to believe in what I do. To my sons, Jeffery and Johnathan Griggs: I love you and thank God for what He's doing in your lives.

To my sister Danette Dial and my brother Terence Davis: Thank you for those times when I look up and see you at a book signing or one of my speaking engagements. That blesses my heart more than you'll ever know. To my sister Arlinda Davis and brother Emmanuel Davis: keep reaching for your dreams! I love my family!

To my granddaughters, Asia Bolden and Ashlynn Griggs: The two of you bring me so much joy and so many smiles, I can't begin to tell you how much I love you! I pray that God continues to bless you as you grow into who God is calling you to be.

To Vanessa L. Rice and Linda H. Jones: who knew that from your reading one of my books we would have become the friends that we have. You both always bless me with your feedback after reading my latest work. I enjoy the in-depth conversations we have about the characters who absolutely come alive for us. Thank you. To Zelda Oliver-Miles: I hope you know how much I love you! Now, get going on that book you're working on. To Regina Biddings: you're a special person indeed.

Thanks, Greg Minard, for what you do to help keep my books on some shelves for those searching for them. To Troy Johnson of AALBC: thank you for the page you put up on your Web site (please thank your mother for me . . . wink, wink!). To Edna Curry of EDC Creations: you bless so many, from authors to readers. To Cydney Rax of Book Remarks: thanks for what you do to let others know what books are scheduled for release. To APOOO, RAWSISTAZ, Black Expressions, MOSAIC: what would we authors and readers do without you?!

I've been blessed by so many of you, whether it was through book clubs, church groups, or individually as you've read my books, sent e-mails, and told others, "You've got to read her books!" To each and every one of you, whatever you've done or are doing—large or small—I thank you from my heart and pray God's blessings upon you.

It's a privilege to be able to do what I do. Thank you for welcoming me into your time and into your space. I'm honored, and I don't and won't take this opportunity *or* you for granted. Enjoy the read, and be sure to tell someone else so that we can both continue doing what we do—writer and readers in ministry together. To God be the glory!

Vanessa Davis Griggs

www.VanessaDavisGriggs.com

Ray of Hope

Chapter 1

There shall not any man be able to stand before thee all the days of thy life: as I was with Moses, so I will be with thee: I will not fail thee, nor forsake thee.

—Joshua 1:5

Rayna "Ma Ray" Towers had fallen asleep on the couch in the den. She'd called herself staying up to watch *The Tonight Show,* but in the end, it appeared some other show—muted—was watching her. Still, at age seventy-five, Ma Ray's senses were keen. That's why she heard sounds of someone breaking in. A few folks she personally knew had had their homes broken into just this year alone. Her granddaughters, Sahara and Crystal Nichols, were staying with her for the summer. Ma Ray quickly got up and went to the hall closet where she kept a twelve-gauge, double-barrel shotgun. She quietly loaded it.

A man who appeared to be around eighteen years old, dressed in washed-out blue jeans and a black Sean John shirt, started up the stairs. She pointed the gun, then pulled back the hammer, causing it to make a metallic clicking sound. "Freeze," she said. "Don't take another step. Put your hands up, or I promise I'll blow you away!"

Six steps up, the young man stopped and raised his hands. "Lady, please don't shoot." He glanced back, looking like a deer caught in headlights. "Please put that down."

Ma Ray glanced out of the side of her eyes toward the table with the telephone on it. She needed to call the police at this point while making sure he didn't somehow manage to escape. "Turn around . . . slowly," she said, repeating what most associate with a good law-and-order-type show.

Standing at five foot five in her stocking feet, a blue flowered cotton nightgown, and a baby blue satin scarf wrapped around her roller-filled head, Ma Ray raised the twelve-gauge shotgun even higher, aiming it squarely at the young man's scrawny chest. A woman who had shot her share of snakes, Ma Ray wanted to be sure that, should she have a need to pull the trigger, she wouldn't miss this target, either.

The young man raised his trembling hands higher. "Lady, are you crazy?" he said. "Look," he said, sweating so hard Ma Ray could now see clear beads forming on his forehead before a few drops began to slowly make their way down his face. "If you'll just put that thing down"—he nodded toward the gun— "I'm sure we can straighten all of this out in no time. I know we can."

"Ma Ray, don't hurt him," seventeen-year-old Sahara said as she ran and stood at the top of the stairs dressed in light blue skinny jeans and a see-through, black-laced shirt. "Please, don't hurt him."

"See, lady," the young man said. "I'm not here to hurt nobody. Listen to Sahara. Listen to your granddaughter"—he began to stutter—"sh-sh-she'll vouch for me." He glanced up at Sahara as though he were now mentally pleading for her to fully back him up. "Sahara was the one who told me to come here like this. Tell her, Sahara."

"Ma Ray, please . . . just put the gun down." Sahara walked toward the intruder.

"Yeah, Ma Ray. *Please* put the gun down." The young man pleaded with his hands still high in the air. "This is all just one big misunderstanding. You'll see."

Ma Ray motioned with the barrel of the gun for him to step down to the floor; he obeyed. Lowering the barrel of the gun, she pointed it at the floor. Cautiously, he lowered his hands. Sahara made her way to the bottom step, looked at Ma Ray, and stopped.

"What's your name?" Ma Ray asked him.

His voice squeaked when he spoke. "B-Man." Then again, but stronger. "B-Man."

Ma Ray lifted the gun back up slightly, pointing it at his shoes.

"Bradley," he said hastily, his eyes fixed on the long, steel barrel of the shotgun. "But everybody calls me B-Man."

Ma Ray lowered the gun again. "Bradley, huh? And did you happen to come with a last name?"

"It's Crenshaw. . . . Bradley Crenshaw."

"I take it you're not from around these parts," Ma Ray said.

"No."

"*No?*" she said, clearly indicating she had a problem with his answer.

"No, ma'am," Sahara hurriedly added, looking at her friend to clearly let him know he didn't need to do anything more at this point to provoke her grandmother.

"I'm talking to him," Ma Ray said, nodding at Bradley.

"No, ma'am," he said. "I live more in the city."

"You say that like you have a problem with the country or something." Ma Ray tapped the gun several times with her trigger finger.

"No. I mean, no, ma'am. I was just saying that I live more in the city, that's all, ma'am. That's all I was saying." His voice sounded like he was on the verge of tears.

"So why are you so far from home this time of night?" Ma Ray asked him.

"I-I-I was bringing something to Sahara."

"Is that right?"

"Yes, ma'am."

"Something that couldn't wait for a decent hour? It must be good, then. So you can give me what you came to give Sahara." Ma Ray took a step toward him.

His eyes widened. "Ma'am?"

"I said you can give *me* what you came here to give Sahara." She glanced down, peering over her wire-rimmed glasses. "And will you *please* pull your pants up! Walking around with your pants hanging down like that. I tell you that just don't make no sense, no sense at all," Ma Ray said.

He quickly grabbed his pants by the waistband and pulled them up.

Ma Ray nodded as she watched him hold up his pants to keep them from falling down again. "You need on a belt. Or maybe you should buy pants the right size to begin with. Okay, Mister Man . . . now give me what you came to give my grand-daughter."

"But-but—"

"But-but nothing." She raised the shotgun once again, pointing its barrel at the hardwood floor in front of him instead of directly *at* him.

He quickly looked down at the gun, then back into her face. "Ma'am, I'm sorry for having come up in your house like this. I promise you I am."

"The correct terminology is breaking and entering. And honestly, by right, were I to have felt me or my family's life were in danger whatsoever, I would have been well within my legal rights to have shot you on sight, no questions asked, with my actions most certainly to be ruled as justified."

"Yes, ma'am. And I really am sorry, Ms. . . . Ma Ray . . . ma'am. Now, if you don't mind, may I go? I really need to be getting on home. All of a sudden, I don't feel so well." The look on his face said it all.

"It depends"—Ma Ray lowered the gun and softly put the hammer back in place, taking it off ready—"on whether you intend to do anything like this again."

"Ms. Ray . . . Ma Ray, ma'am, I promise you: after I leave here, you won't *ever* have to worry about seeing my face in your house without your permission again. *Ever.*"

Ma Ray nodded. "Then I suppose you can go." She went to the front door, opened it, and escorted him out. "Young man, let me give you some good advice. You need to do something more constructive with your life. You got off this time. But the next time, you may not be so lucky. And I'm not talking about with just me. Bradley, folks don't play now and days. And ending up dead is nothing to play *with*. It's not like in the movies or those video games y'all play, where you press a *replay* button and start all over as though nothing has happened. Now, you chew on what almost happened and on what I just said."

"Yes, ma'am. And thank you, ma'am." Bradley stumbled off the wraparound wooden porch, stopping and throwing up in Ma Ray's beautiful flower garden. Holding up his pants, he jogged down the road where he'd left his car, not once looking back.

Ma Ray walked into the house, unloaded the shells from the shotgun, and safely put it back in the closet. Fifteen-year-old Crystal now stood in the den next to her sister.

"Ma Ray—" Sahara said as she stood as still as a framed scene on pause.

"You and I will talk in the morning," Ma Ray said as she started to her bedroom.

"But, Ma Ray—"

Ma Ray stopped without turning around. "I said, we'll talk in the daylight."

Chapter 2

"Ma, Sahara called me a little after two o'clock this morning crying, saying that you pulled a gun . . . a gun on one of her little friends," thirty-eight-year-old Lenora Nichols Stanford said to Ma Ray as soon as her mother answered. "I started to call you after I hung up with her, but it was so late that I didn't want to wake you. Ma, you know you can't go around pulling guns on people like that. You can't."

"And a top of the morning to you, too, daughter," Ma Ray said.

"I'm sorry. Good morning, Ma. But did you hear what I said?"

"Oh, I heard you just fine. And for the record: when you're an old woman who lives in the country alone, it's perfectly okay to pull a shotgun on someone when that someone happens to be illegally breaking into your house."

"*What?*"

"Oh, I guess Sahara left that little part out. And you didn't happen to put two and two together—the fact that she called you after two in the morning," Ma Ray said. "Well, that little 'friend' of hers broke into my house. But then again, in my defense, when I saw him sneaking up the stairs like some cat burglar, I didn't know he was Sahara's friend. I just knew someone had come into my house, uninvited, and whoever that person was, as far as *I* was concerned, they were a threat. And since I'd specifically told both Sahara and Crystal when they got here that there would be none of that sneaking out or sneaking anyone in while they were staying with me, I could only *assume* we were in danger of an intruder. I mentioned to you some months back we've had a few break-ins around here."

"I don't know, Ma. Maybe I made the wrong decision to let them come and stay with you for the summer," Lenora said. "Perhaps I should come and get them and see if their having been with you this week hasn't shown them that I'm serious about them straightening up and acting right."

"Lenora, who was the one that called here hollering and crying about how out of control Sahara and Crystal are? I believe your exact words were, 'Ma, I can't take this anymore! I'm about two seconds away from either strangling them or shipping them off to a boot camp somewhere.' That *was* you, was it not?"

"Yes, it was me. I admit that I was having a bad day, a *really* bad day."

"And I told you then, and I'm telling you now: I believe I can handle a seventeen-year-old and a fifteen-year-old just fine. I raised you and your brother all right, didn't I?"

"But let's be real: you were younger then. And Daddy was there to help you. Children are different these days. Some of the things they do are totally unexplainable. After I told Sahara and Crystal they would be going to your house to stay for a little while, I overheard Sahara asking Crystal what could you do that someone half your age couldn't." Lenora purposely left out the part Sahara had said about *her* having a college degree where their grandmother did not.

"I'll tell you what. For the time being, you worry about taking care of Kyle and Nia and leave your other two children to me, at least for the rest of the summer. We'll be fine. Between me and God, we're going to work this out. And you know how much I love Sahara and Crystal."

"And they love you, too, Ma. They love you a lot. But I keep telling you that teenagers are different now. They're not as respectful as we were back in our day. There's a lot more peer pressure on them. Sure there were things I had to deal with when I was growing up, but it's nowhere near the level that these kids deal with these days," Lenora said.

"Yeah, well. I'll give them that much. They do have things neither you nor I had to deal with when we were coming up. At least, not in the exact same vein. But you know what I always say."

"Yeah, Ma, I know. 'There's nothing new under the sun.' I know. But I feel bad that I can't control my own children any better than I've been able to." Lenora began to cry a little. "Let's face it: I'm an awful mother."

"You're not an awful mother."

"Okay, then. I'm a terrible daughter. I mean, what kind of a daughter pushes her delinquent-acting children off on their senior-citizen mother?"

"You're not an awful mother and you're not a terrible daughter. And I was the one who insisted that you bring Sahara and Crystal here for the summer. They used to love coming here to visit and spending time with me," Ma Ray said.

"Yeah, but that was when they were young. Now they don't seem to want to have anything to do with any of us, let alone hang around us for any extended period of time. I suppose we're too old fogey for them. We're not fun anymore. Ma, you know how teenagers are."

"Yeah, I know. You went through the exact same phase. You didn't want to be around me or your father. Every chance you got, you were off somewhere with your friends. There were times when you thought you were grown and you got a little too big for your britches. But we made it through all of that."

"We did. One might conclude that I'm reaping some of what I've sown. Talking back to you, staying out past the time you told me to be home. It's all coming back on me, big-time. But in truth, I was nothing compared to Sahara and Crystal. Nothing. And they won't admit it to me, but I'm pretty sure they're having sex. Granted, I did have sex when I was in high school, going totally against everything you told me, I might add. But at least it was only with Quinton, my boyfriend, and not with God-only-knows who or how many guys. And yes, I admit there were times when I did just what I wanted regardless of the consequences." Lenora let out a sigh.

"I also believe Sahara and Crystal are experimenting with drugs, even though I've spoken with them about this until I was blue in the face," Lenora said. "I've explained the dangers of sex before marriage, as well as the dangers of drugs. Sahara just throws the hypocrisy of me taking prescription drugs for my depression back in my face. My legalized 'uppers,' she calls them. I just don't know, Ma. Where did I go wrong?"

"Lenora, will you please stop beating yourself up. However we find ourselves now, the fact remains: we're here. And God is going to help us through this."

"But sex can be deadly in this day and time. When I was being rebellious, the worst I had to worry about was an unplanned pregnancy or contracting a venereal disease. Now that AIDS is on the scene, people hardly ever mention VD anymore. People now can get things that can kill them." Lenora's sniffling began to subside. "Kill them."

"Well, every generation has something. My generation dealt with shame, being an outcast . . . sometimes ostracized—"

"And Sahara's report card this past school year contained nothing but Ds and Fs," Lenora said, quickly moving on to a different topic. "She barely passed the eleventh grade, only because her Ds outweighed her Fs. I just knew she was going to have to go to summer school. Edmond and I told her she's never going to get into college with those grades. But she doesn't miss an opportunity to remind Edmond that he's merely her stepfather and she could care less *what* he has to say about anything. She doesn't care about her grades, since she wants to drop out of school, anyway. All she talks about is becoming a model. She thinks school is just a waste of her time. I don't know, Ma."

Ma Ray let out a slight chuckle. "Since she was knee-high to a grasshopper, Sahara has been playing dress-up. That child would get in my closet and find my Sunday's best and my high heels. Oh, that child . . . she loves herself some shoes, even more than I do. And at what . . . five eleven, she's certainly tall enough and pretty enough to be a model. Got those high cheekbones from the Choctaw blood that runs in our family. But regardless, Sahara needs schooling."

"I know this. The problem is getting *Sahara* to see this. And Crystal, who has always been a bit envious and intrigued by her big sister, is being influenced by Sahara's bad actions. So, of course, whatever Sahara is doing, Crystal wants to do it, too. I blame a lot of this on Quinton. He has been such a deadbeat father pretty much all of their lives. He hasn't helped either one of them with their self-esteem *or* their daddy issues."

"For sure Quinton hasn't been the best father. I get that he has his own issues, many of his own making. I've told him that very thing myself. But that's still no excuse for Sahara and Crystal to act out the way they have lately."

"Well, my poor Edmond has been doing all he can. He was the one who found that boot camp set up for out-of-control teenagers. He strongly suggested that we think seriously about sending them to it or something like it."

"Oh, those girls don't need to be put in a boot camp. They're going to be okay. And just how *is* my son-in-law?" Ma Ray asked.

"He's fine. We'll be celebrating our tenth anniversary on the tenth of July. And of course, Nia has him completely wrapped around her little finger. I don't know how a two-year-old can wield so much power over a forty-year-old grown man. Edmond and Kyle are going fishing today, and Nia keeps asking why she can't go with them. It's hard to explain to a toddler that her seven-year-old brother is not as much trouble as a two-year-old. Or that the boys need boy time together. Truthfully, Edmond has a hard time trying to take care of them when he takes them fishing at the same time. So he alternates between them."

"Then why don't you go so she can go with them?"

"Ma, you know I don't like to fish. I don't care to sit in that little canoe Edmond calls a boat, in the hot sun I might add, casting a line into the water, just so I can further sit and watch absolutely nothing happen. Fishing is just not my thing."

"But it's something Edmond likes to do. And it's something the whole family can do together. I think you should go with them and make it a family affair."

"Well, I've told Edmond that I'm not interested, so *that* won't be happening. He and Kyle can go and have a great time. Nia will be all right. Maybe she and I will go shopping or something. We'll find something fun to do while they're gone."

"All right, daughter. Listen, I'm going to get off this phone now. I need to finish cooking breakfast. Then Sahara and I are going to have a nice little chat."

"Ma, look. I appreciate you wanting to help me and the girls and everything. But if this is too much on you—"

"Honey, no matter the weight of a thing, love can hold up anything. So don't you worry your pretty little head about me *or* these daughters of yours. Somehow or other, we'll find a breakthrough through all of this."

"Well, if you need me to come and get them, just let me know. I'm feeling better, now that I've gotten a little break. It was just getting too much, and I guess I broke down. But should they get too much out of hand with you, call me, and I'll come get them."

"Lenora, all I need for you to do now is to pray. Two things I know for sure is that prayer changes things and nothing is too hard for our God. Nothing. I've told you we're going to get through this together, and I mean *just* that." Ma Ray suddenly stopped talking. "Good morning, Crystal . . . morning, Sahara," Ma Ray said in a pleasant voice.

"Sahara's there?" Lenora asked.

"Yes," Ma Ray said in an even tone.

"Well, put her on the phone. I want her to know that I don't appreciate that little stunt she just pulled. I don't appreciate it at all."

"Not a good idea," Ma Ray said, continuing to speak in a code-like manner.

"But Ma, she called me in the middle of the night . . . two

o'clock in the morning, to be exact, telling me that you're pulling guns on folks, while conveniently leaving out *her* devilment in all of it. Sahara needs to know that things like this are not acceptable and they won't be tolerated." Lenora's phone beeped to indicate another call was coming in.

"And that will most certainly happen," Ma Ray said. "Sounds like someone is trying to get you."

Lenora looked at her caller ID. "It's your favorite son," she said.

"Okay. I'm going to get off now. Say hello to Beau for me."

"But Ma—"

"I'll talk with you later, dear." Ma Ray hung up before Lenora could protest further.

Chapter 3

This book of the law shall not depart out of thy mouth; but thou shalt meditate therein day and night, that thou mayest observe to do according to all that is written therein: for then thou shalt make thy way prosperous, and then thou shalt have good success.

—Joshua 1:8

Lenora looked at the phone and thought about letting the call go and calling her mother back instead. But she had to trust that her mother knew what she was doing. "Hi, Boaz," Lenora said when she clicked over. "What's up?"

"Lenora, why do you insist upon calling me Boaz?" her brother asked.

"Because, Beau Azra Towers, Boaz is what I grew up calling you. And just because you think you're so important now that you want everybody to call you Beau, it's no reason for you to expect *me* to up and change," Lenora said. "Oh, and Ma said to tell you hello."

"When did you talk to her?"

"I just hung up with her."

"Well, our mother is the reason that I called. I want to talk to you about Sahara and Crystal. They've been with Ma for about a week now."

Lenora sat down on the bar stool in her kitchen. Her brother's voice had that tone to it. Two years her senior, Beau was going to give more of a lecture than a simple talk.

"Lenora, are you still there?" Boaz asked.

"Yeah, I'm still here."

"Then why aren't you saying anything?"

"Because you said you wanted to talk about Sahara and Crystal. I'm waiting to hear what you have to say."

"Lenora, I know you're having your share of troubles with Sahara and Crystal, more Sahara than Crystal. I get that. But Ma is old. She doesn't get around the way she used to. Your teenage daughters have been with her for at least a week now, and when I asked Ma the other day when you were planning to get them, she quickly changed the subject. I can always tell when Ma is covering up something—she just changes the subject. Since Ma doesn't want to tell me what's going on, I decided to call you and find out." Boaz paused. "So, how long are they planning on being over there?"

"I don't know, Boaz."

"You don't know?"

"No. I *don't* know," Lenora said with attitude.

"So, is the plan for them to stay there until they get on Ma's nerve, until they *force* you to come and get them, until you feel like being bothered with them again? What?"

"See, that's why you make me mad. First of all, this really is none of your business. And yet, as always, there you are, sticking your nose in it. This is between me and my mother. Ma wants them over there with her, and it's really not up to whether you approve or not."

"Ma is keeping them because you don't know what else to do with them," Boaz said. "Lenora, everybody knows Sahara and Crystal are completely out of control. Now Owen and Freda—"

"So what, Boaz. Okay, they're out of control. Just because you have the perfect little family, with Ruth, your perfect little wife, and your equally perfect, not-so-little children who seem to have never given you a day of trouble in their little lives, that doesn't make you some kind of an expert. You and Ruth raised Owen and Freda without any problems, it seems. Great! I get that," Lenora said.

"Len, where is all of this hostility coming from?"

Lenora paused, then let out a sigh. She knew she'd hit a nerve when her brother called her Len. "I'm sorry, Boaz. I'm sorry. It's just I'm tired of hearing—directly or indirectly—how wonderful Owen and Freda are and how bad my kids are. I'm glad Owen and Freda are maintaining 4.0 averages in college. I'm proud that Owen is at Harvard and Freda is at Yale. That's fantastic. You have reason to be proud. Yet, here I am, as always, struggling. I'm struggling to make it, struggling to convince Sahara that she needs to stay in, let alone finish, high school. Sahara makes Ds and Fs, and it doesn't seem to faze her one bit. Not one bit. Then there's Crystal, who has decided to make Sahara her role model. Not someone working hard to make something of their life. But Sahara. Yes, I'm tired, Boaz. I'm tired of feeling like a complete failure. And frankly, you're not helping much right now."

"Lenora, nobody's perfect. And you're not a *complete* failure."

"Oh, you're trying to be funny now, huh? What are you trying to say? That I even fail at being a *complete* failure?"

"Look, you're just having a hard time, that's all," Boaz said. "And you, of all people, know that everything isn't, and hasn't always been, perfect over here. So don't even try playing that card with me. Ruth and I have our challenges—our ups and downs—just like everybody else does. But I'm not going to apologize for the way my children have turned out. Owen at twenty-one and Freda at nineteen have set concrete goals for themselves. Do I talk of their accomplishments and brag about them a little too much? Well, from your reaction right now, apparently I do."

"Yeah, well, what else should I expect from the golden child?" Lenora said.

"Golden child?"

"Yeah, Beau. You're Ma's heart, her favorite child, and everybody knows that."

"Ma doesn't have a favorite child. She loves me and you the same. If anything, she's done more for *you* than she's *ever* done for *me*. If anybody should be jealous or envious, it should be me."

"Oh, please. You could have kept that," Lenora said.

"Okay, Lenora. Case in point: when Daddy died, what did Ma do for you?"

Lenora clenched her jaw. Somehow, she knew when they started down this path that this is where the two of them would end up, yet again. "Can we just change the subject to something else? How's your business? Have you gotten any new big contracts lately, Mister Big Shot Entrepreneur?"

"No, we won't change the subject. When Daddy died, what did Ma do?"

"You know why she did what she did. You know I was having a hard time. It's not because she loves me more than you. She just knew you were doing okay and that I was sinking big-time. This was two years ago. Why are you bringing it up *yet* again?"

"Because, Lenora Tracey Towers Nichols Stanford, I want you to see how *our* mother always bails *you* out. Daddy had money from his days as an officer. And when Ma got that money, what did she do with it? Did she keep it for herself? Divide what she was going to give away equally between you and me? No. She gave you pretty much all of it."

"Because she knew how much I desperately needed it," Lenora said. "You were doing fine. You really didn't need any of Daddy's money. Ma's house and car were paid for. She gets a monthly check. She said she had all that she needed to live on. Besides, I do plan to give it back to her when I get back on my feet."

Boaz started laughing. "I'm sorry. I don't mean to laugh. But you do this every single time. I don't care what it is, you seriously don't seem to get it. I know you believe what you're saying, but you need to stop just once, step outside of yourself, and see *you* the way the rest of the real world sees you."

"What do you mean by that?"

"I mean, dear sister, you really need to grow up and stop acting like the world owes you something. You can't continue to run to Ma for her to fix every little thing for you. You need to grow up."

"I don't run to Ma. I was handling my problems myself. Ma was the one who insisted on giving me that money. I didn't ask her for it." Lenora felt tears begin to sting her eyes.

"Yeah, but you moan enough about your problems that she

can't help but worry about you and want to do what she can to ease your pain. Lenora, you know how much Ma loves us. And there's nothing she won't do for *either* of us, if it's at all within her powers to do it. She knows that, financially, you struggle. You and Quinton, that grubby little first hubby of yours, started *off* behind the eight ball. I tried to tell you when you were getting that big house and two expensive cars that it was too much, too soon. But both of you thought you knew everything, and nobody could tell you anything."

"Listen, Boaz, I really don't want to go down this road with you, okay?"

"Of course you don't. This is what you always do. When someone tries to bring a little light to your situation, you run away like you're on fire instead of taking the time to stop, drop, and roll."

"I'm not running. I just don't see where you're going with this. You want me to admit you were right about me and Quinton? All right, I admit it: you were right. And after Quinton went to prison for robbery, and he and I divorced, I married Edmond. Unfortunately, Edmond's credit was about as jacked up as mine. We both were trying to dig ourselves out of a deep hole. Ma got a large sum of money. She wanted to help me. You didn't need anything with your little perfect life—"

Boaz started laughing. "There you go again."

"What?"

"Being sarcastic. You're right. I didn't need the money the way you did. But let me ask you something . . . " he said, then just as quickly, stopped talking completely.

"What?" Lenora asked after moments of silence. "What do you want to ask me?"

"You know, Lenora, you're right. Let's just forget this. Whatever you and Ma are doing is up to you and her. I just wish you would think about *her* instead of always seeming to think only about yourself. When you need money, she gets it for you. When you need help, she steps in. That brand-new Cadillac she purchased over a year ago, you know, like I do, that Ma actually bought it for Sahara. That was before Sahara started acting so terribly, and Ma changed her mind and decided to keep it instead. At least until Sahara started doing better. But you . . . you try to make everybody believe you're doing everything on your own. Okay, you can't handle Sahara and Crystal, and Ma gets them for who knows how long. Forget that she's seventy-five. You need Ma, and she's right there putting herself out for you. Who cares how it might be affecting her or her life."

"Boaz, I think you and I had better hang up the phone before one of us ends up saying something we can't take back. Because if you're implying that I don't care about our mother, or that I'm using her, then you're going to provoke me to say something I know is going to hurt your feelings."

"Fine, Len. I've said most of what I needed to say, anyway. But you know how Sahara and Crystal are, especially lately. They certainly aren't listening to me when I tell them anything. They don't need to be over there with Ma for too long, getting on her nerves, worrying her to death. But that's just my opinion, which I do plan on expressing to Ma as soon as I get the chance. Then I'm through with it. And both of you can take it for whatever it's worth."

"Yeah, okay," Lenora said as though what he was saying didn't matter. "Message delivered; message received. I'll talk to you later." She hung up before he could say anything else, then immediately burst into tears.

Chapter 4

And they answered Joshua, saying, All that thou commandest us we will do, and whithersoever thou sendest us, we will go.

—Joshua 1:16

Sahara picked at her breakfast as she and Crystal sat at the table with Ma Ray. Crystal wanted only pancakes. She hurried through her stack. Ma Ray sipped her coffee, frowning at its slightly bitter taste before adding another pack of artificial sweetener to it.

"I let the coffee brew too long," Ma Ray said. Neither of the girls said anything.

Crystal put the last bit of pancake in her mouth. "Can I go watch TV now?"

Ma Ray leaned back against her chair. "It's may I, not can. Can is asking if you're able to. Yes, you may, after you make up your bed and clean up the upstairs bathroom."

Crystal smiled, then left. Sahara continued to rake through the scrambled eggs on her plate.

"Are your eggs not to your liking?" Ma Ray asked.

Sahara didn't bother to look up. "They're fine. I told you when you insisted that I get up that I wasn't hungry."

"I know what you said, but you need to eat breakfast. Everybody should start their day off with a good, hearty breakfast. Breakfast jump-starts the brain. Eating breakfast actually breaks a fast. That's how they came up with the word breakfast. Your body needs to know there's still food available so it won't mess with you by trying to conserve energy believing that food's not available—"

"May I *please* just go back to bed? I *really* don't feel well."

Ma Ray reached over and placed the back of her hand on Sahara's forehead. "Well, you don't have a fever."

Sahara pulled her head back from Ma Ray's hand. "I don't have to have a fever not to feel well."

"True." Ma Ray sat back up straight. "So what seems to be ailing you?"

"Nothing specifically. I just don't feel well."

Ma Ray laughed. "You know, when I was growing up and we didn't feel well, my mother would give us a spoonful of castor oil or Black Draught."

Sahara promptly looked at Ma Ray with horror in her eyes.

Ma Ray smiled as she leaned in toward Sahara. "I hated that stuff, both of them. But they sure did seem to have a way of curing whatever ailed you. They were *so* effective, it got to where just the *mention* of them instantly cured you."

"I don't need any medicine or anything else. I'll be fine. I just need to go back to bed."

"Oh, child, I wasn't planning on giving you any castor oil. But you know, sometimes you'll find you have to take what doesn't taste so good in order to right what's wrong. Stuff like castor oil and Black Draught definitely did the trick back in my day. For sure, it made me, my sisters, and brothers think twice about saying we were sick."

Sahara rested her chin on her fist (held up by her elbow) as though she were bored as Ma Ray continued on.

"You and I need to talk," Ma Ray said.

Sahara kept her eyes down. "Ma Ray, I was wrong. I know I was wrong. I admit it, okay? I'm sorry." She released her fork; it made a clinking sound as it fell into the plate. "Can I please go now?"

"Look at me," Ma Ray said. Sahara didn't move. "Honey, I said look at me." Ma Ray's voice was stern.

Sahara slowly lifted her eyes and looked at Ma Ray.

"I know you think that no one understands you. You've become this young woman, a beautiful young woman at that. But Sahara, you have too much going on for yourself to ruin your life the way you seem to be bent on doing." Ma Ray leaned in closer to her granddaughter's face. "You know I love you, right?"

Sahara's face softened. "Sure. I know you love me."

"And you know that your mother loves you."

Sahara's jaw seemed to tighten. She rolled her eyes. "Yeah, right. She loves me."

Ma Ray frowned. "Well, she does."

"She loves me and Crystal because that's what a *good* mother is supposed to do."

"What do you mean by that?"

Sahara looked hard at her grandmother. "My mother doesn't want you or anyone else to think badly of her, so of course she does what's expected of her. Mama adores Kyle and Nia, her golden children. Me and Crystal are the troublemaking ones . . . the children that are the root cause of all her past and now even present troubles."

Ma Ray reached over and squeezed Sahara's hand. "Sahara, that's not true."

"It is true, Ma Ray." Sahara gently wiggled her hand from her grandmother's grasp. "My mother got pregnant with me before she was married. She *had* to marry my father—"

"Where did you get that from?" Ma Ray asked.

Sahara picked up her fork, speared some of the scrambled eggs, and shoved the forkful into her mouth. She chewed hard and swallowed hard before she spoke again. "Ma Ray, I happen to know when I was born. And I know that at seven pounds and three ounces, I wasn't born prematurely. I know the date my mother and father got married. And contrary to what people and my grades may say about me, I really *do* know how to perform mathematical equations." Sahara shoved more of the scrambled eggs into her mouth and chewed with even more emphasis than before.

Ma Ray nodded. "So from that, you've concluded that you're the source of all your mother's problems?"

"Besides, Mama has said as much. More than a few times, she's told me that she wishes I'd never been born."

"Oh, now I don't believe that for one second." Ma Ray fell hard against the back of her chair. She stared at Sahara until their eyes finally locked. "Did your mother say those *exact* words?"

Sahara stared back at Ma Ray with her own smidgen of defiance. "No. Not in those *exact* words. But she's said things like how different her life would be had I not been born. That if she hadn't had me, her life would have turned out *way* differently than it ended up."

Ma Ray stood up, leaned down, and hugged Sahara. "That doesn't mean your mother didn't want you. I happen to know for a fact that your mother wanted you. More than you'll ever know." Ma Ray let go. "Look, sweetheart, people get frustrated. They say things they don't really mean, or things don't come out exactly the way they meant for them to. But your mother loves you." She hugged Sahara again. "She does."

When Ma Ray let go, Sahara gently placed the last of her eggs in her mouth, hurriedly drank her orange juice, picked up the lone sausage patty left on her plate, partially wrapped it in a napkin, then bit it. "I'm finished. Now may I *please* go up to my room?"

Ma Ray shook her head. "No. We're not finished talking—" There was a knock at the door.

"Someone's at your door," Sahara said, jumping to her feet. "I'll get it." She quickly started for the front door.

"Sahara, we're not finished—"

"Coming!" Sahara said, not looking back at Ma Ray as she rushed toward the front of the house.

Ma Ray shook her head. "Lord, that child is hurting something fierce. More than any of us even realize. Please help me do right by her. Help me get through to her. I need to show her *Your* love. I can see now that her mother's and my love are not going to be enough to break through to her. In Jesus' precious name I pray. Amen."

Chapter 5

"Yoo, hoo! Ma Ray, you in the kitchen?" a voice called out from the living room.

Ma Ray came in. "Tootsie, you're up and at 'em mighty early this morning," Ma Ray said to her longtime friend, Priscilla Holt, whom everybody called Tootsie.

"You know what they say about the early bird getting the worm," sixty-five-year-old Tootsie said.

Ma Ray chuckled. "I know what that says about being the early worm."

Tootsie walked over to Ma Ray with a small brown bag in her hand as the two women hugged, then sat down on the sofa.

"What you got there, Tootsie?" Ma Ray asked, noticing the bag.

Tootsie opened the bag and took out a hunk of wrapped cake and some type of liquid in a jar. "I brought you a piece of friendship cake"—she then handed the jar of liquid to Ma Ray—"and two cups of starter juice for you to make your own cake. You'll just need to start the cake within the next three days or else freeze the juice."

Ma Ray set the cake on the coffee table, then took the jar. "We did this a few years back."

"Yeah, but Marva gave me some starter juice about a month ago. So here we go again."

"How is Marvelous Marva?" Ma Ray asked about their friend, more Tootsie's than hers. "Don't see her much since she moved to the city with her banker son."

"Marva's doing okay. You know she got that knee replacement about a year ago, but she's doing well. As well as you can expect, considering she's staying with that son and his wife, who are both as fruity, coconut flaky, and about as nutty as what's used to bake that there cake. The devil is certainly busy, certainly busy. That's for sure."

"Looks like everybody is dealing with something these days. But while everybody may be talking about how busy the devil is, I keep telling them that the devil might be busy, but our God is busier. That's the only thing that is keeping me going," Ma Ray said. "Knowing that God is still on the case. You and I both know where the Lord brought us from."

"Girl, now don't go getting me started. You gonna mess around here and make me have to get up and shout right here in your living room," Tootsie said.

"Two of my grandchildren are here with me," Ma Ray said. "My daughter's two oldest children. Looks like they're going to be spending the rest of the summer with me."

"Yeah, I spoke to that one that answered the door a few minutes ago. But all she did was grunt when I said hello. Young folks these days are something else, that's for sure. Something else. Listen, Ma Ray, I also want to remind you that the twins are picking up our bushels of purple hull peas, corn, tomatoes, cucumbers, and peaches today. They'll be bringing yours by shortly."

"That *is* today, isn't it? With everything that's been going on this morning, I almost forgot that this is the day they're bringing them. It's already been a busy morning for me. Girl, would you believe I had to bring out ole Charlie."

"Oh, no. Not ole Charlie?"

"Yep, ole Charlie."

"Was it a snake, a coyote, what?"

"Oh, it was a snake, all right—a snake of the two-legged persuasion. Pants hanging all off his skinny little behind. He didn't even have the good sense to have his pants hanging with a belt. Some of them that hang at least wear a belt with it."

"Chile, now don't go there. I told those twins of mine that I'd better not *ever* catch them with their britches down like that. Or else I'm gonna pull them all the way down to their knees and make them walk around with their pants that way for the rest of the day. Let them see how something like *that* looks and feels. I bet *that* will stop that mess."

"Tootsie, don't do that. You may end up starting another crazy trend," Ma Ray said. "But you won't have a problem like that with them. You've done a fine job with those twins, a fine job."

"Oh, you know it hasn't been easy, now. But I refuse to let the devil have those two," Tootsie said. She stood up and started for the door. "So . . . you gonna get your granddaughters to help with your bushels?"

"Probably," Ma Ray said.

"You want to shell our peas together today?"

"Now, that's an idea. You know I always love your company."

"Well, I'll tell the twins to keep my bushel of purple hull peas on the truck and bring them over here. We'll just shell peas together," Tootsie said. "Have us a little purple hull peas shelling party."

"Sounds like a plan to me." Ma Ray opened the door and stepped outside on the porch with Tootsie. "I'll see you later on then? Around noon?"

"Noon sounds good."

Ma Ray stood on the porch and watched as Tootsie got in her own tank of a car and drove slowly away.

Chapter 6

And Joshua the son of Nun sent out of Shittim two men to spy secretly, saying, Go view the land, even Jericho. And they went, and came into a harlot's house, named Rahab, and lodged there.

—Joshua 2:1

"They're all tripping," Sahara said on the phone to a guy named Dollar. "If they think I'm going to be stuck out here in the sticks and the boonies without being able to go anywhere or have any fun, they all have vastly underestimated me. I can barely get and keep reception on my cell phone. You have to literally find, then stand in, just the right spot and not move if you don't want your call dropped. That's why I had to call you back on this phone. This is ridiculous!"

"So, when can you get away?" Dollar asked. "I want to see you. You know I'm missing you something fierce." He made a smacking sound.

"Dollar, you need to stop. You don't miss nobody. I haven't heard from you in what? Three months now."

"That's because I've been busy trying to secure better things for you and me. I told you: what I'm doing now ain't what I plan on doing for the rest of my life. Just like other folks, I got dreams and goals. And I've told you that I want you to be part of it."

"So . . . how is Brandy?"

"What? Who?"

"Brandy. You know, the girl you've been busy trying to *secure* for your future these past three months."

He snickered. "Oh, so you heard about that?"

"Yeah, I *heard* about that."

"Look, that don't mean I don't love you. Brandy's folks got bang. Brandy wants me, so why not tap into the free flow of all their dollars to increase the Dollar. If she wants to transfer her folks' Benjamins, as well as other stuff, my way so I can do some things I want, there's no reason for either of us to hate, right? I'm telling you: the girl's folks got big bank. But, Shawty, you know how I feel about you. I don't care who else you hear may be getting at me or with me, you're always going to be my dime. You're my heart. And that's the real deal right there, baby. Real talk. That's what's up."

"Yeah, okay, Dollar. But I hope you know I'm not buying any of what you call yourself selling," Sahara said.

Dollar laughed. "Oh, now, I know you got your own stallions. So don't be trying to front on me, now. I'm not the only one folks are bumping their gums about. Oh, yeah, I hear Miss Sahara is putting it down and taking no prisoners. At least, that's what my homies tell me. But you don't see me tripping or hating on you, now, do you? That's 'cause I know you loves you some Dollar. And you know that I'm *seriously* missing you right now. Seriously. That's why I've been trying to get in touch with you for almost a week now. I miss you. You feel me? I want to see you. But given your present situation, how do you and I make that happen?"

"I don't know. My grandmother is proving to be a tad bit trickier than I thought. She wants to talk, and she seems to have ears like a bat and eyes like an eagle. Truthfully, I was faring better with my mother. I can't shake Ma Ray. But I'll figure something out."

"I thought old people were supposed to go to bed with the chickens and sleep like rocks," Dollar said. "Besides, you're old enough to go out. You shouldn't be all cooped up in some backward country town. Tell your grandmother this is the twenty-first century and she needs to get with the program. Why don't you tell her you're going to spend the night with a girlfriend or something the way you used to do with your mother? Then you and I can have a time like I'm sure you haven't had in a long time. You feeling me?"

"Sahara! Crystal! I need you down here to come help me!" Ma Ray yelled.

"Look, Ma Ray is calling me. I have to go. I wonder what *fun* she has on tap for us today. She woke me up for breakfast, gospel playing softly in the background. I told her I wasn't feeling well, but did she care? No. Anyway, I'll call you later, and we'll see what we can do to get together." Sahara hung up the phone and looked toward the ceiling.

It was close to noon and hot both inside the house and out. Sahara found Crystal and Ma Ray sitting outside on the porch.

Unlike some still in her community, Ma Ray had central air-conditioning. But for some reason Sahara didn't understand, Ma Ray either didn't like turning it on or, if she turned it on, kept it on eighty degrees. Cooler than outside for sure, but not cool enough to make much of a difference to Sahara. On the other end of the spectrum, Sahara's mother kept their air conditioner set on seventy, causing it to be chilly in their house. Sometimes, they had to wear a jacket in the summertime just to keep warm.

Ma Ray said she liked God's natural air better and preferred that to being shut up in some stuffy house with artificial air blowing everywhere. When the air was off, Ma Ray would open up the doors and windows in the house, keeping the unwanted things out (like flying bugs and creeping critters) with screened windows and doors.

Sahara saw the truck full of produce as soon as she stepped out on the porch. She'd grown up with Ma Ray and knew what a bushel was. When she was little, she loved seeing this sight. Now that she was seventeen, and definitely not thrilled about being there, she was anything *but* excited.

Her attention quickly moved from the bushels to the two guys at the truck. One guy was on the bed of the truck handing down the bushels to a mirror image of himself standing on the ground. Once the truck was completely unloaded, they began to bring one bushel at a time to the porch.

"Good afternoon," both guys said in harmony to Ma Ray, Crystal, and Sahara, stepping up on the porch, each carrying a twenty-five-pound bushel of purple hull peas.

"Afternoon, Andre and Aaron," Ma Ray said with a nod.

"Hi." Crystal sang the word as she stood straighter, curving her back just a tad.

"Hi," Sahara mumbled.

Ma Ray looked at her granddaughters, then back to the twins. "One of those bushels of peas is Tootsie's."

"Yes, ma'am. She told us to leave it here. She says she'll be here shortly," Andre Woods (the elder twin by twenty minutes) said. "Where would you like for us to put them?"

"Those look *really* heavy," Crystal said. She smiled at the twin named Aaron.

"Oh, we're fine. I lift way more than this at the gym," Aaron said as he smiled back at Crystal.

"Oh," Crystal said, blushing.

"Tell you what. Why don't you leave the purple hull peas on the porch? That way we can shell them out here. The other things you can take in the house and put in my back room for me. I'll get to them another time."

"Will do, Ma Ray," Andre said.

He and Aaron set the peas on the porch near the wooden, slightly slanted chairs. They went back two trips and got the bushels of peaches, corn, cucumbers, and tomatoes.

"Sahara, will you give them a hand for me?" Ma Ray said.

"I'll help them," Crystal said, practically bouncing up and down.

"I asked Sahara to do it," Ma Ray said with a small smile as she tilted her head.

Sahara shuffled her feet as she walked toward the screen door. She held it open for them as they brought the bushels of corn and tomatoes inside. When the twins cleared the doorway, Sahara stepped in slowly and headed toward the back room where her grandmother kept her stashes of homemade canned goods, to open *that* door for them.

"Thanks," Andre said when he'd cleared the opened back

room door. "By the way, in case you didn't pick it up from your grandmother, I'm Andre."

"And I'm Aaron."

"Yeah, okay," Sahara said, clearly letting them know she really didn't care.

"Your name is Sahara?" Andre asked as he set the bushel of corn down.

Sahara folded her arms and released a loud sigh. "Yes."

"Okay," Aaron said with a slight snicker. "I'm going to get my other bushel."

Andre stood back and smiled at Sahara. "So what's your story?"

She blew out another loud sigh. "What?"

"Why are you so upset? I mean, I haven't been here long enough to do anything to make you mad, so I don't think it's me."

"Don't you have another something to pick up and bring back here?" She turned to walk out.

"Sahara is a pretty name," he said.

"Yeah, well. You can tell my mother since she was the one who named me and I didn't have one thing to do with it." She walked to the front as though she was in a hurry. She held open the screen door as Aaron came in with the bushel of cucumbers.

Andre stepped out and got the bushel of peaches.

"Those peaches look good," Ma Ray said. "I sure hope they're as sweet as they appear to be."

"Oh, they are," Andre said. "Aaron and I already tested them out." He walked past Sahara. "There's nothing Grandma Tootsie hates more than a peach that *looks* good on the outside but ends up with a sour *bite* to it on the inside."

Sahara squinted her eyes at him. She let the screen door go before he cleared it all the way. It hit him, but not as hard as she would have liked. She was well aware when someone was trying to throw off at her. More than aware.

Chapter 7

And it was told the king of Jericho, saying, Behold, there came men in hither tonight of the children of Israel to search out the country.

—Joshua 2:2

Tootsie arrived shortly after Andre and Aaron came from taking the last bushel in the back room for Ma Ray. Ma Ray went inside and got the glass pitcher of homemade lemonade and some tall glasses. She set them on the little, round white table she kept out there just for these purposes. Ma Ray went back and returned shortly with six large, deep metal pans. Andre was handing his grandmother one of the pans he'd taken out of the backseat of her car.

"I got my own pans," Tootsie said to Ma Ray, holding up hers. "No need in me borrowing your pans when I knew we were doing this and I have plenty of my own."

"That's fine. But you know I don't mind when I have something you need," Ma Ray said, putting the extra pans to the side. "Unlike some, you return what you borrow."

"Can I go back in the house now?" Sahara asked.

"In the house?" Tootsie said. "Oh, honey chile, we're about to do some major damage out here with these purple hull peas."

"I'm not shelling peas," Sahara said, putting her hand on her hip.

"Me either," Crystal said.

"Oh, is that right?" Ma Ray said.

"Well, if my grandsons, who are young men I might add, can

shell peas, I don't see why you two young ladies can't," Tootsie said as she looked at both girls.

"I didn't say I *couldn't*, I said I *wasn't*. I don't want to," Sahara said.

"Well, it's plenty of things as adults that we do that we don't want to," Ma Ray said. "So pull up a chair if you'd like or grab a spot on the steps there if you prefer." She handed a pan to Sahara, then one to Crystal. Crystal took her pan with more enthusiasm than Sahara.

Tootsie adjusted the pillow underneath her better as she eyed the two girls. Ma Ray knew Tootsie was biting her tongue to keep from saying what she was really thinking. There was no way they would have ever allowed their own children to talk back to them like that. No way. But Ma Ray had decided to handle things differently.

Crystal sat on the top step next to Aaron. Ma Ray smiled as she saw how much fun the two of them were having shelling their portion of peas. Sahara opted to sit on the swing with her stash of unshelled peas. Ma Ray noted how Sahara was purposely shelling slowly—a tried-and-true method that would normally cause her to be dismissed.

"Do you need me to show you how to shell peas again?" Ma Ray said.

"No, ma'am," Sahara said, emphasizing each word.

Tootsie glanced over at Andre, who sat in a chair near the swing. "Andre, you're going through your bunch like Speedy Gonzales."

"Just want to get through," Andre said. "I have some other things I'd like to do today."

"Oh, I'm sorry," Ma Ray said. "You young men have been so wonderful already. Getting up early and going to pick up all these things for me and Tootsie. And now we have you here shelling peas."

"Oh, it's okay," Aaron said, stealing a glance at Crystal and smiling. "I used to love shelling peas when I was a little boy."

"Yeah, well, just don't be shooting nobody with a zip of peas the way you used to do," Tootsie said. "That boy used to take his finger and go zip." Tootsie demonstrated the act using her thumb as she stripped peas with one swift action into her pan. She laughed. "Only instead of his peas going into the bowl, he would aim it at his twin brother."

"Yeah, and you would make me pick up every one of them and go wash them off," Aaron said. "Even though you were going to just wash them later, anyway."

"Absolutely," Tootsie said. "We weren't wasting no food or effort. Not then, not now." She looked at Andre again. "Andre, are you all right?"

Andre looked up. "Yes, ma'am. I'm fine."

Sahara took out her cell phone and looked at it.

"You can get a signal out here?" Andre asked her.

"No," Sahara said, then snapped her phone shut and put it back in her pocket.

"The church is having something for the young folks in a couple of weeks," Tootsie said. "It sounds like it's going to be an interesting event. Andre and Aaron are signed up to go. You two girls are certainly welcome to sign up as well."

"Something for the young people?" Crystal said. "What is it?"

"A weekend youth conference with what sounds like some great speakers and all sorts of things we young folks care about," Aaron said. "On Saturday, the last day of the conference, there's going to be something called a purity ceremony with a live band and a reception following it."

Crystal smiled as she zipped peas into her pan. "That does sound like fun."

"Andre is working with the committee," Tootsie said. "He can get you two signed up—"

"We likely won't be here in a couple of weeks," Sahara said, cutting her off.

"Is that right?" Tootsie said.

"Andre, if you don't mind, I'd like for you to get Sahara and Crystal signed up for me," Ma Ray said.

Sahara looked at Ma Ray. "But, Ma Ray, I'm telling you: we'll likely be back home by then. Besides, it sounds like something for children."

Ma Ray shrugged. "Well, for now, we'll get you signed up. If you happen to be gone, you can always come back for it."

"If she doesn't want to go, I wouldn't worry about it," Andre said. "A thing like this really works better when people *want* to do it."

"There's plenty that I *want* to do," Sahara said, shooting Andre a hard look.

"Yeah, well—" Andre said.

"Andre, just get my granddaughters signed up for me," Ma Ray said. "Let me know my total cost, and I'll take care of things from there."

Sahara let out an audible sigh as she readjusted her body. Ma Ray tried to keep from smiling as, out of the corner of her eye, she watched Sahara begin to shell that much faster.

Chapter 8

And the king of Jericho sent unto Rahab, saying, Bring forth the men that are come to thee, which are entered into thine house: for they be come to search out all the country.

—Joshua 2:3

Tootsie and her grandsons left after about two hours of shelling peas. Ma Ray had given the twin brothers each a ten-dollar tip for bringing her produce in the house. Sahara had gone in the house after shelling only a handful of peas and hadn't returned—leaving her pan on the swing. Ma Ray picked up the mostly empty pan and poured those few shelled peas into Crystal's almost full pan.

"You did good," Ma Ray said to Crystal.

"Thank you," Crystal said with a huge grin and a slight curtsy. "That was fun!"

"Oh, really now." Ma Ray opened the screen door and held it open for Crystal to walk through. "Wonder why you had so much fun doing something you used to act like you hated doing when you were younger? I don't know. You think maybe you were trying to impress somebody or something?"

They walked to the kitchen. Crystal set her pan on the kitchen counter next to the sink before turning around and smiling at Ma Ray. "Aaron is nice. *Really* nice."

"Yes, he seems to be a fine young man. I must admit: you don't find too many young folks these days willing to sit with us old folks and help us do something like shell peas. And young men at that." She shook her head. "Nope. Not these days."

Crystal took Ma Ray's pan and set it down next to hers. "I thought that was something myself. None of the guys I know would have ever done anything like that," Crystal said. "Aaron is not only strong, but he sure was fast at zipping those peas out of their hulls. So, are they staying with their grandmother for the summer, too?"

"No. They're living with her now." Ma Ray closed the drainer in the sink and dumped a pan of peas in it. She turned the faucet on full force, pelting the peas with water before the sink began to fill up.

"Did something happen with their parents?"

"No one knows who their daddy is, and their mother is totally strung out on drugs now. It's a sad situation, sad. It's been tough on all of them. I keep them in my prayers."

"I have a friend at school whose mother is strung out like that. She's going through the same thing, only she's in a foster home," Crystal said.

"It's definitely hard on children. I just wish parents would think about the children when they're making decisions to do drugs. But it does help when there's family who can step up. Not everybody has family who will step in." Ma Ray turned off the water. "So tell me." She looked Crystal squarely in her eyes. "What's going on with you?"

"What do you mean?"

"Why have you been acting like you have?" Ma Ray dried her hands on a towel and sat down at the kitchen table. She patted the place next to her. Crystal obeyed her unspoken command and sat down in the seat next to her. "Talk to me."

Crystal looked down at her hands and began to rub her one thumb with the other. "What is there to talk about?"

"For starters, why you're giving your mother and Edmond such a hard time when all they're trying to do is to tell you right?" Ma Ray touched Crystal's hands to stop her from fidgeting.

Crystal looked up at Ma Ray and shrugged. "I don't know. Maybe I'm just acting like teenagers are *supposed* to act."

"According to whom?"

"According to everybody who acts like they know what we're going through. When we don't want to talk, they label us as moody. When we disagree with an adult, we're being rebellious. But Ma Ray, sometimes we're just dealing with stuff we don't want to talk about."

"I understand."

"That's what everybody says. They say they understand, but if they really did, why do they do things that make stuff worse?"

"I'm listening." Ma Ray smiled.

Crystal looked at her and twisted her mouth.

"What?" Ma Ray asked.

"I don't want to hurt your feelings, Ma Ray. But I don't think you'll really get what I'm saying. You're kind of . . . old. You know? Now, there's nothing wrong with that. And then, you're a churchgoing woman. You wouldn't really have a clue what I'm talking about."

Ma Ray smiled a little. "I feel you. Why don't you try me?"

Crystal started laughing. "What do you know about feeling somebody?"

"I'm hipped. . . . I'm down. So try me."

Crystal laughed harder. "That's what Mama says, but when I've tried her, she doesn't get it. She doesn't have a clue."

Ma Ray squeezed Crystal's hand. "Seriously, though, sometimes just talking about it can help. Let's say that I really don't get it. At least having a sounding board may help you."

"A sounding board? See, that's what I mean. You and Mama say stuff that nobody understands. What's a sounding board?"

"It's when you say something, it hits a solid mass, and it bounces back to you. That way you get to hear it in a different way. I've found that when I can say something out loud, it takes on a different shape than when it's rattling around inside my head. That's why the devil has such a field day with folks. He tries to get us to keep things inside so we don't really get to see it as it is. What I've learned is that, when you get it out, it's not as big or as bad as it seems when you keep it bottled in." Ma Ray shrugged. "Hey, what do you have to lose? Why not give it a shot?"

"I'm ugly and dorky and, if you really want to know the truth, nobody likes me."

"Wow."

She fell back against the chair. "See, Ma Ray. I *knew* you wouldn't understand."

"Baby, I understand. Somehow, as beautiful and as smart and as talented as you are, you've decided you're not pretty enough or cool enough."

Crystal laughed. "*Cool*, Ma Ray? Cool? Who says cool much these days?"

"Oh. Now you're making fun of your old grandma." Ma Ray pretended to pout.

"No. But of course you think I'm pretty and cool and—"

"Smart. I think you're a very smart young lady."

"Ma Ray, I'm not smart. I struggle in school. I'm not like Sahara. Sahara is beautiful *and* she's smart. She really doesn't have to study to get good grades the way I have to. And she makes friends so easily. The only reason that people even act like they like me is because I'm her sister."

"Oh, Crystal, that's not true. Do you have any idea how much you have going on for you?"

"Ma Ray, of course you're going to say that. You're my grandmother. Sure you think I'm great. You're supposed to encourage me. That's a grandmother's job. That's what grandmothers do." Crystal began to wipe her eyes.

Ma Ray stood up and opened her arms. "Come here."

"Ma Ray, I don't want to be treated like I'm some kind of a baby."

"Come here," Ma Ray said again, smiling.

Crystal stood and fell into her arms. "Ma Ray, why can't I be popular? Why can't I be like other people?"

"Because, baby girl, God made you a designer's original. He made you unique. You weren't created to be a copy of anyone else. You're special. God created you special because you're valuable to Him. We all are."

Crystal pressed in even closer to Ma Ray. "I'm sorry, Ma Ray.

I'm sorry I've been giving Mama such a hard time. But Mama doesn't care about me."

Ma Ray pushed Crystal away from her so she could look her in her eyes. "Yes, she does."

"She cares, but not really. My mother doesn't see me. She's too busy fixing whatever Sahara might be dealing with at the time or doing things for Nia or Kyle. And good old Edmond always takes his children's sides about everything. It doesn't matter what's going on, he automatically assumes either me or Sahara was the one who did something wrong to them. I'm just tired of being caught in the middle."

Ma Ray pulled her in closer again. "So, you act out."

"I'm not *trying* to act out. I'm just tired of being the good girl. When you're the good one, for some reason, you become virtually invisible."

Ma Ray began to squeeze her. "Why . . . you don't feel invisible." She pulled back slightly and grinned. "And you don't look invisible, at least not to me."

"That's because you have a way of making us feel like we exist."

Ma Ray sat back down, pulling Crystal down with her. "You're being a little hard on your mother, don't you think?"

"No, I'm just telling you what I feel."

There was a knock on the front screen door. Ma Ray looked toward the front room. "Wonder who that could be?"

Crystal turned toward the front as well. "You want me to get it for you?"

"No. No. I'll do it." Ma Ray stood back up. She hobbled a little when she first starting walking. Her right knee was beginning to bother her again. She made her way to the front door and immediately began to grin.

"Hey, Ma," the six-foot-seven gentleman said as he peeped through the screen.

"Beau!" Ma Ray said. "What a nice surprise! I didn't know you were coming this way." She quickly unlocked, then opened the screen door. He grabbed her up after he stepped inside, her feet dangling off the floor as he hugged her. "Boy, put me down," she said after he dangled her for about a minute. "You always do that. I've told you about grabbing me up like that."

"Oh, Ma, you know you like it." He eased her down until her feet rested flatly on the floor.

"Yeah, well." She smiled. "Come on in, come on in."

"My goodness, Ma, it's hot in here," Boaz said. "Why don't you turn on the air conditioner?"

"Oh, I will. You sound just like Sahara. All y'all care about is that fake air. Personally, I like God's natural breeze. And I try to put off closing off the place for as long as I can."

"Well, I've told you: God gave man the knowledge to come up with air conditioners. So that tells me that He desires for us to be comfortable."

"I'm comfortable. You city folks are the ones acting like you're going to die from the summer heat. That's why I keep telling folks they'd better be sure they're saved. Because this is nothing compared to Hell. Last I heard, there are no air conditioners, fans, or even access to cold water down there. And we all know that Hell is a real place. I don't care what some folks want to try and say. Just like Heaven is a real place, so is Hell."

"Yeah, well, Ma, there's no reason for you to practice being hot when you don't need to, since we all know that you're going to Heaven when you leave this place."

"That's where I'm aiming. When I move from this old building, by the way that has started to lean and slant more and more here lately, I want to make my home in Heaven." Ma Ray led Boaz to the kitchen.

Crystal turned around. "Hey, Uncle Boaz." She had both hands submerged in the sink of water. She looked like she was playing with the shelled purple hull peas instead of washing them. "Look at you—all *g'd* up."

"Hi there, Crissy," Boaz said. "G'd up?"

"Yeah, g'd up. You know, it means you look good in your threads. And I've told you that I don't go by Crissy anymore. It's Crystal."

"Oh, you mean the way I keep telling people I don't go by Boaz, but for some *reason* they still insist upon calling me that?"

"Uncle Beau, you know you'll always be Uncle Boaz to me. Old habits are hard to break."

Boaz walked over to her and gave her a big hug. "Are you helping Ma?"

"Yeah," Crystal said. "Look at all these peas." She picked up both hands filled with peas. "And we have another pan to wash over there." She pointed her head toward the peas still in the large pan.

"I remember these days," Boaz said. "Ma would get us to help her shell peas. I even remember when we tried our hands at farming for those few years. We had to reap our fruits and vegetables ourselves. That was backbreaking hard work. That's how I ended up meeting your aunt Ruth. She was out in our field 'gleaning,' as my father called it."

"Gleaning?" Crystal asked as she dried her hands.

"Yeah," Boaz said. "That's when people come behind you after you've picked what you're planning on getting. They get to reap whatever you leave behind. That was Daddy's way of giving to those who were struggling or in need. Just needing a little hand up, not so much, just a handout. I was in charge of things this particular day. I saw this beautiful young woman out there trying to see what she could find. She didn't realize it at the time, but I told one of our workers to tell her to come back the next day. And on the next day, I instructed the workers to purposely leave handfuls of things for her to have."

"Oh, you must have *really* liked Aunt Ruth from jump street," Crystal said.

"Yeah. And my love has only multiplied each and every year since that time."

Crystal sat down in the chair at the kitchen table. "I wish someone felt that way about me. Maybe someday, but I really doubt it. Things have changed a lot since you came along. Guys are mostly jerks now."

"Not so," Ma Ray said. "Many may not know how to act or

treat a *real* lady these days. But that's why a *real* lady must teach him how she *will* be treated."

"So, where's Sahara?" Boaz glanced around as though he was looking for her.

"In her room. Probably asleep," Crystal said. "She kind of had a long night. Then Ma Ray got us up early for breakfast. Then she made us shell peas."

"Oh. What happened last night?" Boaz said.

"Nothing that concerns you," Ma Ray said quickly to Boaz and before Crystal could say anything more. "Crystal, if you like, you can go do something you want to do. You've been a great help to me today. I'll finish up down here."

Crystal smiled as she got up to leave. "Thanks."

After she was gone, Boaz cleared his throat. "So, are you planning on telling me what happened that caused Sahara to have a long night?"

"No."

"Ma—"

"I have fresh peaches in the back room. You know how you love peaches."

"There you go again. Why do you always do that?"

"Do what?"

"Try to change the subject when you don't want to talk about something?"

She smiled. "Boaz," she said, purposely calling him that, "now when have I *ever* had to answer to you about anything I do?"

"Ma, I talked with Lenora this morning."

"I know you called. I was on the phone with her when you beeped in. Want something to drink? I have fresh lemonade in the refrigerator. Just the way you like it."

"Why do you do this?" Boaz said.

Ma Ray began to fan herself with her hand. "You know, it *is* a bit heated in here. Maybe I *will* turn on the air conditioner. Help me close all the doors and windows down here, will you?" She closed the door and windows in the kitchen before walking out of the kitchen to the hall where the thermostat was located. She called Crystal and told her to close all of the windows upstairs. Boaz closed off the windows and doors in the front of the house. The house began to cool off rather quickly.

"Want to go outside on the porch?" Ma Ray said to Boaz after they finished.

"Sure," Boaz said. "We cool the house down, and then go outside in the heat. Makes perfect sense to *me*. I'll get the pitcher of lemonade, glasses, and lots of ice."

Ma Ray knew this was going to be one of those serious conversations. She could tell whenever Boaz was in that "place" where she wouldn't be able to avoid it or somehow conveniently be able to change the subject.

Chapter 9

And the woman took the two men, and hid them, and said thus, There came men unto me, but I wist not whence they were.

—Joshua 2:4

"Sahara, you woke?" Crystal said in a whisper with the door cracked open.

Sahara's first instinct was to pretend she was asleep. But she knew Crystal didn't care if she was or not. "I'm awake," Sahara said.

Crystal opened the door wider and walked in. "Are you okay?"

Sahara sat up completely. "Looks like Ma Ray finally decided to turn on the air. I thought I was going to die from all of this heat."

"Yeah, that's what I was coming to do. Make sure your window was closed. You know how Ma Ray feels when she *does* turn on the air."

Sahara laughed a little. "Yeah, I know. She fusses about cooling off the outside." Sahara sat up straighter. "So what made her decide to turn on the air?"

"Uncle Boaz is here."

"He is?"

"Yep. He looks good, too. Has on this G-macking outfit. You know how he always dresses up. Well, even when he dresses casual, he's dressed to the nines."

"I suppose you can do that kind of stuff when you're rolling in dough," Sahara said.

"You sound just like Mama now."

"Maybe Mama's right about them. Sometimes they do act like they're better than everybody else. It's always 'We this. We that.' 'Freda this' and 'Owen that.' I get so sick of hearing about all of them and how great and wonderful they all are."

Crystal sat on the bed, her foot underneath her leg. "Better watch it. Your PHD is showing."

"Crystal, don't be funny. I'm not in the mood. And I don't have a Playa Hata Degree. I just want to get out of this place. It's so boring here!"

"Ma Ray said we could borrow her car if we want to go to a movie or something. We *could* go to Walmart."

"Oh, joy! We can drive Ma Ray's car to the movies. That car is so old, I'm afraid to drive it anywhere. We could get out and push it and I believe it would go faster than when we're riding inside of it."

Crystal started laughing. "You wrong for that. You need to leave Ma Ray's deuce and a quarter alone," she said, referring to the dark blue Electra 225.

Sahara laughed, too. "I don't even think they make that car brand anymore."

"Well, you know she's not going to let you drive her Cadillac."

"Of course not. That's the newer car, and she has to wait until it's old to really decide to drive it. I don't understand people. Then they have the nerve to act like teenagers are the ones with the problems. They buy stuff and don't want people to touch it until it becomes really old. Like it's supposed to last forever or something."

"At least Ma Ray doesn't keep plastic on her furniture," Crystal said. "And to be fair, Ma Ray is not like most people. She doesn't care about people using her stuff."

"Yeah, right," Sahara said. "It's just the deuce needs to get its workout so it will keep running. It's such a huge car, though. Can you imagine how much gas that thing uses up? I think we should report Ma Ray to the environmental protectionist or something."

"So, do you want to talk about last night?"

"Not really." Sahara stood up and walked over to the vanity. She picked up a pair of earrings and put them on.

"Ma Ray could have killed somebody."

"Yeah, well, how was I to know she was going to do something like that? It's this stupid area and these stupid cell phones. When B-Man got here, his phone wouldn't pick up a signal. So what does he decide to do? Break in. Which probably wouldn't have been a problem if Ma Ray had been in her own room asleep the way old people should."

Crystal stood up and walked over to Sahara. "I don't think you should do that."

"Do what?"

"Talk about Ma Ray like that. She really does love us. She would do anything for us. You know Edmond was trying to get Mama to send us away to some boot camp for out-of-control teenagers. Ma Ray actually did us a favor by stepping in like this."

Sahara went and gingerly sat back down on the bed. "So, you're trying to blame me for all of this?"

"No, it's not just you. I've been doing my share as well," Crystal said. "But Ma Ray and I were talking a little while ago, and I think she really does understand."

"How many times do I have to tell you that adults don't understand? They say they do, but things aren't anything like it was when they were growing up. Ma Ray didn't even have television when she was young. She's been in church probably all of her life. She was married to a cop who later became a preacher. They had a farm where they grew stuff. Uncle Boaz took it over, then sold that land for a nice price. Then there's Mama. . . . You know what? I don't even want to *talk* about Mama."

"Hey, don't stop. Ma Ray says it's good to get things out of you," Crystal said.

"Mama is so busy trying to find the right everything. She wants us to believe she and Edmond are doing fine, but they're not. They fight about everything. And I'll bet you money that Edmond has another woman on the side. And that stupid church we go to, I'm sick of all those phony people. Everybody trying to act like they have it together when they're just as messed up, if not more so, than the world they claim to be separated from. The preacher's wife is the one running the church while the preacher is sitting back just letting her. All you hear from him is an appeal for money. And there's Mama trying her best to keep up with everything they're saying you have to do in order to prove to God that you love Him." Sahara sat against the headboard. "I'll tell you: I can't *wait* until I'm grown. I'm never stepping foot in another church as long as I live. I promise you *that!*"

Crystal came and sat beside Sahara. "That's a bit harsh, don't you think? I mean, there are lots of churches to choose from. If you go to one you don't like, you keep trying until you find one."

"What's the point? How many churches have we been a member of already?" Sahara asked. "Huh?"

"That's because every time we get deeply involved, Mama finds out stuff she didn't know they believed in the beginning. Then folks start messing with her, and she becomes so miserable she has to go somewhere else. Honestly, I like church. And I'm looking forward to going to this youth conference with Aaron and Andre."

Sahara started smiling. "Oh, you just like Aaron."

Crystal blushed a bit. "Well, he seems to be a nice guy. Both of them seem nice."

"Oh, yeah. Cletus One and Cletus Two. Wonder Twin powers." Sahara laughed.

Crystal didn't laugh. "Stop calling them Cletus. They're neither tacky nor country backward. I think they're both peng."

"You think they're both peng? You do know what peng is, right?"

"Yes," Crystal said with a big smile. "They are attractive, physically fit, and really *quite* sexy."

"See, that's a problem right there," Sahara said. "I think you need to pump your brakes. You shouldn't be thinking sex or sexy at all. The reason we're here right now is because our mother thinks we're sex crazed and out of control. Oh, and she thinks I'm a bad influence on you."

"Don't you think Andre is hot? I think Aaron is hot. They're identical twins."

"Andre is not my type. I prefer my men to be grown. Any guy who will allow his grandmother to have him hauling fruits and vegetables around to other old folks, and then make him sit and shell peas with her, is not strong enough to wrap his arm in mine."

"Well, I see it differently," Crystal said with a big smile.

"Of course you do. Real talk: weak people *need* weak people. I am *too* strong of a woman to be with someone who will shell peas and then be excited about going to some church youth conference. Then again, maybe I *should* talk to him while I'm here. See if I can't open his eyes to the real world. Show him how to have some *real* fun. That way, he won't be some lost country bumpkin if and when he ever gets out of this place."

"Well, I think they're both really great guys. And personally, I'm looking forward to seeing Aaron again."

"I wouldn't go there if I were you. I'm telling you, Crystal. It's people like Andre and Aaron you need to be the most leery of. They pretend they're these nice guys, when in truth, they're really bad boys in disguise. Hey . . . maybe you're right. Maybe I *should* check out Andre. If nothing else, it would be something to pass the time while I'm sentenced to this slow-Internet, no-cell-connection-keeping place." Sahara picked up the novel on her nightstand and opened it to her bookmarked page.

Crystal stood up, then shrugged. "Just try to stay out of trouble, will you? Ma Ray really *does* care about us. And I don't think it's right for us to give her so much trouble. She deserves better than that. Much better than that."

"Close the door on your way out, all right?" Sahara said, rushing her sister out of her room.

"Sure," Crystal said. Then, as instructed, she pulled the door closed behind her.

Chapter 10

And it came to pass about the time of shutting of the gate, when it was dark, that the men went out: whither the men went I wot not: pursue after them quickly; for ye shall overtake them.

—Joshua 2:5

"Is she gone?" came a voice from underneath Sahara's bed.

"Yeah," Sahara said with a sigh. She put the novel back on her nightstand.

The guy got up and flopped down hard on her bed. "Wow! That was close!"

"Yeah. That's why I told you that you shouldn't have come up here. What if that had been my grandmother instead of my sister? My grandmother doesn't always knock before she comes barging in." And after what happened last night, Sahara knew her grandmother would be even more on her toes when it came to her.

"I'm just glad somebody finally got the good sense to turn the air on in this bad boy," Junebug said. "It was starting to get ridiculous in here. But when I saw you walking out there earlier today, my heart literally did a backflip. Girl, you make all this sweating *more* than worth it. It's been years since I've seen you. You were like twelve or thirteen, something like that. You're as fine as wine that seems to only be getting better with time. But back then, you would hardly give me the time of day." He shook his head as he bit down on his bottom lip. "You look *so* good— a real dime piece. Nothing like these chicken heads around here. And that's fo' sheezy. So, how old are you *now?*"

"Seventeen," Sahara said.

Junebug lived with his folks up the dirt road from Ma Ray's. He was twenty, and from what Sahara had learned from their conversation so far, he'd dropped out of high school at age sixteen but still lived with his parents, having given them his word that he was working toward getting his GED. He really wasn't, since he had a pretty good hustle going on that brought in more money than any minimum-wage job ever could. And staying with his good Christian folks, in a country place, was a perfect cover for all of his mischief. He could do all of the dirt he wanted, come back to the "woods" as he called it, and no one was the wiser.

"So, what were you doing down there near that natural area?" Junebug asked.

"My grandmother had us shelling peas," Sahara said. "I just couldn't take it anymore. That's why I was out there. I guess they thought I was up here resting or something. But who can rest in all of this heat? I had sneaked out the back, and before I knew it, I ended up down there. I've always liked that place. It's so peaceful down there. I heard something, thought it might be a wild animal or something, looked up—"

"And there I was thinking I *had* to be dreaming," Junebug said. "You, wearing those sweet little short-shorts, your legs looking like they go on for days." He glanced down at her legs. She put her hands on her thighs as though that would be enough to cover them from his gawking.

"Listen, Junebug. It was good seeing you and all. But now I need to figure out a way to get you out of here. Crystal just said my uncle Boaz is here. And he's even worse than my grandmother. If he catches you up here in my room, who knows how he'll go off. And I'm about one mistake away from being sent off to a boot camp or something."

"Well, trust me, I'm sure boot camp is a whole lot better than juvie. That's where I ended up for a few months. I wish my folks had been nice enough to put me in some place like some chomp boot camp."

"How are we going to get you out of here without anyone seeing or hearing you?" Sahara asked as she stood up and pulled the hem of her shorts down in another attempt to divert his ever-gawking attention from her legs.

He smacked his lips a few times. "What if I don't want to go?"

"Well, you have to. I'm not going to get into any more trouble, at least not today."

"You've already been in trouble today? Aren't you a little too old to be getting in trouble? You're seventeen. At seventeen my mother was already married with my oldest sister on the way."

"Do you think you can climb out of the window? Make your way to the tree and shimmy down."

"What? Climb out of this window." He started laughing. "I'm not climbing out of no window, and I sure ain't about to shimmy down no tree."

"Well, I need to get you out of here."

"Well, then, you'd better come up with a better plan than that. If your room was on the ground floor, climbing out of the window might be an option. Two floors up, nope. Not me."

"Okay, okay. I'll think of something."

"When can I see you again?"

"You can stop by anytime. Just ring the doorbell and it will be fine. My grandmother knows you and your folks. The way she acts about all of you, she'll welcome you in with open arms. She seems to love for us to have company. As long as they do it the right way."

"The problem is your grandmother *does* know me. And believe me: she will not be welcoming *me* with open arms. She's made that perfectly clear on more than a few occasions. The last time, she told me she was from a place called Hope."

Sahara frowned. "A place called Hope?"

He laughed. "Yeah. But it's not at all what you're thinking. She said that she *hopes* I don't ever step foot on her property ever again, because her *hope* for me is for *me* to be able to walk away under my own powers. It was that cousin of yours that caused her to say all of those things to me. What's her name? Freda, yeah, that's her name: Miss Prim and Proper Freda. Ma Ray was saying that she *hopes* I get my life together and *hopes* I come to know Jesus in the free pardon of my sin before I meet my maker. I wanted to tell her that nothing in life is ever free. It always cost somebody something. But she had that look that told me it was best that I keep my big mouth shut. So, I did."

"My grandmother? You're talking about *my* grandmother. Ma Ray said *that?*"

"Yeah, I'm talking about your grandmother: Ray of Hope. She told me she had a lot of *hope* for me. And the first thing I could do to ensure some of her hopes for me came true was for me to never step foot in her place without her permission ever again."

"And yet . . . here you are, in my room, no less," Sahara teased him, then grinned.

"Well, when I saw you today, looking on fire at the top of that bank, with that water flowing down below us, I wouldn't have been able to look myself in the mirror had I let you come back here *all by your lonesome.*"

"Like I said . . . *we* need to get *you* out of here before Ray of Hope or Ray of Hope's son finds you here and gives you a *sting*ray of hope. Then we'll both find ourselves up a creek, trying to row our boats, without a paddle."

"When can I see you again?" He walked up close to Sahara. Sahara tried to step back, but he grabbed her around the waist to let her know he was also quite strong. "And don't tell me to ring your grandmother's doorbell. I want to show you some real fun. I'm sure you're not seeing much of that hanging around all of these deadbeats. I have access to stuff. You know what I mean? So maybe you can sneak away; that way, you won't have to worry about anybody looking for you to be home at a certain time."

"I'll let you know," Sahara said. "But for now, you have to leave." She pushed him away and walked toward the door. "Listen out for my cue, okay? And when it sounds like the coast is clear for you to leave, I want you to make your way down the steps and out of the front door. Quietly, if you don't mind."

He smiled and bit down on his bottom lip again. "All right. But you owe me. And I *always* collect on my debts. Always."

Chapter 11

But she had brought them up to the roof of the house, and hid them with the stalks of flax, which she had laid in order upon the roof.

—Joshua 2:6

"Hi, Uncle Boaz," Sahara said when she walked into the den. She went over and hugged him. "Crystal told me you were here."

Boaz hugged her back. "Hi, Sahara. Shorts are a little short, don't you think?"

Sahara forced a smile. "Do you have any idea how hot it's been in this house? Ma Ray says she hates artificial air, so we all have to figure a way to make do."

"Well, the air conditioner is on now," Ma Ray said. "I don't know what the fuss is all about. Before we had air conditioners, we managed to live and not die. We survived it just fine. Now y'all act like the world is coming to an end if you can't have things just the way you think it ought to be."

"I'm hungry. Is anybody else hungry besides me? Why don't we all go in the kitchen and fix something fun to eat. You know, Ma Ray. The way we used to all pitch in and do it. I think it will be fun."

"We've eaten already. There's plenty left in there," Ma Ray said. "Go in there and get as much as you want."

"Oh, Ma Ray. I knew you'd cooked something already. But I really would like to do something fun. It's been so long since we've all done something, together as a family, in the kitchen. I know—let's bake some cookies. Uncle Boaz, you know how much you love Ma Ray's cookies, oatmeal . . . chocolate chips with those big old chips she chips herself. You know, Ma Ray, how you take a large block of chocolate and just hack away. Then the cookies bake, and those large pieces of chocolate just melts and gets all ooey and gooey. When you pull them apart, all soft, hot out of the oven, the pieces of chocolate stretch from one broken piece to the other, making a string of chocolate. Then, we hold up one broken piece and let the warm chocolate settle on our tongues—"

"Okay, I'm sold," Boaz said. "Girl, you know you have a way with words. I can't believe you're not acing English in school."

"She writes a lot of poetry and short stories," Crystal said. "She's really good, too. And I'm not just saying that because she's my sister."

"Poetry and short stories, huh?" Boaz said.

"I just play around. I like playing around with words. I like the music that can be made just by placing certain words in certain places," Sahara said. She got up and started for the kitchen, glancing up the stairs as she passed them.

Ma Ray saw her when she glanced that way. Ma Ray wasn't sure what was going on, but deep down in her knowing, she knew Sahara was up to something.

"Ma, are you coming?" Boaz asked. "You know, you're the cooking expert. We're just following your lead."

Ma Ray smiled. "Coming," she said, scampering to catch up.

Chapter 12

Just as Ma Ray was taking out the first batch of cookies, the doorbell rang. Sahara jumped.

"Why are you so jumpy?" Boaz asked Sahara.

"No reason," Sahara said. "I just wasn't expecting the doorbell to ring, that's all." She looked at the entranceway.

Boaz got up from the kitchen table to go answer it. Ma Ray could hear who it was as soon as he opened the door. She hurriedly wiped her hands on the apron with the cartoon baker on it that Sahara and Crystal had given her for a Mother's Day gift when they were little bitty girls, and started toward the front.

"I knew that was you," Ma Ray said as she hugged Lenora, then Kyle and Nia. "What great timing. We just finished making homemade chocolate chip cookies. In fact, I just took a batch out of the oven."

"Cookies!" Kyle said. "I'm Cookie Monster! *Raowl.*" He made a roaring sound, then started for the kitchen.

"Wait on your sister," Lenora said.

"Nia, come on. We're going to get Ma Ray's big cookies!"

Nia ran to her brother, who quickly grabbed her hand and practically dragged her along.

Lenora looked at Boaz. Ma Ray immediately felt the tension between them.

"So what are you doing here?" Lenora asked Boaz.

"Came to see our mother," Boaz said.

"Why today?" Lenora asked.

"Why not?"

"What's going on with you two?" Ma Ray asked.

"Nothing," Boaz said.

Lenora walked over and set her purse down on the sofa. "He's just jealous."

Boaz turned toward Lenora. "Jealous?"

"Yeah, Ma. Boaz is jealous."

"What does he have to be jealous about?" Ma Ray asked.

"Okay, maybe jealous isn't the right word." Lenora flopped down on the sofa. "But I'm sure he's expressed his displeasure that Sahara and Crystal are staying here with you for who knows how long. And I'm sure you've painfully explained to him how you had to step in to help me because I'm so incompetent when it comes to taking care of my own. Boaz likely finessed somewhere in the conversation how all I ever do is skillfully take advantage of you, which I don't. Then he probably further emphasized, in his own sneaky way, how much better of a child he's always been, and a parent he is now, than I will *ever* come close to even dreaming of being. I don't know why Boaz feels he always has to make me look bad. I don't."

"Wow, that was really good, Len," Boaz said.

Lenora flashed him a hard look. "What? Did I interrupt before you were finished trashing me to Ma? Should I have called to let Ma know I was coming so you could have thrown your rocks and hid your hand by being out of here before I arrived?"

"Lenora, what has gotten into you?" Ma Ray said, her hand on her chest. "My goodness."

Boaz smiled. "It's okay, Ma." He leaned down and kissed his mother. "I'm going to get a few cookies to take home and get out of here."

"Please don't leave on my account," Lenora said.

"Lenora, stop it!" Ma Ray said.

Boaz smiled as he shook his head. "I enjoyed the visit today."

Ma Ray smiled back. "So did I, son. Don't let it be too long before we do it again." Boaz hugged Ma Ray as she rubbed his back, then patted it softly. "Take Ruth some cookies."

"Oh, I'm sure Ruth doesn't eat cookies. That's why she's able to stay in such great shape," Lenora said.

Boaz flashed Lenora another look but didn't say anything back. He went to the kitchen. Ma Ray could hear all of the children telling him good-bye. He came back, hugged her as he told her good-bye. "See, you around, Lenora," Boaz said. "Take care."

"Likewise," Lenora said, barely looking at him.

Ma Ray sat down next to Lenora. "Okay, what was that all about?"

"What was *what* all about?"

"What's the problem you're having with your brother?"

"I'm not the one having the problem." Lenora blinked her eyes several times. "So . . . how long was he here?"

"About two...two-and-a-half hours."

"And in that time, how many times did my name come up?"

"Let's see," Ma Ray said, looking toward the ceiling. "I believe the correct number would be . . . zero. Your name didn't come up at all. He came in. He and I and Crystal talked for a little while. He talked me into turning on the air conditioner. Crystal went upstairs and talked to Sahara. He and I went out on the porch for about thirty minutes. Came back in the house. Sahara came downstairs shortly after Crystal came back. Sahara spoke to her uncle. She wanted to make cookies. Let's see, now—I don't want to leave anything out. I let them do all the mixing for the cookies while I washed, then blanched the purple hull peas we shelled today."

"Okay, Ma. I see. So Boaz didn't say one word about the girls staying here with you? He didn't ask how long they were planning on being here. He didn't mention that he thought you were too old to have to be bothered with *my* troubled teens? Didn't say anything like that to you or to the girls? Nothing at all?"

Ma Ray smiled as she took Lenora's hand and patted it. "No. We merely had an enjoyable time, and then you showed up."

"Oh." Lenora pulled her hand out of Ma Ray's. "You were having an enjoyable time until I showed up."

Ma Ray let her body go limp from exasperation. "What? Who said anything about *until* you showed up? I said *then* you showed up. Then! Not *until* you showed up. Then."

"Same thing. I came in and ruined everything as usual. You were having a wonderful time, then I showed up."

"Well, you do have a chip on your shoulders, and I don't quite understand why. So if you have something you want to get off your chest, by all means dump it."

Lenora took her hands and rubbed from her cheeks up toward her forehead, then down her face, raking over her eyes, and ending at her mouth. She then crossed her hands and pressed them against her chest. "It's me. I was wrong. Once again, I was wrong." She took her hands down. "I saw Boaz's car when I drove up. Then him standing there at the door like he's *the man,* and I lost it. . . . I just lost it. He and I spoke earlier today. He was trying to find out why the girls were here, and how long they would be staying."

"Well, that's really not any of his business or concern," Ma Ray said.

"Exactly! And that's exactly what I told him. But he made it clear he intended to let you know what he felt about my incompetence—"

"Is that what he said? Your incompetence?"

"No. No, he didn't say that word *exactly.* That's my shorthand for cutting through all the noise of what he means but doesn't say. He does think that I take advantage of you. But, Ma"—she turned squarely to her mother and grabbed both her hands—"I don't. I would never *purposely* do anything to hurt you. Never purposely. You've been my rock. You're been so wonderful to me. I promise you, when I do things that hurt you or look like I'm trying to get over on you, I'm not doing it intentionally."

Ma Ray took one of her hands and patted Lenora's a few times. "Oh, I know."

"Mama! Ma Ray! You want a cookie?" Nia said as she walked

into the room with one large cookie in her hand and chocolate smeared all over her face.

"Oh, baby, look at you! Come here," Lenora said with her arms open. She picked Nia up and sat her on her lap.

"There's a *whole* bunch of them," Nia said, raising her hands as though to show how high the cookies reached. "Sahara and Crystal keep making more and more and more." She wiggled a little, readjusting her body more comfortably on her mother's lap.

"That *many?*" Lenora said, smiling. "Well, I suppose Ma Ray and I need to get in there and get us one or two."

"You'd better. Before Kyle eats them all up," Nia said, nodding. "He thinks he's Cookie Monster."

"Oh, my, I guess we'd really *better* get in there, then," Ma Ray said as she leaned her mouth down close to Nia's cookie.

"You want a bite, Ma Ray?" Nia said.

Ma Ray smiled, then took a little nibble. "Thank you, precious," she said.

"You welcome," Nia said, then jumped down and ran back to the kitchen.

Chapter 13

And before they were laid down, she came up unto them upon the roof.

—Joshua 2:8

Sahara went upstairs to her room as soon as her mother came in the kitchen to get cookies. She checked under her bed and in the closet to be sure Junebug was not there. He was gone. She slowly let out a sigh of relief.

She really didn't want to be around her mother. Uncle Boaz had been really great, better than she thought he would be. But she was glad he'd left shortly after her mother arrived. She could tell he wanted to talk to her . . . alone . . . and she really didn't want him trying out his psychobabble junk on her. She already knew she was being rebellious. She knew she was giving everybody a hard time. She knew she was wrong about most of the decisions she was making lately. But for some reason, she just couldn't help herself.

At seventeen, she absolutely hated being stuck in the country with her grandmother and deprived of all the real comforts of life. Ma Ray didn't have a video game system. Their mother wouldn't let them bring theirs, because Kyle liked playing it too much to be without it. Ma Ray didn't have a computer, although their mother had offered to buy her one as a present. She and Crystal both laughed when they heard their mother discussing a computer for Ma Ray. Ma Ray flat out asked her,

"What on God's green earth, pray tell, do I need with a computer?"

Their mother tried to tell her how she could e-mail people. How they could instantly send her pictures of the family. She could see Nia and Kyle practically grow up before her in real time. Ma Ray told her daughter she could save her money on that foolish waste. She'd rather see the family in person and they could bring her copies of their photos.

Edmond, their stepfather, told their mother what Ma Ray was *really* trying to say to her. "Your mother was probably politely saying: how can you spend money to buy me a gift of a computer when you owe me money, lots of money at that? She would, in all probability, prefer being paid back some of what you owe her instead of you spending more of *her* money on something *she* doesn't want or need."

Well, that small statement started another blowup between the happy couple. But that was nothing new for Sahara. No matter why an argument appeared to start in their house, the central theme always came back to money. Or more to the point: the lack thereof. But that never stopped their mother from spending and throwing it away "like it grows on trees." That's what Edmond had told her more than a few dozen times.

Edmond really got upset with their mother whenever she put money in church instead of paying a bill that was due—or worse, past due. That always pushed him over the edge. Sahara often heard Edmond telling their mother how stupid she was to put money in church when the power company had already sent a final disconnect notice. But their mother would keep doing it, saying how she didn't want to be cursed with a curse. That God would rebuke the devourer. Then she'd turn to Ma Ray to bail her out, yet *again.*

And Ma Ray never let their mother down. Which was why she and Crystal were over there in the first place. Edmond had made it perfectly clear that he was fed up with trying to figure them out. She didn't care how much he tried telling them he couldn't love them any more had they been of his own flesh,

Sahara knew his fuse was shorter with her and Crystal because they weren't his biological children.

That's what made her the maddest about all of this. No one told the real truth. Their words said one thing, while their actions spoke an entirely different truth. Edmond always took the side of Kyle and Nia, his children. It didn't matter what was going on; if they cried, he would run in and say to her or Crystal, "What did you do?"

It didn't matter that Kyle was about to stick a case knife in the electrical socket after having taken the childproof protectors out and she'd just yanked the knife out of his hand. It didn't matter that Nia had uncapped a marker and was in ready position to draw pictures on the wall just before she snatched the marker out of her hand. It didn't matter that Nia had put something in her mouth she'd just picked up off the floor and Sahara had reached inside and pulled it out before she swallowed it. Sahara was sure plenty of babies had eaten pennies and junk off the floor before anyone stopped them. But she'd done her best to at least *limit* her little sister's "junk" food consumption.

Edmond, and even her mother, always came barreling in with fixed frowns on their faces as they practically yelled, with spit flying everywhere, "What did *you* do?"

At school, as long as she was making straight As, no one paid her any attention. It was always the ones who needed extra help that got any acknowledgment that they even existed. The first C she made on her report card caused her mother to go into overtime damage-control mode. For the first time in a long time, she acknowledged Sahara was there. And it wasn't that she purposely tried to make bad grades after that . . . because of that. Then again, or maybe on some subconscious level, she did. All of a sudden, the popular boys in school began paying attention to her. She was no longer being treated like an L7 (a square), and it felt really good to belong.

The girls with power invited her into their inner circle. She was glad she was no longer alone. Then there was this party where all the special people would be. She'd asked her mother about going. Of course, if her mother didn't know the family, she wasn't going to let her attend. Her mother said, "No," which should have been the end of it. But then came along a six-foot-three hunk of a hunk named Dollar.

Dollar was every girl's dream. He still was, the way women of all ages flocked to him. At the time, Dollar was a seventeen-year-old with women twice his age chasing him. That was evident when he had one of the teachers giving him private tutoring lessons after school, in her home, no less. He let everybody know that he'd learned how to "do the laundry" a new and better way, which was no big deal for Sahara, since she occasionally did the laundry at home herself.

"No, he's beatin' dem cakes," one of the girls in her newfound group explained.

"Well, okay," Sahara said. "That's generally how you *make* a cake. We use an electric beater, but my grandmother said before electric beaters came along, they would hold the bowl and use a wooden spoon to beat their batter for their cakes."

That caused all of the girls to burst into a full-blown laugh.

"So, I suppose you don't know what 'jeepin'' is or 'making cookies'?" Gina said.

That's when it hit her how out of the loop on the latest teen language she was. All of these phrases were codes for "having sex." Words and phrases teenagers used to keep their parents and the older generation from knowing what they were talking about.

So when Dollar showed an interest in her and told her he would like to "hit it" sooner rather than later, her brains took a total leave of absence. All she knew was that someone made her feel like she was wanted. And *that* was what was missing in her life. Whenever Dollar saw her walking his way, he would shift his weight onto his back leg and, with his piercing brown eyes, scale her body from head to toe as though she were his favorite dessert coming his way. Even the way he smacked his lips, which should have been insulting, made her feel like she was special.

He wore down her logical thinking by telling her how much she was "off the chain," "off the heezy," "off the hizzle," and "off the hook." He called her "jiggy," which she learned meant he thought she was hot, attractive, and most definitely sexy. *What girl doesn't want to feel like she can command someone's attention in that way?*

Dollar convinced her to find a way to "come to the most crackalackin' party of the year." Even if it meant defying her mother. Sahara hadn't quite reached the place of defiance at that time. So she devised a plan to spend the night at one of her friends' house where they would be doing wonderful things like Bible Trivia and eating chili hot dogs.

Sahara's mother believed her; she had no reason not to. Only, Sahara didn't go to the friend's house. In fact, Sahara learned a valuable lesson from all of this: *If you're going to tell your folks you're spending the night with a friend, make* sure *you let that friend in on the plan so she doesn't call your house and ask your mother if she can speak to you, then proceed to say, "What* spend *the night? She's not over here with* me."

Needless to say, Sahara and Sheila were no longer friends. That friendship was severed . . . lost that night, as was something else that had been a treasure to her. She'd given up her pearls. And if she could go back and live that night over again, she would most assuredly not have given up something so precious. It wasn't worth it. Dollar wasn't worth it. And all those who said, and continued to say, differently, she soon learned, merely lied because they—like she now—could never go back. Not ever again. And as Ma Ray had often told her, "Misery loves company. When folks are miserable and can't change something, they want others to be miserable, too."

Those were *some* of the lessons she learned that night in losing her virginity. Still, for whatever reason, she couldn't manage to find her way out of this rabbit's hole.

Sahara pulled out her laptop that her mother let her bring, wishing she could connect to the Web and at least chat with a few friends, check e-mails, maybe play a few games online. But with Ma Ray having only dial-up connection, if you used the phone line, it wasn't even worth the effort to try. Just then, the house phone rang.

After a few minutes, Ma Ray hollered up the stairs, "Sahara, phone's for you!"

"I got it!" Sahara yelled back. She picked up the receiver of the phone while wondering who, besides her mother, could be calling her on Ma Ray's line. "Hello."

"Hi, this is Andre Woods. Were you busy?"

Sahara sat back against the headboard of her bed. "What's up?"

"If you're busy, I can call back later. Or you can call me when it's a good time for you."

"I'm fine. What do you want?" she said. She then noticed she was mindlessly twirling her index finger around the black cord attached to the Mickey Mouse telephone she was using.

Puzzled at why she'd done that, Sahara quickly yanked her finger loose and sighed loud enough that she was pretty sure he most likely heard her.

Chapter 14

And she said unto the men, I know that the Lord hath given you the land, and that your terror is fallen upon us, and that all the inhabitants of the land faint because of you.

—Joshua 2:9

"Your grandmother asked me to get you and Crystal signed up for the youth conference our church is putting on in a couple of weeks," Andre said. "But truthfully, it is abundantly clear that you're not interested in attending."

"It's like I said, I don't think we'll even be here in two weeks."

"Yeah, well, I'm calling because I didn't want to go to the trouble of setting things up and having your grandmother pay for it if you're not planning on going."

Sahara sat up straighter. "What's it to you? I mean, if you sign us up and we don't go, they can refund my grandmother's money."

"It's nonrefundable," Andre said.

"Nonrefundable? What kind of a scam is *that?*"

"Not a scam. It's what they're doing to keep people from signing up and then backing out later. When you're paying a hundred and twenty dollars to attend an event like this, you'll be sure to fulfill your commitment if you know you can't back out at the last minute. Besides, there is a lot of expense associated with this. Breakfast and lunch provided for two days. They have people they're paying to come in to give workshops and to speak. There are workbooks, other books, and things they put in the packages for each attendee. There's the purity ring that's included along with the things for the ceremony that's scheduled to take place. Oh, and there's the reception that follows the purity ceremony on Saturday evening, after the conference concludes, with a live band and everything."

"Yee-hi," Sahara said dryly.

"See. You know . . . "

"What?"

"That's okay. Just forget it."

"No, what were you going to say?"

"Sahara, you're a beautiful girl, a very beautiful girl—"

"And?"

"Not and . . . but."

"*But?*"

"Yes. You are a very beautiful girl, *but* your attitude is bugly."

"Bugly?" Sahara started laughing. "Bugly? Are you trying to be hip and trying to say fugly?"

"No. I'm trying to say just what I said: bugly."

"Still, you're trying to call my attitude ugly?"

"If the Prada fits," Andre said.

She laughed some more. "Like I even care what you think or have to say, Cletus."

"My name is not Cletus; it's Andre. Andre Woods."

"Yeah, same thing. Cletus meaning country . . . backward. You know, like living out in the woods. And Woods like . . . out in the woods. Cletus."

"Oh, I see you're just full of it."

"Oooh, look at Cletus. Trying to make your way to this century with your comebacks, huh?"

"No, I'm just keeping it 100 . . . just telling the truth."

"Wow, you must have a book that tells you all of the crisp things to say. How else would someone like you know about anything new like 'keeping it 100'?"

"You know what? I'm glad you're not coming to the youth conference."

"Who says I'm not coming? Oh, I'm coming. Me and my sister will be there. So you can do whatever you need to do to make it happen and let them know that Sahara will be in the house. A'ight. Peace out," she said, then slammed down the phone. Sahara fell facedown onto the bed. "Oh, God, what did I just do?"

"Sahara?" Ma Ray said as she tapped softly on the door.

Sahara sat up and tried to wipe the frown off her face. "Yes."

Ma Ray walked in. "Did you give Andre all the information he needed for the youth conference?"

"Ma Ray, I don't know why you want to throw away your money on that stupid conference. You know it's going to be boring. You've given enough money to our family. I don't think you ought to waste it on something lame like this."

"Lame? Honey, I don't think something that will probably turn out to bless you, be beneficial to you and your sister, and contrary to what you think right now, just might turn out to be more fun than you believe, is lame."

"Of course you don't, Ma Ray. You don't know what real life is like out there. You live in your little la-la land of church and 'Jesus making ways out of no ways.' You live in a place where all you do is pray to and praise God. You don't have a clue what's out there in the real everyday world."

"I know that Satan is still going to and fro, like a roaring lion, trying to see who he can devour. I know that was the way it was in my day, and I'm sure it's even more so today. But if you think just because I'm old now that I arrived here this old—"

"Ma Ray, I'm not a child. I know you have your problems, too. And I know you were a teenager just like Mama was a teenager, just like my daddy was a teenager, just like Edmond was a teenager 'once upon a time.' But when you were coming up, y'all could marry at thirteen and fourteen. You didn't have all the pressures we have to stay pure and keep it together. You could see someone you wanted to be with and marry them, skipping some of the temptations we have to fend off. That's what I'm talking about. Then we get put on blast—"

Ma Ray looked confused.

"Put on blast . . . called out in public," Sahara said.

"Oh," Ma Ray said with a smile.

"We get put on blast because we fall and we fail and we're

bad kids. Because we don't live up to other people's expecta-
tions or even worse: because we don't fulfill the dreams that
were someone else's foiled or aborted dreams. I don't want to
be a lawyer or a doctor. I want to be a model. But who cares
what I want? It's only *my* life."

"I care. Your mother cares. Edmond cares. Even your father
cares."

"See, that's why I keep telling y'all that none of you understand. My mother cares because that's what mothers are supposed to do to be good mothers."

"Sahara, that's not fair to your mother."

"Okay, you're right. My mother cares, she just doesn't care
enough. And Edmond will be happy when I'm out of their
house and their hair. The only reason he's afraid I won't gradu-
ate or get into a college is because that would mean I'll be stuck
at their house that much longer. And my father, oh, I don't
even want to go there. He hardly ever calls. He doesn't pay
child support, which incidentally means more to Mama than it
does to me. I know she needs the money, but I'd be happy just
knowing that I . . . that *we* were important enough to *our* father
that he wants to spend some time with us. Is that too much to
ask?"

"Well, now, your father truly is dealing with a lot of stuff.
Stuff that's definitely not your or your sister's fault."

"Yes, I know that he went to jail. Which means he now has a
record. That makes it harder for him to get a job or at least a
decent job because of his record. Mama has had him picked up
for failure to pay child support and getting behind in his pay-
ments. Then he can't work because he's in jail. He loses the
piece of a job that he had. So he can't pay child support. It's
just one vicious cycle. People who mess up are told they should
be productive in society, but then everything is stacked against
them having that opportunity. And as young people, we're supposed to understand what grown folks sure don't seem to be
able to? It's just . . . not . . . fair!" Sahara wiped her tears.

"Sahara, we're all here for you. We're here for you and for
Crystal. Granted, as adults, we're looked at to have all the an-

swers. But the truth is: we don't always. But I'll tell you what I *do* know. I know that each and every one of us is doing the best we know how. And when we mess up, we try our best to fix it. That's all we're asking of you. You're a smart young lady with so much potential . . . so much potential. But you're squandering it. And for what? Because you want to be part of some lame group."

"Lame, Ma Ray?"

"Yes, lame. A crowd of underachievers. You need to find the group that's supposed to be cool or whatever the right word is now."

Sahara began to laugh. "It's crunk."

"Crunk?"

"Yes, crunk. Or poppin'. Poppin's good."

"What about ghetto fabulous?" Ma Ray asked.

"No. Ghetto fabulous is not really good. Ghetto fabulous is people who are trying to have a rich look without the real wealth to sustain it."

"Then that sounds *exactly* like the word I'm looking for when it comes to some of the people you're stooping down to be a part of. They're trying to have a rich look in character when they really don't have the true wealth to pull it off. They're spiritually and morally bankrupted—morally ghetto fabulous."

"Ooh, good one, Ma Ray."

"Maybe you should join *my* club." Ma Ray playfully bumped Sahara.

Sahara bumped back. "What's the name of your club? The Sanctified Sisters?"

"Some might call us The Saints That Really Ain't, or better yet, The Saints That Weren't Always. Because, Sahara, despite what you see now, none of us have walked a perfect line all of our lives. I don't care what people may show you. We've all teetered or faltered on that line at some point. Everyone has a scar or two somewhere, everyone. Some scars are seen; some hidden. From the parking lot to the pulpit, everyone."

"Sure, Ma Ray. I'm pretty sure that God, long ago, forgave

you for that piece of bubble gum you stole when you were four years old."

"How did you know about that?" Ma Ray said. She started laughing. "I'm just teasing. But don't be fooled, now. All of us are human. That's no excuse, but there comes a time when, in order to save another, we have to show our own scars. Jesus was nailed to the cross, though not for sins of His own. Those were our sins on Him up on that cross."

"I know, I know, Ma Ray. It was for you and me. Please, can we not have a Bible study right now. I'm seriously *not* in the mood for a sermon."

"And I wasn't going to preach one. But what I was *trying* to say before I was so rudely interrupted is that Jesus had scars from what He went through. And Thomas, one of His hand-picked disciples, refused to believe it was really Jesus until he could see and feel the scars for himself. Jesus allowed old doubting Thomas to see and touch the scars just so we, who wouldn't be able to do so but believed just the same, might be blessed."

"Okay, Ma Ray. I get it. You can pay for me to go to that youth conference. I'll show that little *smug* Andre not to mess with me."

"I think Andre is a nice young man. You could learn a lot from him."

"You know, he's not as nice as he tries to pretend to be, right?"

"From all I know of him, he is. Has he done anything that proves otherwise?"

"No. It's just the nice acting ones are usually the ones you really need to watch out for. They put on these great acts in front of folks, but behind closed doors, they're nothing like what they let the world see."

"Well, I don't get that from either of the twins. I think Ms. Tootsie has done and *is* doing a fine job with them. Now, about what happened with that Bradley fellow. Do you realize the danger you put everybody in this house in?"

Sahara pressed her back against the headboard of the bed and laid her head back. "I didn't, until I saw you with that shotgun." She looked square at Ma Ray. "That was going a little overboard, don't you think?"

"Sahara, I heard someone breaking in my house. You and Crystal are the most valuable things in this house right now. If I feel you're in danger, I'm going to do whatever I need to protect you. That's just a fact."

"Well, I don't see what the big deal was about him being here."

"There is no big deal about him being here. If you want to invite your friends over, do it the right way. Tell them to come at a decent hour and preferably to ring the front doorbell. I don't have a problem with that. But *you,* trying to sneak some guy in, or *you,* trying to sneak out of the house in the dead of night, is *not* acceptable. It's just not. If you want to go out, tell the guy to pick you up at the front door. And I want to look in his eyes before you leave here with him. That's all I'm saying. I'm not trying to treat you like a baby. But there are lots of wolves in sheep's clothing roaming around out there. And you young folks need all the help you can get navigating around them."

Sahara leaned over, picked up a speck from the pink chenille bedspread, and dropped the white speck onto the floor. "But B-Man is not a bad guy."

"Then why would he disrespect you by sneaking up in here at two o'clock in the morning?" Ma Ray asked. "Huh?"

"That was partly my fault. He wanted to see me. I didn't feel like going through drama with you, so I told him to come over after midnight. I figured you would be asleep by then. I'd planned on meeting him outside. But he lost his signal on his cell phone."

"But he was in the house on his way up the stairs," Ma Ray said.

"Yeah, now that was sort of bad on his part. I'd told him which room I stayed in. I suppose when he made it to the house, he found a way in and was coming to my room."

Ma Ray tilted her head. "He *found* a way in? *Found* a way in?

Sahara, I hope you don't really believe I'm accepting, as truth, all of this bologna you're trying to feed me."

"Okay, I *may* have left a door unlocked. But you leave doors and windows open for fresh air all the time. I told him which room I stayed in. But I thought he'd have been here before two. That's the truth, Ma Ray. I had no intentions of him coming here at two in the morning. He just wanted to see me. And frankly, I didn't see any harm in it."

"As I've said, your friends are welcome to come visit. As long as it's a decent hour when they arrive, and as long as they are respectful enough to come through my front door *when* a responsible adult is here." Ma Ray smiled as she looked at Sahara. "Do we have an understanding?"

"Sure. Yeah. No problem. Your house, your rules."

"Honey, no one has rules to hurt you. Rules are there to protect you. I know you want to have fun, but with everything in life, there are consequences. Sometimes, what may have seemed like fun can turn into tragedy in a heartbeat. Folks who love you like me, your mother, Edmond, even your father . . . we all want the best for you. And if you ever want to talk about anything, and I do mean anything, I'm here for you. Okay?"

Sahara smiled. "Sure. Sure, Ma Ray." And just as quickly, her smile faded.

Chapter 15

For we have heard how the Lord dried up the water
of the Red Sea for you, when ye came out of Egypt;
and what ye did unto the two kings of the Amorites,
that were on the other side Jordan, Sihon and Og,
whom ye utterly destroyed.

—Joshua 2:10

Ma Ray looked again in her jewelry box. The diamond watch she wore to church every Sunday was not there. She knew she'd put it in there when she came home from church last Sunday. It was a ritual she did without thinking about it. She would get home from church, take off the watch, put it in the jewelry box, then deal with changing into more comfortable clothes. It was that way every single time. So there's no way she could have misplaced it.

The watch was more than valuable from a monetary standpoint. It had sentimental value. Her beloved husband, Sal, had given it to her on their thirtieth wedding anniversary. She'd thought it was a bit extravagant; he'd said she was worth it and so much more. Sal had been a policeman, an undercover detective. That's how she'd met him, though nothing like people may have thought. Later, he became a preacher. And she played the piano for the small church he was called to pastor. They'd bought this house to be closer to the church and to get away from the hustle and bustle of the city life. For a few years, he even tried his hand at farming, though that just as quickly went by the wayside.

Ma Ray had loved every minute of being married to Sal. Because of him, her whole life had changed. He was the one who brought her to the Lord. After years of being told she would never be able to conceive, she found out she was indeed blessed to be pregnant—a miracle. Beau Azra Towers (Boaz for short, named after Sal's longtime partner killed in the line of duty) was born, and two years later, Lenora Tracey Towers— proving just how much God really can do the impossible. Like the way God dried up a roadway for the children of Israel to cross the Red Sea without them getting stuck in the muck, when Pharaoh's army was about to overtake them. That's how God is.

That's what Ma Ray loved about the Lord. Not only could you read about the history of what God has done for others, but there was your own history of what God has done for you to lean on for encouragement. A person could do as David did when he was about to fight Goliath, who he called an uncir-cumcised Philistine—a giant that had the nerve to defy the armies of the living God. When King Saul told David, a youth, he wasn't able to fight against Goliath—"a man of war from his youth"—David recalled his history while keeping his father's sheep. How there'd come a lion and a bear that took a lamb out of the flock, and how he'd defeated them. *What was this giant to God?*

Ma Ray had a history. Not many knew of her *true* history, but she knew. She knew what and where God had brought her from. And if she found that she would need to show her scars to save her granddaughters, then that's what she would do. But for now, she was doing whatever she could to reach them, whatever tools at her disposal.

Sahara walked into Ma Ray's bedroom. Ma Ray snapped out of her thoughts and looked up. "You need to put on the skirt to that top, and hurry up. It's time for us to leave for church."

"What skirt?" Sahara asked, glancing down at herself.

"The skirt that I'm sure goes with that shirt you have on."

"Ma Ray, this is a dress." Sahara looked down again. "This is it. All of it."

"Oh, no, it's not. You're not going out of this house with just *that* on. Does your mother know you have *that?*"

"Know? She was the one who bought it for me."

"She must not have looked at it good when she bought it. Or maybe she thought it was a shirt. Whatever, I can tell you that you're not going out of this house with just *that* on." Ma Ray made a vertical gesture with a slightly crooked index finger. "And you're *especially* not going to the church house wearing *that.*"

"This is the style, Ma Ray. This is what people are wearing. You need to get with the times."

"Oh, I'm with the times, all right. And it's time you make your way back up to your room and find something to add under that, with it, or find something else that covers more than what that *thing* is covering now."

Sahara let out a loud sigh. "Ma Ray—"

"Sahara," Ma Ray said, mimicking back the same tone. "Listen, if you walk up in our church house with that on, Sister Thomas will *personally* grab you, time you step through the door, and carry you straight to the altar. Then she will proceed to get some oil and start praying the lust demons out of you—"

"Okay . . . all right. I'll change. I don't want any drama today."

Ma Ray closed the drawer of the jewelry box. "Sahara, you wouldn't by chance have seen my watch, have you?"

"You mean the diamond watch you wear on Sundays?"

"Yeah. That one."

"No, ma'am. I haven't. Did you lose it or something?"

"No. I'm pretty certain that I put it in here." Ma Ray nodded toward the jewelry box. She turned back to Sahara and forced a smile. "Hurry up now and change. I hate being late for church, even if they *don't* ever start on time."

The church building was modestly full. Reverend Pettaway preached a blistering sermon about the three Hebrew boys in the fiery furnace. Ma Ray concluded that was one of his favorite passages to preach from since he preached it at least once a year, most times during the scorching summertime.

When collection time came, Ma Ray opened her wallet. There were only five one-dollar bills and a five-dollar bill in there. She looked in other compartments of the wallet and then inside various parts of her purse. She'd had one hundred dollars on Saturday. She'd given the twins ten dollars each for them bringing the fruits and vegetables in the house since she'd already paid for them prior to them being picked up. Ma Ray was meticulous about where she kept her money. She kept her bills in one place, her change in her change purse. One place— never anywhere else. It was evident: someone had been in her purse and stolen the other seventy dollars. She gave Sahara and Crystal both two dollars each to put in the collection plate. She took out the other five and placed it in the plate for herself. Ma Ray began to rock her body slightly as she silently prayed.

After service, Crystal came over to Ma Ray. "Ma Ray, can Sahara and I have fifty cents to buy a drink from Old Man Miller? We left our money at home."

Where other churches may have had vending machines, Old Man Miller sold off-brand sodas out of a cooler he kept in the trunk of his car. That was the highlight for the members, especially the children, when church dismissed: to buy a drink from Old Man Miller. He'd buy the drinks for about twenty cents and sell them for fifty. No one minded paying that, since it was convenient having him there, particularly during the heated summertime.

Ma Ray pulled out her last dollar bill and handed it to Crystal. "Oh, and Crystal, it's Mister Miller for us; we call him Mister Miller."

"Well, I was just calling him what all the others call him," Crystal said.

Ma Ray smiled. "I know, sweetheart. But we're different. *Mister* Miller."

"Would you like one, Ma Ray?" Crystal asked.

Ma Ray smiled. "No, dear. But thank you for asking."

Crystal smiled, then hurried away.

Ma Ray closed her purse and patted the outside of it a few times. She then said yet another prayer.

Chapter 16

And as soon as we had heard these things, our hearts did melt, neither did there remain any more courage in any man, because of you: for the Lord your God, he is God in heaven above, and in earth beneath.

—Joshua 2:11

When Ma Ray got home from church, she looked to see what else might be missing that she hadn't noticed before. The one-carat, diamond, heart-shaped necklace Boaz had given her was not there. But other than those things, she didn't notice anything else.

Ma Ray generally cooked on Saturday nights for Sunday, but with all of the traffic in and out, she didn't get a chance to fix anything but a pot of purple hull peas. Having fresh vegetables in the back waiting to be put up helped a bit with a few more things she could prepare. The girls liked salads, and it would be especially good since the tomatoes and cucumbers were so fresh. Creamed corn was another one of her specialties. And instead of a peach cobbler, she decided she could make peach turnovers.

Before she could even get started, there was a knock on her front door. Tootsie stood with her grandsons. Tootsie rarely ever rang Ma Ray's doorbell when she visited.

"Tootsie, what are you doing here?" Ma Ray said as she opened the front door.

"I thought you'd likely not have cooked like you normally do. So I decided to do the neighborly thing and bring you some of what I fixed. Besides, it's no fun eating a fabulous meal without some fabulous company. It's been a while since we've broken bread together, and I'm sure our grandchildren will enjoy each other's company. So here I am."

"Also, I brought your package for the youth conference," Andre said as he walked in with the big box of prepared food. "I was going to bring it over today since the deadline to turn things in is Wednesday."

"I'm sure that's heavy. You can take it on back to the kitchen," Ma Ray said.

"That's nothing for that boy," Tootsie said, handing Ma Ray the large envelope with the youth conference information inside. "We'll need to heat up everything, since I fixed it all last night. I was about to put things in and on the stove when it dawned on me that it would be fun just to come here and make it a day."

"Well, the Lord is good, because I sure didn't cook last night like I normally would," Ma Ray said, taking the envelope. "I was just about to make a fresh salad and fix some other stuff. I *did* cook a pot of purple hull peas last night, but that was only because I blanched and put up those purple hull peas we shelled yesterday."

"The chicken needs frying," Tootsie said. "I cut it up, seasoned it, and let it marinate overnight like I generally do. I don't care much for reheated fried chicken. I like mine dripping hot, fresh out of the grease. It's just not the same when it's reheated. I thought about baking it, but you know kids prefer their food fried to baked."

"Tell me about it," Ma Ray said. "Well, you know I have plenty of grease. So, we'll just heat the grease up and get things to popping. I sure do appreciate you for thinking about us like this. You're a true friend, Tootsie. A true friend to the end. You really are."

"Just giving back to one who has given so much . . . to so many. You know you've been there for me. Don't *even* get me started."

"Excuse me, Ma Ray," Aaron said, "but is Crystal around?"

Ma Ray smiled. "Of course. They're both upstairs changing out of their church clothes. She and Sahara will be down shortly. If you like, you can holler upstairs to let her know you're down here. Then you and Andre are welcome to go in the den and watch television while me and your grandmother finish up Sunday's dinner."

"It won't be long until we eat," Tootsie said. "Isn't there some game or something y'all want to watch on TV?"

"Yes, ma'am. I'm sure there's *something* on television. Although the pickings get slim during the summertime," Aaron said.

Ma Ray pointed. "The den's in there. I'll let Crystal know you're here."

In a few minutes, Andre came out of the kitchen. "Where's Aaron?"

"In the den, finding something to watch on TV," Tootsie said, pointing toward the den.

"First, how much do I owe for the youth conference?" Ma Ray asked Andre.

"It's two hundred and twenty dollars. It's actually a hundred and twenty dollars each, but they give a discount when multiple people in the same family sign up."

"I told them that price is a bit steep for some folks," Tootsie said. "But I believe it's worth it. Some folks spend *that* amount to lay away a pair of Jordan shoes."

"I'll give you a check before you leave," Ma Ray said. Andre headed to the den.

Ma Ray and Tootsie went to the kitchen to finish up. Ma Ray turned on the deep fryer and filled it with shortening. Tootsie pulled out a nice pot of turnip greens, candied yams, creamed corn, and a huge pan of her legendary ooey gooey macaroni and cheese from the box Andre had placed on the counter.

"How was church service today?" Tootsie asked Ma Ray as she set the pots on the stove and turned on the corresponding eyes.

"It was okay. You know my pastor is from the old school. Not like your little young pastor. We get the pretty predictable sermons, but our pastor is consistent." Ma Ray watched the shortening melt.

"Okay, Ray." Tootsie stepped up to her. "What's on your mind?"

"What makes you think something is on my mind?"

"Because you're not your usual self. Your body's here, but your mind is working someplace else. Is it your granddaughters?"

"No. Not really. Well, I'm not sure," Ma Ray said. Ma Ray was trying to decide whether she wanted to share any of her present thoughts or situation at this juncture.

"Come on, Ray. Since when have you and I kept anything back from the other when we were truly troubled? I spill my guts to you all the time. So, tell me what's tumbling around inside of your head right now."

"There are a few things in my house that have all of a sudden grown legs and walked off. They've gone missing," Ma Ray said.

"Missing? Like what?"

"Like my diamond watch and diamond necklace. And when I went to church, I found all but ten of what should have been eighty dollars gone from my purse. And that's just what I've been able to figure out. The Lord only knows what else is missing."

"So, what are you thinking?"

"I don't know. And truthfully, I don't think I really want to *think* right now, because I don't like where my thoughts may be leading me."

"You think it's one of your grands?"

"I don't want to think that. Those are my babies. Sure, they're my daughter's children, but they're mine, you know."

"I know. I felt the same way when it came to my own daughter. I tried to turn a blind eye to what was going on around me. And my child was literally stealing me blind trying to finance her drug habit. First you think you just may have misplaced it or been mistaken about how much you had. Then you think maybe you hid it and just forgot where you hid it. That if you keep looking and thinking hard enough, you'll eventually find it. But then, you run out of excuses and you have to face some hard truths. Truths that will have family turning on you like you were the one who did the wrong."

Ma Ray took the bowl of floured, ready-to-fry chicken pieces and placed them into the rolling, hot oil. The sound of frying immediately began to overtake the room.

"So do I accuse them without having real proof and see if the one responsible will step forward and confess? And what if it wasn't one of them? I could ruin any chance of helping them by alienating them forever, especially if neither of them is responsible."

"Let's see. Was there anyone else who could have done it during the time frame you're looking at?" Tootsie asked.

"The missing money had to have happened Saturday after the noon hour, since it was there, for sure, Saturday when I gave Andre and Aaron ten dollars each for bringing my fruits and vegetables in the house."

"Well, I know me and my grandsons were here during that time. But I believe the only time they went inside of your house was to take in your vegetables and stuff."

"And Sahara walked them back there and they came straight back out and stayed out here the rest of the time they were here," Ma Ray said. "Tootsie, I sincerely hope you're not thinking that I'm trying to accuse your grandsons."

"In this day and time, none of us can be excused. Everybody is a suspect, including *me*. I had a friend a few years back who would call me to take her to the store. Her physical mobility was limited. This one time I got out of the car to help her take in her bags. I left her in the car so she could take her time getting out. When I got back in my car, I noticed coins all over the car floor, but I didn't think much about it. I'd left my purse when I'd gotten out. Would you believe when I got home I learned she'd stolen my cash right out of my purse? Like I wouldn't figure out it was her."

"You're kidding," Ma Ray said, chuckling a little.

"No, I'm *not* kidding. I never took her anywhere else ever again. And you can believe *that*. Christian or no, that was the last time I gave her a ride anywhere."

"Well, I need to pray about what to do next," Ma Ray said. "The Lord knows I want to help these children. I know it couldn't have been that boy that broke in here early Saturday morning, because he didn't get any farther than the steps. I just don't know."

"Hi, Ms. Tootsie," Crystal said as she walked quickly into the kitchen.

"Hi, Crystal."

"Ma Ray, may I get us all something to drink?" Crystal asked.

"Sure. And because Ms. Tootsie was so generous in thinking of us, dinner will be ready shortly."

"Oh, I'm not really all that hungry. We don't ever eat at home on Sundays until around five," Crystal said as she opened the refrigerator door.

"Five?" Tootsie said. "O'clock? On a Sunday?"

"Yes, ma'am. Mama generally doesn't cook until we get home from church. And our church service can last until almost one-thirty on Sundays. Mama likes to go out to eat, but that doesn't always work so well when you have six mouths to feed. So, by the time she's finished cooking, it's about five o'clock."

"Well, do you and your sister help her cook?" Tootsie asked.

"Help? Her cook?" Crystal said.

"Yeah. Help your mother cook and clean the house for that matter," Tootsie said.

"Not if we can help it," Crystal said with a laugh. She took out three cans of sodas and closed the refrigerator door.

"Well, you *should* help," Ma Ray said. She looked down at the cans. "Three? Where's Sahara?"

"Upstairs . . . looking at solitaire on her laptop wishing that you had a high-speed connection so she could at least surf the Internet instead of slow dripping it."

"Well, tell her we have company, and she needs to come down here," Ma Ray said.

"I already told her," Crystal said.

"Then tell her again. And this time tell her that *I* said it," Ma Ray said.

Crystal smiled and nodded. "Okay"—she sang the word—"I'll tell her." She then sashayed out of the kitchen with an overly exaggerated switch in her hips.

Chapter 17

Now therefore, I pray you, swear unto me by the Lord, since I have showed you kindness, that ye will also show kindness unto my father's house, and give me a true token.

—Joshua 2:12

Sahara came downstairs.

"Hi, Sahara," Andre said, standing when she entered the den.

Sahara threw up a nonchalant wave and flopped down in an overstuffed chair. Aaron and Crystal were talking and didn't bother to look up or say anything to her.

"How was church today?" Andre asked.

"Church was church: boring as always."

"Not where we go. We always have a wonderful time," Andre said.

"Yeah, I bet you do. I bet you get a *kick* out of watching ice melt, too."

"Excuse me?" Andre said, pulling his head back a tad.

"Why are you here?" Sahara said with a deliberate smirk.

Andre forced a smile. "Maybe because *my* grandmother and *your* grandmother are such great friends. Or maybe because of something I've been asked to do by your grandmother. Or just maybe . . . maybe it's because I absolutely *adore* your company."

Sahara squinted at him, then got up and snatched the remote control off the coffee table. She started changing the channels.

"Hey, we were watching that," Crystal said.

"Yeah," Aaron said. "We were watching that."

"Didn't look like you were watching anything but each other to me," Sahara said to Crystal and Aaron as she kept clicking to another station.

"Turn it back!" Crystal yelled. "You're being rude, Sahara. Aaron and Andre are company, and they wanted to watch that. You can't just come into a room and change the channel without asking if it's okay. Mama has told you about that."

"Why should I ask if it's okay?" Sahara continued scanning through the channels. "I was doing fine upstairs in my room until I was *told* to come down here. If I have to be down here, then I have just as much right to watch what I want as any of you. And I don't want to watch what was on. I'm tired of the male-ego world where we women have to be ladylike and let the men have control over everything, including the remote."

"I'm telling Ma Ray. Just because you're mad at her for making you come down here doesn't mean you have to be evil to us." Crystal got up and left the room.

"Frankly, I don't care if you change the channel. I don't care about television all that much, anyway. I have better things to do with my mind," Andre said with a fake smile.

"Yeah, I bet you're a real brainiac. A knockoff Einstein or something. I'm not at all surprised that we *peons* down here bore you," Sahara said.

"Why do you do that?" Andre said.

"Do what?"

"Why do you put yourself down like that? Do you have any idea how special you really are?"

"Oh, I'm *quite* aware of how special I am. That's why so many want to get with this." She used her hand to showcase her own body the way models showcase things on programs such as *The Price Is Right.*

"I wasn't talking about special *that* way. And the ones you're bragging about who want to get with you don't care about the true you. All they care about is what they can get from you," Andre said.

"Like you don't," Sahara said with a slight chuckle just to further antagonize him.

"Oh, believe me, I have high standards. I'm not interested in bargain basement deals. God created you fearfully and wonderfully, and you're cheapening and marking yourself down."

"You don't know anything about me," Sahara said.

"I know—"

"Dinner's ready," Ma Ray said as she walked into the den. "Y'all go on in and wash up. We're eating in the dining room. Sahara, escort our guests to the washroom."

"It's that way," Sahara said, pointing in the direction of the half bathroom near the den.

"Sahara, please *take* them and *show* them as I just asked you to do," Ma Ray said sternly.

Sahara blew out a defiant sigh as she clicked off the television and gently threw the remote control on the coffee table. She stood up. "Come on," she said to Aaron and Andre, as she walked painfully slow most of the short way.

Chapter 18

And that ye will save alive my father, and my mother, and my brethren, and my sisters, and all that they have, and deliver our lives from death.

—Joshua 2:13

"**W**hy don't you kids go to the movies or something?" Tootsie said. Ma Ray looked like she was completely caught off guard by that.

"I was just about to ask if we could do that," Aaron said.

"I don't think that's a good idea," Ma Ray said, looking at Sahara. "At least, not today."

"Why not?" Tootsie said, looking at Ma Ray.

"Because I don't *want* to go to the movies," Sahara said, looking at Tootsie. She knew better than to *totally* embarrass her grandmother by saying what she really wanted to say, which was she didn't want to go to the movies with *these two*.

"Well, I have some extra cash. It would be my treat," Tootsie said.

"It's not the money," Sahara said. "I have my own cash. I'm quite capable of paying my own way."

"She wasn't saying that we weren't," Ma Ray said to Sahara with a tone that spoke to her *own* tone.

"May we go outside?" Sahara said to Ma Ray, forcing a fake smile.

"Sure. I don't keep you in here," Ma Ray said.

Sahara jumped up. "Come on, y'all. Let's go outside." She headed out the back way instead of toward the front. Crystal,

Aaron, and Andre followed, though Sahara was walking faster than all of them.

"What's up with you?" Crystal said as soon as they walked down the back porch steps and were completely out of earshot.

Sahara was still walking briskly. She didn't stop to answer her sister.

"Sahara!" Crystal grabbed her sister by the arm and spun her around. "We could have gone to the movies and you had to ruin it. You ruined it for all of us."

"I didn't ruin anything," Sahara said.

"Yeah, you did. Because you know there's no way Ma Ray is going to let me go to the movies with Aaron by myself. Not until I turn sixteen. If you don't go, I can't go. And you know that. All you had to do was go along. Why can't you think about anybody other than yourself?"

"Who said I even wanted to go with her?" Andre said, chiming in.

"You see, both of y'all are selfish," Aaron said. "I wanted to go to the movies with Crystal. This could have been fun. It doesn't mean it's a date. But we could have been doing something other than sitting around this place doing pretty much nothing."

"Go in there and tell Ma Ray that you want to date, Crystal, and see where that gets you. Maybe she'll let you go with Aaron without me," Sahara said. "But there's no way I want to go *any-where* with *somebody* who thinks he's too *good* for me."

"Who said I thought I was too good for you?" Andre asked.

"When we were in the den, you said it. Not that I really care," Sahara said.

"What I said was that you ought to think better about the value of yourself. I was trying to tell you how awesome God made you. That's where I was going. What I said is: you are cheapening and marking yourself down."

"You don't know anything about me," Sahara said, stepping up to his face. "You're just like most Christians. You like judging other folks. I suppose it makes you feel all warm and fuzzy inside, comparing yourself to others who don't quite measure up in your sight. Well, Mister Choir Boy, maybe you don't measure up in *my* sight. Maybe while you're busy looking at how deficient I am, you need to take inventory of your own self and your own sad, pathetic life. Maybe you should work on saving your own self, instead of worrying so much about me!"

Sahara turned and marched down toward the natural area and the stream.

Chapter 19

Then she let them down by a cord through the win-
dow: for her house was upon the town wall, and she
dwelt upon the wall.

— Joshua 2:15

Sahara walked past a huge oak tree. It reminded her of an old man with bent knotty elbows, knobby knees, and thin arthritic fingers that seemed to stretch and point toward the indigo sky as it played around . . . sporting one of Ma Ray's straw hats (the ones with the green plants sprouting out of their tops). Lavender blooms were all around hanging down, looking like bunches of grapes. She walked past the natural area, past the clearing, to the edge of the bank. She grabbed a vine that hung from a tree and held it as she scaled halfway down the steep bank where a stream lazily flowed below. Sahara sat down on the ground and hugged her knees.

"Hey." She heard a voice from someone standing at the top of the bank behind her.

She turned around to look. "Go away," she said, then turned back around.

"I'm sorry," Andre said. "I'm sorry, okay?"

"Why don't you just leave me alone? I'm not bothering you."

"I'm not trying to bother you. How did you manage to get down there so quickly and easily, anyway?"

She looked back to make sure he saw her when she rolled her eyes at him.

"Come on. Quit being difficult," Andre said, trying to strategically place his feet in places safely so he could get where she was without sliding, falling, or rolling down.

"That cord right there," she said, pointing at the vine.

"You mean this *vine?*"

"See, that's why I don't care to be bothered with you. Cord . . . vine . . . whatever."

He grabbed the vine and slowly walked down. "You're right. I can be too smart for my own good sometimes." He stood above her. "This is nice," he said, looking around.

"Yeah. I've always loved it here."

"You like nature?"

"Nope. I just like the way I feel when I'm out here. It's . . . peaceful . . . serene."

"Yeah. I have a place sort of like this over at my grand-mother's. There's no water near it like this, but it's peaceful. It's a place where I can go out and feel like it's just me and the Lord, spending time together."

Sahara bent her head back. "Please don't start with church stuff again. I *really* don't want to hear it."

"I'm not talking church stuff. I'm talking about a relation-ship with God. Have you ever thought about that, Sahara? I mean *really* thought about what that means?" Andre sat down beside her.

Sahara picked up a twig off the ground and started breaking it up into little bitty pieces and chunking it. "Not really."

Andre glanced over her way. "Think about it. There's this big powerful God, right? He's so huge that He starts speaking words, and the next thing you know . . . the things He's speak-ing start showing up for real. The heavens and the earth. And when I say heavens, I mean it with an *s*. There are galaxies be-yond galaxies, farther than man will ever be able to see. And God did it all. And to think, He created us."

Sahara looked over at him.

Andre smiled at her. "We were so important to God that He made you and me. Look at your hand." He held out his own hand and began to look at it. "Look at the details of every sin-gle part of it." He reached over and took her hand. Sahara pulled back. "I'm not going to do anything to you." He took her hand again and held it, palm up, next to his. "See. Look at how alike, yet different, our hands are."

Sahara looked at her hand. "I know. No two fingerprints are alike," she said.

"Wow, check you out," Andre said, his hand still lightly touching hers.

"I'm a lot smarter than I pretend to be sometimes," she said.

"I know. I know pretty much what you're going through." He nodded at her.

Sahara snatched her hand away from his. "What do you want? Why do you keep following me?"

"Because I think you're special. But I guess even more to the point, because *God* thinks you're special."

Sahara laughed. "Oh, I get it. You're God's gift to women, and so you're letting me know that *I'm* special because you're giving me the time of day. Well, isn't *that* special?!"

Andre leaned back a little. "No. Not where I was going at all. God thinks you're special because He made you. For Him, just Him creating you is enough to make you special. He fashioned and designed you. God just doesn't want you to continue to sell yourself short. So, regardless of how much I *don't* want to be bothered with someone who obviously doesn't want to be bothered with me, it's not about me. God created you for a purpose. And you need to know and to understand that."

Sahara looked up at the sun playing peekaboo through the wooded trees. And for just a second, she felt as though God were pecking her softly all over her face with sun kisses while playing a special song just for her, using the trickling, calming sounds of the stream.

Chapter 20

And she said unto them, Get you to the mountain, lest the pursuers meet you; and hide yourselves there three days, until the pursuers be returned: and afterward may ye go your way.

—Joshua 2:16

"Are you planning on staying out here long?" Andre asked as he got to his feet, grabbing the vine to help him stay up.

"Don't worry about me," Sahara said. "I know my way back to the house."

"Yes, I'm sure you do. I just don't like the idea of you being out here, this far away from your grandmother's house, by yourself," Andre said. "Why don't you come on back with me?"

"I'm fine, thank you. I'll be along shortly."

"Sahara—"

"Listen, Andre. I enjoyed the short talk and all, but don't go getting this twisted. You're not my type at all. Okay?"

"I never said I was. I happen to have someone I'm talking to already."

"Then why are you here bothering me instead of trying to figure out how to be there with her?"

"Look, all I was going to say to you is to be careful. That's it."

She smiled at him. "Well, I've done just fine taking care of myself all these years without your help. I believe I'll be just fine when you leave me alone."

Andre pulled himself back up to the top of the bank, using the vine, and left Sahara. She picked up a pebble and threw it at the stream. She loved hearing the *plop* or *blip* when the rock hit the water. She picked up a few more pebbles and repeated the exercise.

"Hey," a male voice said.

Startled, she turned quickly, looked up, then just as quickly turned back around.

"So, you're not going to respond?"

"Junebug, are you spying on me?"

He laughed. "Don't flatter yourself."

"Then if you're not spying on me, why is it you seem to show up here whenever I come down here?"

He started down and immediately began to slide. "Whoa!" he yelled as he fell, grabbing Sahara to break his fall, then held on to her.

She shrugged him off of her. "Should have used the cord," she said with a smirk.

"What cord?" Junebug asked, dusting his hands off.

She pointed. "*That* vine."

He merely gazed at her. "I declare: you look more beautiful each time I see you."

"Is that right?"

"Yeah, that's right. And I know beautiful when I see it. You really should be gracing magazine covers or something."

Sahara blushed. "That's what I want to be—a model."

"Well, you've got the goods," he said, looking at her as though she were a mouthwatering dish being served on a platter. "That's the real deal. Maybe I can hook you up with the right folks and see if we can't make that happen."

She twisted her mouth. "Like you really can do that."

"Don't underestimate my reach. Just because I'm from the country doesn't mean my reach is limited to this place alone. In fact, I have some contacts in California. I'll put some feelers out there and see what comes back attached."

"You'd do that for *me?*"

He scaled her body with his eyes. "Absolutely. But the question is: what are you willing to do for *me?*"

She grunted, then laughed. "Do for *you?*"

"Yeah." He leaned down to kiss her.

Sahara turned away. "I've not gotten anything yet. So, I guess that means I don't owe you anything until *after* you've delivered something."

"Ooh, check you out. Quite the businesswoman. I can see you're going to be a tough negotiator. Look out, world: Sahara is coming!" He tried to kiss her again.

She shoved him away, this time harder. "Stop," she said.

"Stop?" Junebug grinned. "You don't really want me to stop, now, *do* you?"

"If I say stop, then that means I really want you to stop. I don't play games."

He laughed. "Yeah, right. You women love to play games. You love to tease, to egg us on. But I'm not mad at 'cha. I like a good game myself." He pulled her in to him.

Sahara struggled and pulled herself out of his grasp. She stood up, grabbed the vine, and started back up the bank.

"Hey! Where you going?"

"Back to the house," Sahara said.

He scrambled to stand up. "Don't leave me." He hurriedly grabbed her.

"Let go," she said. "Get off of me. You're going to make me break the vine."

He just held on that much tighter.

"Let go of me!" Sahara said as she tried to walk back up the bank using the vine with him groping her as he continued to hold on to her.

"Let her go!" Andre said from the top of the bank.

Junebug looked up. "What? Mind your own business."

"That's exactly what I'm doing," Andre said. "So let her go like she asked you to."

"Look, youngblood. There's nothing to see here. She and I have this under control. I'm just trying to get from down here just like she's trying to."

"Then be a man and let the lady go first." Andre stretched his hand out to Sahara.

Sahara yanked her body out of Junebug's grip. She walked

back up the bank, taking Andre's hand when she was close to the top.

"Now, throw the vine back down here," Junebug said, his hand stretched toward her.

Sahara slung the vine back at him and stomped off.

Andre trotted past the tall weeds, trying to catch up with her. "Hey. Wait up."

Sahara glanced over her shoulder, then back around, refusing to even slow down her stride.

Chapter 21

And the men said unto her, We will be blameless of
this thine oath which thou hast made us swear.

—Joshua 2:17

Ma Ray was in the kitchen gathering the leftovers together for Tootsie to take home. She just happened to be looking out of the kitchen window to the backyard and saw Sahara jogging as she got closer to the house. Andre was taking long strides as though he was trying to hurry and catch up with her. Crystal and Aaron had come inside a few minutes earlier and were out on the front porch swing. Sahara flung open the door, then saw Ma Ray and Tootsie.

"What's wrong?" Ma Ray asked.

"Nothing," Sahara said, and continued past her without breaking her stride.

Andre tapped on the door. "Come on," Ma Ray said.

"Which way did Sahara go?" Andre asked.

"What's going on with her?" Ma Ray asked him.

Andre twisted his bottom lip a little. "I don't know. I really don't."

"Did you two have an argument or something?" Tootsie asked.

"No, ma'am." He released a sigh. "I promise, Grandma . . . Ma Ray, I would never do anything to hurt her. Not on purpose." He looked at his grandmother. "Are you ready to go?"

"Yes. In fact, we just finished putting some of the leftovers in the box for you boys to carry out to the car. I was just about to call for you," Tootsie said.

"Fine. I'll take it out for you," Andre said.

"Are you sure everything is okay?" Ma Ray asked.

"Yes," he said.

"I hope you know my granddaughter doesn't *mean* to do things to offend. I know you're trying to be nice to her, but she's been having a difficult time of things of late," Ma Ray said.

"It's okay. I'm used to it." Andre picked up the box. "But never let it be said that I didn't try." He walked out of the kitchen with the box.

"Hold up. I'll get the front door for you," Ma Ray said, trying to rush ahead of him. She opened the front door. That also gave her a chance to check on Crystal and Aaron. They were playing the game where they would count to three as they said, "Rock . . . paper . . . scissors," then freeze with their fingers and hands in some position. She hadn't seen anybody play that game in a long time.

Crystal sat up straight when she looked over and saw Ma Ray standing there.

"It's time to go?" Aaron asked, disappointment lacing his words.

"Yep," Tootsie said, coming up from behind Ma Ray. "It's time to go."

"But you're welcome to come and visit again," Ma Ray said to Aaron. "Just as long as I'm here when you come."

Aaron began to smile. "Thanks." He stood up. Crystal stood up as well. They walked slowly toward the steps. "I'll call you," Aaron said.

Crystal smiled. "I hope you're not just saying that and then you chicken out."

"I promise. I'll call you." He grinned, then squeezed her hand.

Chapter 22

Behold, when we come into the land, thou shalt bind this line of scarlet thread in the window which thou didst let us down by: and thou shalt bring thy father, and thy mother, and thy brethren, and all thy father's household, home unto thee.

—Joshua 2:18

Aaron called Crystal just like he'd said he would. They'd talked for about an hour, mostly about life and what they both wanted out of it. Crystal told Sahara she felt comfortable talking to Aaron. He came over to see Crystal on Tuesday. Crystal had told Sahara how much she *really* liked Aaron. Sahara told her she wasn't impressed. So when Aaron showed up on the porch around six that evening with flowers for Crystal that he'd picked from his grandmother's garden, Sahara couldn't take it anymore.

"I'm going outside," Sahara said to Ma Ray as she passed through the kitchen, out through the back door.

Sahara knew Ma Ray wanted to protest, but she didn't slow down enough for her to get started. Ma Ray had been trying to talk to Sahara since Sunday night when things had quieted down. Sahara didn't want to talk. All she wanted was to get back to her real life and hook up with the people she liked hanging out with. Upon Ma Ray's insistence, she'd met the pastor's seventeen-year-old daughter at church on Sunday. Ma Ray thought it might help Sahara to make a friend there around her age.

Sahara's first thought was that she definitely didn't want to be friends with a preacher's kid. *You never knew what you'd get with one of them.* They were either the most boringly religious folks you ever want to meet or the chief priests among the sinners. Either way, she wasn't trying to be friends or get to know anyone here.

She walked to her special spot . . . past the tree she knew so well, past wildflowers and the tall weeds. Grabbing the vine, she scaled down the bank. Instead of sitting in her normal spot, this time she went even farther down. She really wanted to be as close to the stream as she could get and still be able to climb back up the embankment.

"Hey, where you going?"

Sahara stopped and looked up. "Junebug, *what* are you doing here?"

"Looking for you," he said. "I got something for you."

"What?"

"Come back up some more and I'll show you," he said.

Sahara looked down at the beckoning stream, then back at Junebug.

"Come on." He smiled, then nodded. "Come on."

Sahara pulled herself back closer to the top. He came down and met her. "What do you have for me?" Sahara asked.

They sat on the ground together. He pulled out a flask of liquor. She shook her head. "Ma Ray would smell that on my breath before I even stepped up on her back porch good," Sahara said.

He unscrewed the top, took several swallows, then screwed the top back on and stuck the flask back in the front of his shirt pocket. Junebug then smiled, pulled out a ziplock bag with white, homemade rolled sticks, and held one of the sticks out to her.

"What makes you think I want *that*, either?" she said, nodding at the marijuana joint.

He continued holding the stick out to her. After staring at it for a minute, she finally took it.

He smiled. "I hope you can see that there's plenty more where that came from." He shook the bag, then put it back up.

"Plen-ty. I got other stuff, too, if you're interested in some stronger things. You just let old Junebug know what you want and, baby"—he scanned her body—"it's yours."

"What do you want, Junebug?" Sahara asked.

"I already told you. I like you." He lit a joint and took a drag. "I want you to be happy. You're not like these chicken heads and gold diggers around here. Everybody here wants something, but nobody wants to do anything for it. Even those holier-than-thou folks at these churches want something. I'm talking about from the benchwarmers to the preachers. They're all looking for something. Reverends and pastors pimping and pushing while so many of them try to look down on folks like me. Like what they're doing is somehow better than what I'm doing. At least I'm honest and up-front about what I do. If you want to feel high, I got what you're looking for, but it's going to cost you. I'm fair with my price. I don't ever try and take *everything* you got. Say you're looking for love; I understand that. And I can help arrange something without you totally having to sell your soul to get it." He held the lit joint out to her.

Sahara looked at it but didn't take it. She looked down at the ground. "Why do you say that about church folks?"

"What? That they're pimping and pushing?" Junebug picked up a rock and chunked it. He then took another hit from his joint. "When I was going to church, all I ever heard from every one of them preachers was something about money. If you loved God, you had to prove it by bringing your money to them. If you wanted to be blessed, you had to bring them some money to get your blessing. And if you *really* wanted to be blessed, they told the story about that widow woman, you know the woman that gave all she had. But what really gets me is how so many of the preachers tell you that if you don't pay your tithes and offerings that you're going to be cursed and all kinds of trouble is going to come down on you. Sounds like the way a whole lot of operations I'm familiar with work. If you want your establishment to be protected, then you have to pay a price to be sure nothing happens to you and yours. If you don't pay, well . . . let's just say, stuff happens."

Sahara shrugged. "I never thought about it like that."

"The more I went to church, the more it sounded like the mob to me. Preachers merely selling woof tickets, if you ask me. I don't think what a lot of them is saying is from God, *really* is coming from God. Not trying to strong-arm and manipulate folks like a lot of them do. Preachers finding Mr. and Mrs. S. T. Rugglin', and they be trying to turn them every which way they can think of but loose. I thought Jesus came to set people free. Maybe I'm wrong, but there's a scent of the mob in play. That's how I feel about it."

"You're not saying that *God* is like the mob, are you?" Sahara said.

"Oh, no. Not at all. In fact, as far as I'm concerned, God and I are cool. It's all these people down here calling themselves representing Him. They're the ones I have problems with. Them coming up with all kinds of scams and schemes—that's what's driving so many folks like me away. Every time you turn around, they're begging for more money. It's embarrassing, really. You see, I figure if God owns everything, then why does He have to ask *me* for money every time I turn around?"

"God doesn't need your money, but it shows Him that you love Him," Sahara said. "That's what my pastor at home always says, anyway. It's to help them finance God's Kingdom down here on earth."

"Yeah, I've heard all of that, too. I ain't buying what they selling, because all I see is those fat-cat preachers living all large and in charge off the money folks supposedly are bringing to the Lord. Riding around in their big, fancy cars, wearing expensive designer suits, diamond rings on this hand and that, while folks like my mama are barely getting by. Christians sitting in the dark with their lights turned off because the power company doesn't accept faith as a payment for services rendered. We've had our power turned off more than a few times while my mama was busy singing that the Lord was going to make a way somehow." Junebug stomped on a large black ant and twisted his foot, causing Sahara to jump at first until she saw what he was doing.

"Well, I figure the Lord already made a way. And I ain't letting no man in a fancy suit holler at me about what God is telling Him to tell me, trying to suck me in. Telling me I ain't blessed because I won't give my money to what they're doing. Let's not even talk about the women they end up messing around with. I'm referring to the ones that *mess* with women. People can believe what they want. I ain't buying it, none of it."

"Aren't you afraid God is going to strike you down?" Sahara said.

"For what? For not letting somebody make a fool out of me? When God made me, He didn't make no fool."

"No. For saying what you're saying about the man of God and Christians who are trying to do what they believe is right?"

"You talking about folks like your grandmother?" Junebug said. "Your grandmother is an all-right woman. She doesn't like me much, though. But honestly, if there were more Christians carrying the banner like Ma Ray and my mama, I might consider buying into some of this religious stuff. But I know the game. I know how the game is played. And believe me: most of the preachers I've seen and heard know how to play the game brilliantly. My motto is and has always been: Don't hate the player, hate the game."

Sahara shrugged. "I'm not talking about any Christians in particular. I just know you're not supposed to act like that about God's stuff. I would be afraid to say some of what you just said."

"So, Miss Sahara. You telling me that you buy into all that church hype?"

Sahara primped her mouth. "Not really the church hype. I guess I really don't have strong feelings about it or them one way or the other. But I believe in God, I do believe. I'm just not sure about all this other stuff folks try to sell in the *name* of God."

"Say, why don't you and I go have some fun?"

"I can't go anywhere while I'm here unless Ma Ray knows with whom and where I'm going. Oh, and as my date, you'd have to ask her permission the first time around."

Junebug frowned. "So, I would have to ask your grandmother if I want to take you somewhere? If I wanted to take you out on a legitimate date? You for real?"

"Yes."

"Oh, Junebug don't do that. First of all, we may not even get back to the house before daylight." He leaned over and smiled. "But now, if you were to sneak out of the house, we could go have all the fun we wanted for as long as we want, and no one would be looking for you, to even know when you should be back."

"That's not going to work. Trust me: Ma Ray will know I'm gone. Somehow, she'll know. She has some kind of radar, special sense, internal alarm, or something. My mother and stepfather are already threatening to send me and my sister away to a boot camp. If I don't act right while I'm here, I know that's *exactly* where I'll end up next."

Junebug leaned over and kissed her. "I really like you, Sahara. You feel me?"

"Yeah, I feel you. I like you, too. But I also understand it's not as simple as you're trying to make it out to be."

He kissed her again. "Look, you could sneak out after your grandmother goes to sleep. I could pick you up a little ways down the road from here. We could go have a great time. I could even have you back before the sun comes up."

"What if Ma Ray comes looking for me and I'm not in my room? You don't understand how difficult it really is doing something like this. It's hard on your nervous system," Sahara said.

"Okay, let's say Ma Ray comes looking for you and you're not there. Let's say she's waiting up for you when you come in the house. Just tell her you came out here to be by yourself. I'm sure she knows you like it down here. You can tell her you couldn't sleep so you decided to go outside for a while. You know, to get in touch with God. She'd believe something like that," Junebug said. "I can even bring you back here through the special way that I come when I come here. That way, when you go back in the house, it would really look like you're telling the truth. I'm telling you, this will work." He kissed her on her lips. "Come on. Let me show you some real fun while you're here. Please." He kissed her on the lips once more, then smiled. "Write your digits down for me so I can call you." He handed her a pen and a small notebook turned to a blank page.

She wrote down her grandmother's number since she really didn't want him having her cell number. Besides, she couldn't get or keep much of a signal, anyway.

"Why don't we do something tonight?" He put the notebook back in his shirt pocket with his flask. "What do you say?"

Sahara smiled. "I'll think about it and let you know. But we would need a plan, a signal, just in case something goes wrong. You can't call that number after ten-thirty. That's my grandmother's number, and she's a really light sleeper. If the phone rings, she'll surely investigate, inquiring as to who was calling at that time of night. That's if she doesn't answer the phone herself."

He started laughing. "What? You're saying we need a *plan* for the *plan?*"

"Don't laugh. Let's say I agree to this. And let's say you're looking for me, but my grandmother doesn't go to bed until late. Or something else comes up, and I can't let you know we need to scrap the plan. Cell phones are definitely unreliable out here, so I can't count on calling you on your cell and letting you know there's a problem."

"So, what do you suggest the plan be?"

"I don't know. I'm thinking." She began to grin. "I know. The red draperies in the front of the house. Ma Ray usually draws them closed at night and opens them during the day. You can see that window easily from the road, even at night. If something happens where I find I can't get out, I'll twist one side, so that it looks like a cord. If you see that, you'll know for sure that something is wrong and that I can't come."

He shrugged. "Sounds like a plan to me. Just don't let your grandmother know you and I are talking. She doesn't care for me *at all*. So, does this mean you'll get away and go out with me tonight around midnight?"

"We can give it a try and see what happens."

"So, I'll ride by the house around midnight."

"Yeah, sounds good."

"So, let me be sure I have this straight in my head. If the red drapes are closed, then I'll look for you a little ways down the road from here."

"Yeah."

"And if it's opened, what does that mean again?"

"That it may still be okay, but that Ma Ray has not gone to bed yet. She generally closes the drapes right before she turns in."

"But if one side of the drapes is twisted like a cord, then that means you're having trouble getting away," Junebug said.

"Right."

"If that turns out to be the case, do you want me to ride back around one o'clock to see if it's all clear then?"

"You can. But if at one it's the same thing, then we'll scrap the plan entirely."

"Fine. Then, I'll roll by here at midnight." He stood up. "Wear something banging, okay. I plan to show you how we do things around these here parts."

Sahara smiled.

He looked up the bank, then back at her. "You're not going to the house yet?"

"No. I'm going to sit here a little while longer."

"A'ight." He handed her his lighter. "Just in case," he said, then nodded. "I'll catch you tonight. Peace out."

"Yeah," she said. "Later."

After he left, she took out the joint he'd given her and looked at it. She looked up toward the sky. The sunlight seemed to, once again, be playing peekaboo with her through the trees. "God, what am I doing? What is *wrong* with me?" She put the joint, along with the lighter, in her short pants pocket. After five minutes, she stood up and left.

Chapter 23

And it shall be, that whosoever shall go out of the doors of thy house into the street, his blood shall be upon his head, and we will be guiltless: and whosoever shall be with thee in the house, his blood shall be on our head, if any hand be upon him.

—Joshua 2:19

"You were outside in your special place?" Ma Ray asked Sahara when she came into the kitchen. Ma Ray was peeling peaches and slicing them up. On the stove, the dark-blue speckled boiler contained tomatoes she was stewing to can later.

"Yes, ma'am," Sahara said.

Ma Ray nodded. "I like being down there as well. It's really a peaceful place."

Sahara went and sat at the table with Ma Ray. "I didn't know you went down there, too."

Ma Ray held out to Sahara a peach slice pressed tightly against the knife she was using. "Oh, there are lots of things you don't know about me." Sahara took the slice and bit it. "Years ago, that was one of my spots I'd go to hide out," Ma Ray said.

"Oh, sure, Ma Ray. I can just see you now, going down there to hide out. And who *exactly* were *you* hiding out from?" Sahara took another slice of peach Ma Ray held out to her.

"Sometimes to get away from your grandfather. Sometimes just to get away from the world." Ma Ray raised a peach slice up to her mouth and ate it. "Good and sweet, huh?" she said, referring to the peach. "You know that oak tree out there?"

"The one that looks like an old man flexing his muscle?"

Ma Ray laughed. "I never thought about it like that. But now that you mention it, it does remind me of your granddaddy when he was past his prime, trying to show off the muscles in his arm." She held out another peach slice; Sahara took it. "That arm you're referring to, that tree limb, it used to hold a swing. I loved sitting on that swing, feeling like I didn't have a care in the world."

"What happened to the swing?" Sahara asked.

"I'm not real sure. I think one of the neighbors' children—an older child, of course—may have come over and cut up the leather seat. The chains with the cut leather were just hanging. Your uncle Boaz took the chains off to keep anyone from accidentally getting hurt. He said he was going to fix it back. I guess he forgot, and I ended up forgetting all about it as well. In fact, I hadn't really thought about it until just now. Maybe I'll mention something about it to him and see if he still plans on having it done."

Ma Ray got up and took the pile of sliced peaches over to the sink. "You want to help me can the tomatoes and then these peaches?"

"Sure. I guess. I don't have anything else *fun* to do today," Sahara said.

"Oh, now. If you're going to act like *that* about it, then don't worry about it." Ma Ray tilted her head as she dried off her hands. "Come here." Ma Ray held her arms open.

"Ma Ray, I'm okay."

"Baby, come here," Ma Ray said again with a warm smile.

Sahara stood and reluctantly walked like a robot into Ma Ray's arms. "I'm not a baby anymore, Ma Ray."

Ma Ray hugged her and rocked her from side to side. "Nonsense! All of us like to be babied every now and then. Even your mother." Ma Ray pulled back and looked at Sahara. She brushed Sahara's hair down with her hand. "That's right. Your mother comes over here from time to time trying to act like she's coming to check on me, when the truth is, she just wants her mother to hug and love on her. I'll let you in on another secret." Ma Ray lowered her voice. "Sometimes, as old as I am, I wish I could fall into *my* mother's arms just one more time, and let her hug and baby and love on *me*. So don't try and act all *fly* with me."

Sahara pulled back and laughed. "Fly, Ma Ray? *Fly?*"

"Okay," Ma Ray said. "School me. What's the word this year?"

"Bobo *could* be a good word. It means fake, not genuine. Although fly is more crunk than bobo."

"Bobo, huh? Well, there's nothing new about that. We used the word bobo in my day. In fact, there was a boy in our community named Bobo. And then, there was Bobo the Clown. He used to come on television. Bobo the Clown, that is."

Sahara laughed. "You're something else, Ma Ray. Just when I think you don't get it, you prove just how much you really do."

"Hey, don't hate—celebrate. I *do* what I *do*." Ma Ray began to move her head like a strutting chicken.

Sahara laughed some more. "You're chron, that's what you are."

"Chron? Okay. I'm not going to even *try* and figure *that* one out."

"It means that you're tight, you're cool . . . you're awesome," Sahara said.

"Ooh, I like that. Ma Ray Chron! I'm chron. Wait until I tell Tootsie. I'm chron."

"Ma Ray, can we have another soda?" Crystal asked when she walked in. "Sorry. I meant to say, *may* we have? Hey, Sahara." She threw up her hand in a lazylike wave.

"Hey," Sahara said back.

"Hmmm, I don't know, Crystal. Y'all need to watch consuming so much sugar. And sodas are full of sugar."

"Come on, Ma Ray. We're young. Didn't you get the e-mail? Young folks live off of sugar." Crystal walked over to Sahara. "What's that about to fall out of your pocket?"

"What?" Sahara said, following Crystal's gaze.

"That right there," Crystal said, pointing at the pocket of Sahara's yellow shorts.

Sahara quickly tried to push the white stick back in her pocket, but in her rush, she flipped it onto the floor instead. She stooped down quickly to pick it up, but Ma Ray's foot beat her to it.

"I got it," Sahara said, trying to pull it out from under Ma Ray's foothold.

"It's okay. I'll get it." Ma Ray bent down and made a slight grunt after picking it up. She rolled it gently between her fingers. "What's this?"

Sahara reached over and quickly took it out of Ma Ray's hand. "It's nothing."

"Oh, it's more than nothing. I know nothing when I see it, or should I say when I *don't* see it. And that is definitely not nothing. Were you out there doing drugs?"

"No, Ma Ray, I was not."

"Then why was that *thing* in your pocket?" Ma Ray pointed at the joint.

"It was in my pocket because I *wasn't* smoking it. Had I smoked it, then it wouldn't have been there at all," Sahara said.

"Did you bring that mess here to my house?" Ma Ray asked. Her voice was not staying in control the way she wanted it to.

"No, ma'am. I wouldn't do something like that," Sahara said as though she'd been insulted.

"Then where did *that* come from?"

"Somebody gave it to me," Sahara said.

"Since you've been here at my house?" Ma Ray asked.

"Yes, but I didn't use it, which is why it was in my pocket."

"Okay, I'm missing something or *something*. You were just outside. Is there a pusher, a dope dealer, or somebody like that in my backyard for you to have gotten that?"

Sahara let out a loud sigh. "See, Ma Ray. That's what I'm talking about. Nobody ever gives me a fair shake. Something happens, and the first thing everybody does is jump to the most negative conclusion."

"I'm not jumping to anything. I'm asking you a question, and frankly, I'm not getting much of a real answer from you. You say you didn't bring drugs with you to my house. I believe you. So the question then comes, if you didn't bring it, then how do you happen to have something like *that* in your possession now? Talk to me, Sahara. Tell me what's going on."

A few tears began to fall. Sahara wiped them away quickly. "Ma Ray, I didn't do anything wrong. You have to believe me!"

"I'm not saying that you did. All I'm asking is, where did that *thing* come from?"

Sahara walked over to the trashcan, ripped the joint up, then threw its remnants in the can. "It's gone! Okay? Now can we just drop this whole thing?"

Aaron came in the kitchen. Sahara looked at him, then stormed out of the room.

Aaron looked at Crystal, then Ma Ray. "What's wrong?"

"Go on and get those sodas you asked for," Ma Ray said to Crystal as she made sure that all the eyes on the stove were completely turned off.

Aaron looked at Crystal as though he wanted to ask the question again. Crystal shook her head quickly to let him know not to ask it.

Ma Ray patted Crystal on her back. "Be good. You all go on back to what you were doing. It's going to be all right."

"Are you sure, Ma Ray?" Crystal asked.

"I'm sure. Go on back, now. I'm going up to check on your sister." Ma Ray left the kitchen and went up the stairs to Sahara's room.

Chapter 24

And if thou utter this our business, then we will be quit of thine oath which thou hast made us to swear.

—Joshua 2:20

Ma Ray knocked on Sahara's bedroom door.

"I really don't feel like talking right now," Sahara said.

Ma Ray pushed the door open and walked in. She gingerly sat down on the bed and began to brush down Sahara's hair with her hand as Sahara lay facedown on the bedspread. Ma Ray began to chuckle a little. "I remember when you were first born. Oh, my goodness, you were such a smart little baby. You were all alert and looking around. Then when you started talking, you were so curious about what everything was. 'What's this? What's that?' I know all children ask questions, but you"—she patted Sahara on her back—"*you* wanted to have *conversations* about it after you found out what it was. You wanted to know how it worked, what it did, what else could it do."

Sahara flipped over and looked up at Ma Ray. "You always do that," Sahara said.

"Do what?"

"You always try to make us feel better by telling us stories about when we were younger. Well, I'm not a little girl anymore."

"Yeah, but, you're still that same curious child. You're independent, and you like to find out things, even if you have to find out all on your own."

Sahara sat up. "Ma Ray, I didn't do anything wrong. Yes, I had that *thing* on me. But I didn't smoke it. I could have, but I didn't. And I know you're probably thinking that maybe I had more than just that one, and I may have smoked it before I came inside. But I didn't. I promise you, I didn't."

"And I believe you," Ma Ray said.

Sahara lowered her head and the tone of her voice. "You believe me?"

"Yes. If you say you didn't smoke anything, I believe you." Ma Ray picked up Sahara's hand and began to pat it. "I asked you where you got it from. It was a simple question. We're way out here in the country. It's not like you have easy access to something like that around here. At least, I wouldn't have thought so."

"Ma Ray, it's not important where I got it from."

"Oh, I beg the difference," Ma Ray said.

"Of course you do."

"The question is: why don't you want to tell me?" Ma Ray released a quiet sigh. "That guy I caught in our house early Saturday morning couldn't have given it to you. I never took my eyes off him. Andre and Aaron have been here. Then there was the time while we were at church."

"I know you couldn't possibly think the Poppins brothers are responsible," Sahara said as though the very thought repulsed her.

"The Poppins brothers?"

"Yeah, you know, like in Mary Poppins. The perfect little gentlemen: Andre and Aaron."

"I wouldn't think either of them did, but I'm not naive enough to put anything past anyone. So did you get it from someone at church?"

Sahara popped her lips. "You mean those folks at *your* church?"

"Well, I know you talked to the pastor's daughter. That girl sort of has a reputation, although I wasn't buying into it. But I wouldn't put too much past anybody. So is that where you got that *thing* from? From her or some other teen at church?"

"No, Ma Ray. Listen, I'm not going to tell you where I got it from. Now, if that gets me in trouble or if you want to call my mother and have her come get me, then do what you have to do." Sahara folded her arms.

Ma Ray reached over and pulled Sahara into her arms. "Baby girl, I have no intentions of calling your mother about this. You say you didn't smoke anything while you were out there, and I'm going to believe you. I just hope you feel free to always tell me the truth. But I'm here for you. I promise you that. I'm here for you. And as long as there is breath inside of me, you have my oath that I'll be here for you. I'm fighting for you right now. I pray for you all the time. I believe somehow God is going to help me get through to your true worth." Ma Ray shook her head. "If only you knew just how valuable you are to God. Well, God didn't give up on me, and I know He's not giving up on you. So if God believes in you, then who am I to argue with the Lord?"

Sahara pulled away and tilted her head upward. "I just keep messing up. I don't know why you believe me or trust me." She looked in Ma Ray's eyes. "I'm certainly not giving you much of a reason to, that's for sure."

"Because"—Ma Ray smiled—"you are fearfully and wonderfully made in the Lord. You're going to figure this all out. We've all messed up and fallen short of the glory of God. And *that's* a fact." She tapped Sahara softly on her nose.

"Even you, Ma Ray? For real? You really think I believe you've ever done anything really wrong or bad?"

Ma Ray laughed. "Oh, you'd be surprised. When I tell you that God will make you into a new creature, you're looking at what God can do. I'm going to say to you what Sarah said—"

"Sarah?"

"Yeah, in the Bible. She was married to Abraham. Had that child in her old age."

"I thought you were talking about a real person," Sahara said.

"She was real. I hope you don't think the Bible is fairy tales. Those things in there are for our benefit. . . . They're recorded to encourage and guide us. So, as I was saying. Sister Sarah asked, 'Is there anything too hard for God?' And I'm going to tell you this. No, there's nothing too hard for God. Not you, not me, not the worst sinner out there who's done the worst thing you can think of. Okay, so, you've gotten off track. God is a God of second chances." Ma Ray stopped. "What say we have a little prayer now."

Sahara shrugged. "Fine with me."

"Do you want to do it?"

"Me?" Sahara's voice squeaked. "Pray?"

"Yes, *you*. Pray."

Sahara shook her head. "No. I don't want to pray. You can do it." Sahara then held Ma Ray's hand, closed her eyes, lowered her head, and waited on Ma Ray to begin.

Chapter 25

And she said, According unto your words, so be it. And she sent them away, and they departed: and she bound the scarlet line in the window.

—Joshua 2:21

The phone rang. Ma Ray answered it. "Sahara!" Ma Ray yelled up the stairs. "Phone's for you."

Sahara picked up the phone. "Hello."

"Hey," the voice said. It wasn't who she was thought it was. To her surprise, Sahara let out a sigh of relief.

"Andre?"

"Did I catch you at a bad time?"

"No. I was just sitting here." She got comfortable in the bed. "What's up?"

He laughed.

"What's so funny?" Sahara asked.

"I'm sorry. I didn't mean to laugh. It's just that I didn't expect you to be nice or polite to me. It feels weird. You kind of caught me off guard."

"What are you trying to say? That I'm not a nice person?"

"No, not at all. I'm sorry. I don't think that came out right. You're a nice enough person. It's just you and I generally don't often have too many *nice* conversations."

"Yeah, well, today . . . is today. So what do you need?"

"I was calling to see if you might be interested in going to Bible study tomorrow night . . . at my church. We're getting ready for the conference. A lot of the people who have signed up will be there. It will give you and Crystal a chance to meet some of the folks. That way you won't feel so out of place. Plus, we have a really great Bible study. That's how Aaron and I ended up becoming members of this church. Our grand-mother was going to another church. Aaron and I visited this church, and it impacted us in such a profound way, Grand-mother decided to go and check it out."

"Check it out? What kind of a church *is* this?"

He laughed a little. "It's a regular church, but you know how older people are. If you're doing anything different than what they're used to, they start thinking the place may be a cult in disguise. Grandmother had never seen me and Aaron excited about going to church. She heard a few things we were talking about that happened at church, and she decided if it was a cult, she was going to squash us going before we got too inducted."

"Wait a minute now," Sahara said. "I didn't agree to come to some crazy place myself."

"It's not like that. That's what my grandmother discovered when she came. We believe in God, we believe in Jesus, we be-lieve in the Holy Spirit. The pastor is in his early thirties, so that kind of threw my grandmother off a little. She's used to old heads who don't ever want to retire or turn things over to the younger folks coming along, as the pastor. But when she vis-ited, she saw that the Gospel of Jesus Christ was being preached and going forth strong in that church. It took her a minute, but within six months, before we knew what was happening, Grand-mother was going up front to join the church. Now, we're all there together, heartily serving the Lord."

"Sounds sweet," Sahara said. "But I'm not really looking for any life-changing experiences. And I'm especially not looking for one at a church. I hope you know that the *only* reason I'm going to this youth conference is to make my grandmother happy."

"Oh, I got that. You've made that much *abundantly* clear. I was just thinking you might like Bible study. Who knows, maybe you'll find what you're looking for before the conference takes place."

"Who says I'm looking for anything?"

"Everything about you says it," Andre said.

"See. *Now* do you get why I act like I do about you? You're so self-righteous. You don't know a thing about me, yet there you are: judging me. That's what you church folks try to do to folks. You know that everybody has something going on in their lives, so you try to find out what it might be and try to exploit it or capitalize on it. Well, Andre Woods, what you're trying to do is not going to work on me. I'm here because my grandmother is convinced she can help me act better, where my own mother has failed. I'm doing my time, and before long, I'll be released and back home. I don't want to upset my grandmother because she's old and, quite honestly, I know she really loves me. I don't want to do anything to hurt or upset her."

"Are you finished?"

"I'll let you know when I'm finished," Sahara snapped back. "I don't need you trying to look down your holier-than-thou nose at me."

"Sahara, I love you—"

"What?" She spat the word out. "What did you just say to me?"

"I said I love you with the love of the Lord. God loves you," Andre said.

"Well, I can't *stand* you. And I don't need you trying to be all sanctimonious with me. I don't need your love."

"God loves you, Sahara. That's what I'm hearing in my spirit right now. God wants you to know how much He loves you. He sees you, and He wants you to know that He loves you."

"Okay, we're done!"

"But you didn't answer my question."

"*What* question?"

"Would you like to go to Bible study tomorrow night?"

"You want an answer to your question? You want me to answer your question? Well, here's your answer, Andre." She slammed the phone down. "That's my answer," she said to the hung-up phone. "Can you hear me now? Can you hear me *now?*"

* * *

After Aaron left around eleven, Sahara went downstairs and sat in the room with the red draperies. Ma Ray came in to close them. "I'll close those for you, Ma Ray," Sahara said. Ma Ray kissed her good night and left. Sahara walked over to the draperies and pulled them closed. She stood there for another two minutes before opening them back. She took one of the draperies and began to twist it to look like a cord.

Sahara sat down on the floor next to the twisted panel and began to cry. "God, please help me. I don't like my life right now. I *do* want things to be different. I really do. I just don't know how. I don't know how to fix things. Please, God. Please, God. Help me."

Chapter 26

And they went, and came unto the mountain, and abode there three days, until the pursuers were returned: and the pursuers sought them throughout all the way, but found them not.

—Joshua 2:22

Crystal had tried talking Sahara into going to Bible study with her. Aaron was coming to pick her up at six-thirty. He'd said Bible study began at seven, and no one liked being late, not even people who normally went through life keeping CPT (Colored People Time) like his grandmother. Sahara could see how excited her sister was. She just wasn't sure if her sister's excitement wasn't more because of Aaron than going to some Bible study.

After Crystal left, the phone rang. Sahara answered it on the second ring, beating Ma Ray to it. Turns out, it was a good thing she did.

"Hey, Sahara, what happened last night?" Junebug said.

"I'm sorry," said Sahara. "I told you I might run into some problems."

"I understand. I knew you said that, but I was still hoping. So what are you doing now?"

"Nothing much. Just finished reading a book."

"Reading a book? Hey, listen, can you get out for a little while?"

"Not really. My grandmother is here. She didn't go to Bible study."

"Doesn't that old bat ever take a nap or go to sleep or something?"

"What did you just say?"

"I'm sorry. I didn't mean anything by it. I'm just frustrated. I was really looking forward to seeing you last night," Junebug said. "So, why don't you meet me at your spot? I can be there in ten."

"I don't know about that. I'm supposed to be helping Ma Ray finish putting up her canning," Sahara lied. "You know how these folks are when it comes to canning. And Ma Ray got bushels of stuff. She's been working on finishing them all this week."

"Let your sister help her. I want to see you. Thirty minutes. That's pretty much all I need. Surely you can get away for about thirty minutes."

"Normally I could. But Ma Ray is counting on me."

"Oh, okay. Well, never let it be said that I forced any woman into doing *anything* she didn't want to. Maybe next time."

Sahara bit down on her bottom lip. "Yeah. Maybe next time." She looked up at the ceiling. "Well, I have to go."

"Sure. I'll hit you up later. Peace out."

"Peace out." Sahara softly placed the phone on the hook. She went downstairs to the kitchen. "Want some help?" she asked Ma Ray.

"Wow. Of course I'd love some help," Ma Ray said. "Grab some of those jars and help me fill them with these stewed tomatoes."

Sahara did as instructed. "These are so pretty," Sahara said as she looked at the bright red through the glass Mason jars.

"Yeah. To be honest, the thing I love most about canning is the therapy I seem to get from doing it. You feel that much closer to God. I mean, you take something He has kissed with His love, and you lovingly put it in a safe place to see, capture, and hold on to that beauty. Even the idea behind canning is to preserve. You take something that could spoil or go bad, and you put it in a place to keep it fresh and beautiful for as long as possible until it's ready for good use."

Sahara smiled. "It sounds like you're talking about me." She looked at Ma Ray. "I guess we could say that my mother sent me and Crystal here so you could can . . . preserve us, in a way."

"Hmmm, I never thought of it that way."

"Ma Ray, I'm really sorry for all the trouble I seem to have caused you since I've been here."

Ma Ray went and kissed her on the forehead. "It's going to be all right. You're going to make me *so* proud one of these days, I just know you are. You're like the plants outside. We plant, we water, we prune, we fertilize, and still the weeds try to take over. Bugs try to infest—ruin the beauty of the blooms. But when we care, we keep pruning, we keep digging up the weeds that would just as well choke out the good we want to thrive. We squash the bugs. The flowers grow and bloom. And if we're blessed, we get to enjoy the fruits of our labor. The Bible says, 'One plants, one waters, but God gives the increase.'"

The doorbell rang. Ma Ray scratched her head. "Wonder who that could be?" She went to the door and came back with a visitor. "Look at what the cat dragged in," Ma Ray said to Sahara.

"Hi, Sahara," the man, dressed to the nines, said.

"Junebug?" Sahara said it as though she hadn't seen him in years. "What are you doing here?"

"I heard you were here. My mother told me. I remembered you from when you were a young girl, and I thought I'd come by to say hello." He walked over and hugged her.

"I haven't seen you in many a moons," Ma Ray said.

"Yes, ma'am, I know."

"You don't attend church anymore. At least not there with your folks," Ma Ray said.

"No, ma'am. I've been trying to get my life together. I keep saying when I get back right, I'm going to come back to the church," Junebug said.

"That's the wrong way to go about it," Ma Ray said. "The way you do it is: you come to the church, and let the *Lord* get you right. And even then, it's an ongoing, lifelong process."

"Yes, ma'am. You're right. In fact, now that you bring it up, I had been thinking about going to this Bible study at this church I heard about. Maybe I should start there."

"The main thing is to start somewhere," Ma Ray said. "You take one step and see if God won't take two."

"Sahara, would you like to go to this Bible study with me tonight?" Junebug said.

"Who *me?*" Sahara said.

"Yeah, *you.* Maybe you'll be the encouragement I need to step out and make a change in my life. I know my mother would be happy. So—what do you say? We could go to Bible study tonight. That's if it's okay with you, Ma Ray?"

Ma Ray looked at him. "Bible study? I think it would be a fine idea. Fine."

"You do?" Sahara said.

Ma Ray looked at Sahara. "Oh, yeah, I think it would be a fine idea. This young man, wanting to get his life together, is looking at going to Bible study on a Wednesday night like this. Of course, I think that's excellent."

"Great!" Junebug said, clapping his hands one time. "So, Sahara, let's do this." Junebug grinned like the cat who just ate the canary.

"But, Ma Ray, don't you need me here to help you finish?" Sahara said to Ma Ray.

"Oh, this will keep. This young man's soul is *way* more important than this canning stuff. Go on up and change into something more appropriate for a Bible study," Ma Ray said. "Junebug, you go on in and have a seat in the living room until she's ready. It shouldn't be long," Ma Ray said. "Oh, I think this is a *fine* idea!"

Sahara went upstairs and changed. She came back down fifteen minutes later.

"Wow, you look good," Junebug said when Sahara walked into the living room. "You ready to go?"

Sahara nodded.

"Just a minute," Ma Ray said, as she rushed into the living room. "I just need to put on my hat, and we'll be *all* set to go."

"Excuse me?" Junebug said, looking at a dressed-up Ma Ray.

Ma Ray set the purple hat on her head and wiggled it until it was sitting *just* right. She turned to Sahara "You like?" she asked, then winked.

Sahara smiled. "Oh, Ma Ray. I like! I *really* like!"

"So, *you're* going?" Junebug asked. "You're going with *us?*"

"Wouldn't miss this for the world. I'm so glad you thought about doing this." Ma Ray walked to the front door and held it open. "Lead the way, Mister Junebug. Lead the way."

Junebug walked out of the door.

Ma Ray locked the door when they were all on the outside. She looked up at the orange evening sky and grinned. "Beautiful evening," Ma Ray said. "Beautiful! Wouldn't you agree?"

Sahara grinned. "Yes, Ma Ray. Beautiful!"

Chapter 27

So the two men returned, and descended from the mountain, and passed over, and came to Joshua the son of Nun, and told him all things that befell them.

—Joshua 2:23

"It was *too* funny," Sahara said to Crystal. "I'm telling you: Ma Ray went and got her hat, you know the purple one she loves to wear with the feathers on top."

"Yeah, Ma Ray adores that hat. She says that's her through-the-week, dress-up hat. Ma Ray knows she loves herself some hats," Crystal said. "Personally, I don't get the hat thing. But she *does* have a lot of them. I might try one of her hats one Sunday."

"So, there Ma Ray was, adjusting that hat on her head, telling Junebug she was all ready to go. You should have seen the look on his face. It was priceless! I did all I could to keep from bursting out laughing, right there on the spot."

"You know, if you were going to go to Bible study, you could have gone with us. Oh, Sahara, I had such a great time at Bible study," Crystal said. "It was so different. It was fun. It was interesting. It's the kind of church that makes you look forward to the next time you go. I've never been to a church like this before. You would love it. I'm telling you. You'll love it."

"Yeah, sure," Sahara said with little conviction.

"For real. I know you think my view is colored because of Aaron. And I will admit, I really, really like Aaron. I really do. But this has nothing to do with him. It helps me understand why he's so grounded and such a gentleman. He's different from other guys. At this church, they seem to really encourage men to step up, do the right thing, and to take responsibility. I'm so used to hearing about how the men are above the women, and how most places make it sound like it's all about the men and we're just some sub something or other down here to make sure the men are happy and taken care of. Forget us and our needs. We don't really count."

"Yeah . . . well, welcome to the *real* world," Sahara said.

"No, that's what I'm saying. This church is different. It encourages the men to be men. For married men to *really* love their wives, the way Christ loves the church. I'm telling you, if I had a man like the way God intended for men to be and treat and take care of women, I would *gladly* submit to that man."

"Okay, it sounds like you've been brainwashed already," Sahara said.

"No, I'm just starting to really understand who I am in the Lord. I'm understanding my value and worth to God."

"All of this from one little Bible study?" Sahara said, making fun of her sister.

"No. Not just from one little Bible study. Aaron and I have been talking. At first I thought he was just trying to pull one over on me. But he's really a nice guy. He really is. And so is Andre."

"Andre? Okay. If you say so."

"Why are you so mean to him? Why do you treat him like you do?" Crystal asked.

"Because I don't like him."

"What did he ever do to you?"

"Nothing. It's just I'm not as easy as you are. You always give people a chance. You want to see the best in folks. Well, I've been around long enough to spot a knockoff, perpetrating wannabe when I see one."

"Well, you might not think much of him, but there are lots of girls at church trying to get his attention."

"Good for them. I'm happy somebody sees something in his high-siding self."

"Wow, you have strong words for Andre. I don't think he's high siding at all. I've never seen him remotely acting like he's better than other folks," Crystal said.

"And that's why you're *you* and *I'm* your big sister. Crystal, you don't see a lot of things."

"Like?"

"Like, maybe Aaron isn't all that he's pretending to be. Maybe he's trying to get with you just because he wants to prove something," Sahara said. "You know what I'm saying?"

"That's not a nice thing to say, Sahara. You're acting like I don't have anything going on at *all* with me. And that all Aaron could *possibly* be after, when it comes to me, is what he thinks he can get from me."

"That's not *exactly* what I was saying. I'm only saying that, between me and you, you're the nice one of us two. And Crystal, you *have* to admit: you *do* give people more of the benefit of the doubt than I do. Crystal, when you meet folks, you put them at one hundred and *then* let them prove whether they deserve to be there or not. Me? Everybody starts at zero, and they determine—by their subsequent actions—whether they gain points toward the positive end of the scale or move into the negative."

"Okay. Well, back to your story. So, how was *your* Bible study?" Crystal said.

Sahara smiled. "The best part of it was watching Junebug try to figure out a church to take us to. Ma Ray insisted on sitting in the backseat. She said she didn't want to impose on us." Sahara snickered. "Junebug didn't have a *clue* where he was going to go with Ma Ray sitting in there. And Ma Ray's church doesn't have a Bible study anymore, so he couldn't even take us there."

"But weren't you upset with Ma Ray for *essentially* crashing your date night?" Crystal asked. "I know all you were doing was trying to sneak out and go do something else. I know you, Sahara."

Sahara shrugged. "Honestly? I wasn't upset at all. In the first place, I didn't really want to go anywhere with Junebug. There's something about him that kind of creeps me out. Truthfully, I was shocked when he showed up here, and a bit put out by his audacity. But he acts like he's terrified of Ma Ray. I think it has something to do with him trying to talk to Freda and something that happened that caused Ma Ray to get up in his grill."

"You talking about our cousin Freda? You think he was trying to talk to Freda?"

"Yeah. But I don't believe she ever gave him a second thought," Sahara said.

"Not Freda. Freda is different from me and you. All Freda has ever cared about is doing the right thing, being the perfect daughter, the perfect student—"

"I know. Freda has always made me sick. You'd think she's *never* done one thing wrong in her life," Sahara said. "That's why Mama is so hard on us. She looks at Freda and Owen and wonders why we can't be self-motivated the way Uncle Boaz's children are. But I bet you, even Saint Freda has a few skeletons hidden away in her closet."

"You think?"

"Oh, I'm sure. Who doesn't have a bone or two lurking around? They may not ever tell it, but everybody has something they're hiding. But I really don't want to talk about Freda. Honestly, talking about her depresses me."

"Okay, so finish telling me where Junebug ended up taking you and Ma Ray."

"Oh, this is funny. He got a call on his cell phone—"

"You mean his cell phone works out here in these boonies?" Crystal asked, widening her eyes.

"It's just like with the rest of ours—sporadic if you get anything at all. You could tell he wasn't getting a good signal. Then he lost his signal about a minute after the call came through. He then claimed there was some huge emergency taking place. He brought me and Ma Ray home in a hurry, so he could 'take care' of it." Sahara curled her fingers to indicate quotes.

Crystal laughed. "The oldest trick in the book!"

Sahara laughed as well. "I know, right? So he brought us home and promised Ma Ray that he would try again some other time. Asked her to keep him in her prayers. Big phony."

"Well, I'm impressed that he got up the nerve to ask Ma Ray about taking you anywhere. You know how strict Ma Ray is. Aaron can come over and 'sofa sit,' as Ma Ray calls it. But he has to leave no later than eleven. The only way she'll let me go anywhere with him is if you go with us."

"I'm not going on a double date with you and Aaron. I'm not."

"Oh, Sahara. What would it hurt? We could go to the movies. It would be fun! At least it's better than sitting around this place doing nothing all day except staying in your room and reading books."

Sahara grabbed her sister's hand. "As much as I hate we're stuck in this boring place, the only thing I can think of that would even be more boring is being stuck somewhere next to Andre. And whether you know it or not, I don't think Ma Ray would let either of us go out with just *anybody*, even from around here. As for my real friends, even if I *could* get any of them to come take me out, there's no *way* they would adhere to Ma Ray's rule of coming to the front door, meeting her, asking for her permission. It's not going to happen. So I'll just bide my time until we go home, and I'll make up for lost time then."

"What if we don't go back home?"

"Child, please. Mama's not going to keep us here past the summer. Uncle Boaz will talk about her so bad that even if she *didn't* want to, she would *have* to take us back."

"Uncle Boaz is all right," Crystal said.

"But he does sort of look down on our mother," Sahara said.

"Can I say one more thing about Andre? Please . . . " Crystal put her hands in a prayerlike position.

"Only if you *just* can't help yourself," Sahara said.

"You really should give him a chance. I'm telling you: all those girls were trying to talk to Andre, and he didn't seem interested in any of them. Not a one of them."

"Maybe he's gay or something."

"No. I've seen him around you. He really likes you. You're just so nasty toward him. If you'd quit being so nasty to him and maybe give him a chance, you might find you really like him, too." Crystal smiled. "You should have heard him expounding on one of the scriptures we were discussing. He then tried to show an example of love, and he talked about his grandmother and folks like Ma Ray and some other woman I've never heard of. He talked about agape love, unconditional love."

"Agape love?"

"Yeah. That's when someone loves you without condition. You don't have to do anything for them to love you nor can you do anything so bad that you could lose their love. Like how God loved us before we ever even knew Him. How He loved us while we were yet sinners. We can't do anything that would even be deserving of God's love. God just loves us. And no matter how much we mess up, we can't mess up enough for Him to fall out of love with us. God's love is not dependent on what we do."

"Oh, you mean like how Craig was trying to tell you that time that if you loved him, you would sleep with him, and if you didn't, that meant you really didn't love him?"

Crystal jerked her body back. "How do you know about *that?*"

"I know. He was bragging about how he cut you loose because you didn't do what he wanted. His love was conditional. As long as you did what he wanted, he loved you. When you didn't, the love was all but gone," Sahara said.

"Right. That's not agape love. It's like a parent that shows love to you as long as you're being obedient. But the moment you mess up, they act like they don't love you anymore. But I found out tonight about agape . . . unconditional love. And Sahara, to be honest, I want that in my life."

"You have it. I agape you. Ma Ray agapes you," Sahara said.

"Why didn't you say that Mama agapes me?" Crystal asked.

Sahara shrugged. "I'm sure Mama agapes us. It's just she *does* have her conditions. So I don't think that *totally* qualifies as agape. If we act right, Mama loves us. If we don't, she looks for ways to get us out of her hair."

"You should have come to Bible study with us tonight," Crystal said. "It would have made you see even *that* in a different light. At least, that's what happened for me. I was upset with

Mama for sending us here like this. Not because I don't love being with Ma Ray. It just felt like we were damaged goods and she didn't want to be bothered with us anymore. But after listening to the preacher tonight, and some of the people who shared during discussion time—and *especially* hearing Andre talk about their mother and grandmother and some of what they've been through—I see just how *much* our mother truly loves us. Mama loves us *so* much, she sent us to the best place she could think of to try and help us. Ma Ray loves us, Sahara. She loves us. She's trying to help us get our lives together. And for once in a long time, I'm actually listening."

"Okay. I'm glad you had a great time at your *Bible* study. I think I'll go to bed now. Maybe I'll start reading a new novel or something."

"Why don't you work on your poems?"

"Maybe I'll do that. I just wish Ma Ray had a faster connection to the Internet other than this redonkulous dial-up, so I could log on. This *really* is the pits!"

"I know it's redonkulous . . . yeah, beyond ridiculous. But you could *still* use dial-up if you really wanted to connect to the Internet that bad," Crystal said. "It might be slow as Christmas—"

"Dial-up kills me. It takes twenty minutes just for one page to load. We'll be home by the time I reach the place on the Internet that I want to go."

"Aaron says there's this café in town that has fast connection. We could go there sometimes and surf the Net."

Sahara smiled as she stood up and held open the door for Crystal to leave. "Now *that,* little sister, sounds like a plan. Bye-bye." She wiggled her fingers in a wave at Crystal as she gently put her out, then closed the door.

Chapter 28

*And they said unto Joshua, Truly the Lord hath de-
livered into our hands all the land; for even all the inhabitants of the country do faint because of us.*

—Joshua 2:24

Andre knocked on the front door. Ma Ray smiled as she
opened it. "Your grandmother called and said you were
on your way over. You must have flown to get here," Ma Ray
said.

"No, ma'am. I drove the speed limit," Andre said.

"Well, come on in. I tell you what. You are such a wonderful
young man. You and your brother both."

"Thank you, Ma Ray."

"Tootsie is so proud of the way you both are turning out," Ma
Ray said. "Just keep your eyes on the prize and keep pressing toward the mark of the high calling in Christ Jesus. Keep your
hand in God's hand, and you're going to be just fine, just fine."

"Yes, ma'am. That's what I strive to do every single day."

"What's *he* doing here?" Sahara said as she stood at the top of
the stairs.

"Sahara, that's not the way we greet company around here,"
Ma Ray said.

"He's not company. Company is someone who visits every
now and then. Every time I turn around, he seems to be here."

"Sahara, apologize for that."

"It's okay, Ma Ray," Andre said.

"No, it's not," Ma Ray said to Andre. She turned back to Sahara. "I said to apologize."

"I'm sorry," Sahara said in a whisper.

"Louder. I can't hear you," Ma Ray said.

"I'm sorry!" Sahara said louder.

"It's fine," Andre said to Sahara. He turned toward Ma Ray. "I'll be out back." He then went back outside through the front door.

"Come down here," Ma Ray said to Sahara.

"But, Ma Ray—"

"Now!"

Sahara walked down the stairs as though this were her final walk before an execution. When she reached the floor, she stood toe-to-toe with Ma Ray.

"And take some of that wind out of your sails," Ma Ray said.

Sahara let the air out of her cheeks.

"Don't you *ever* do anything like that again, do you hear me?" Ma Ray said.

"Ma Ray, I didn't mean to disrespect you or to make you upset. But what is he doing here? Why is he here so much? I'm not interested in anything with him."

"Oh, so everything is all about you, huh, Miss Sahara? The earth was created to revolve around you? Is that what you're trying to say?" Ma Ray said.

"No. I'm just talking about Andre right now. And every time I look up, he seems to be over here. Was he over here like this before we came? So the question is: why is he here so much now? Why?"

Andre strolled back in the house carrying a large leather bag. He nodded at Ma Ray and walked toward the kitchen without saying a word. Sahara heard the back door open, then close.

"What's he doing now?" Sahara asked Ma Ray.

"Why?" Ma Ray said.

"He just walked through your house like he lives here, then went out the back door."

"I guess if you want to know, you can go and ask him your-self," Ma Ray said.

"Quite frankly, I don't really care," Sahara said.

Ma Ray shrugged. "Suit yourself." She left, headed for her bedroom.

Sahara stood there a minute, then went back upstairs.

Chapter 29

And the Lord said unto Joshua, This day will I begin to magnify thee in the sight of all Israel, that they may know that, as I was with Moses, so I will be with thee.

—Joshua 3:7

Sahara stayed in her room for about an hour. Then she got up and went downstairs to the kitchen.

"You need help with anything?" Sahara asked Ma Ray.

"Nope. I have everything all bottled up, and I'm just putting them on the pantry in the back room."

"What about *these* over here?" Sahara said, pointing at three jars segregated on the kitchen table.

"I'm sending those back with Andre when he goes home. I told Tootsie I would send her some chutney. She loves my homemade chutney."

Sahara looked out of the window. "What's he doing out there?"

"Who? Andre? I told you, if you want to know what he's doing, then go ask him yourself."

"But you *do* know?" Sahara said.

Ma Ray nodded. "I know more than most folks think I know. So, yes, I *do* know."

Sahara twisted her mouth a little. She opened the back door and went out.

Andre looked up briefly when he saw her bouncing toward him. He kept on working.

Sahara stopped when she got to the tree.

Andre stood up straight. "It's finished. Would you like to try it out?"

"So this is what you came here to do?" Sahara said.

"Yes."

"How did you know? Did Ma Ray ask you to do this?"

"No, she didn't ask me to do this," Andre said. "I offered to do it. And when I did, she started acting like I was a prophet from God or something." He looked at Sahara more intensely. "So . . . do you want to try it out or not?"

Sahara tried to keep her expression hard. "I guess," she said. Andre held it steady until she took full possession of it. Sahara sat down on the leather part of the swing held up on the tree by strong steel chains. She smiled.

"Whoa, was that a smile I just saw?" Andre asked.

Sahara pushed off and began to swing. Andre stepped back so he wouldn't be in her way.

"Is it okay?" he asked.

She pumped harder and made herself go higher.

"It's perfect," she said as the wind seemed to caress her whole body with each level of height she managed to achieve. She couldn't help but think that this was how birds had to feel as they soared through the air. After about five minutes of swinging, she allowed the swing to come to a rest.

"You're sure it's okay?" Andre asked.

"Positive," she said. She cocked her head and looked into his eyes. "So, this was *your* idea?"

"Yes."

"What made you do it?"

"Why?"

"Look, I'm just curious. But if you don't want to tell me, then keep it to yourself."

He shrugged. "I saw you here the other day. When I saw this tree, I thought it was ideal for a swing. I just decided, since you like this area so much, you might like to have a swing to sit on or swing in sometimes. That was all."

"So you asked Ma Ray about doing this? Did you happen to tell her you were doing it for me?"

"I asked Ma Ray what she thought about me putting an old-fashioned swing out here on this tree and, like I told you, she acted like I was some prophet who was bringing a Word from the Lord down from the mountain. She was so excited. She couldn't believe I 'had the vision to ask to do this,' those being her words, not mine."

Sahara leaned backward, then back straight. She began to move the swing just a little. She twirled it around, then raised her feet off the ground to let it spin her. "Did Ma Ray ask you about anything else?" she asked when it was back straight.

Andre was putting his tools and things back into the leather bag. "Like what?"

"Like, anything else?"

"Would you care to be more specific?" Andre said.

"The only thing you and Ma Ray talked about was you putting up this swing? Did she ask you anything about me?" She sighed. "Did she say anything about *me* to you?"

"Other than you being a difficult child—"

"She did *not* say that," Sahara said. "Did she?"

He laughed. "No, she didn't say that. But she did ask if I happened to know anything about drugs and where a person may have gotten some from around here."

"Are you for real? Did she ask you that for real?"

"Yep. I figured she was maybe talking about you."

"Of course you would."

"See, there you go again. Do you always jump to conclusions or is it just when it comes to me?"

She pretended to be thinking, tapping her index finger against her buttoned lips.

Andre smiled and shook his head. "You're something else, that's for sure."

"So, what did you tell her? About the drugs, I mean?"

"You don't have to worry. I didn't mention Junebug to her at all. I figure if you had drugs, you definitely got them from him, the Pusher Man. And since I happen to know he's been out here with you, if you *had* drugs, he's the one."

"You didn't say anything to Ma Ray about that? About Junebug being here?"

"Nope."

Sahara exhaled slowly. "Thank you. The last thing I need is for Ma Ray to start freaking out like my mother does."

"So, do you want to talk about what's going on or should I keep on minding my own business?" Andre said. "It's your call."

"Junebug was here the other day, and he *did* give me a joint. I didn't smoke it or anything. But like an idiot, I stuck it in my pocket. It fell out. Ma Ray saw it. And even though she said she believed me when I told her I hadn't smoked anything, I know I've raised some red flags in her mind."

"May I tell you something?" Andre said.

"Sure."

"She's also concerned about some missing items."

Sahara frowned. "Who? What missing items?"

"Ma Ray. She told my grandmother that some pieces of jewelry and money have come up missing."

"What kind of jewelry?"

"For starters, a diamond watch and a necklace," Andre said.

"So why hasn't Ma Ray said anything about that to either me or Crystal?"

"I don't know the answer to that."

Sahara shook her head slowly. "She asked me if I'd seen her watch. You think she believes one of us took those things? That me or Crystal would actually *steal* from her?"

"I can't answer that. I just know, from talking to my grandmother, that Ma Ray has officially eliminated me and Aaron from her list of suspects."

"You and Aaron?"

"Yeah. It appears that during the actual time frame of when these items likely went missing, Aaron and I happened to be around."

"When did those things come up missing?"

"You remember when we brought those bushels of fruit and vegetables? Well, it must have been around that same time frame. From what she told my grandmother, things were there Saturday around noon, then gone by Sunday morning," Andre said.

"Wow, so she probably *does* think I may have taken them, then. Because she hasn't said *one word* to me, not one. I'm going to talk to her about this."

"I don't know if that's a good idea," Andre said.

"Why?"

"Well, because she hasn't said anything to you about it yet. Maybe she *doesn't* think it was you or Crystal. Maybe she's trying to figure it out."

"I don't want my grandmother believing that I'm so low that I would actually steal from her. I need to straighten all of this out right now." Sahara stood up and turned toward the house.

Andre touched her arm. She looked down at his hand. He slowly let his hand fall to his side. "If you don't mind me giving you my thoughts about *this* at this point?"

"It hasn't stopped you *so* far."

"Forget it then, Sahara. If you want to be snippy about every-thing—"

"I'm sorry. I'm sorry." She touched his hand. "Please. I'd like to hear your thoughts."

"Okay. If you start this conversation with Ma Ray, are you will-ing to come totally clean about everything with her? What I mean is: you need to tell her about Junebug and him being out here . . . about him giving you that joint. If you're going to talk to her, you can't hold things back. Because then it makes you look like you're not telling the whole truth. People like Ma Ray can sense when you're holding back something. Don't ask me how, but believe me, my grandmother knows when I'm skirting around things. And when people like my grandmother and Ma Ray feel like you're playing them, they *really* come in for the kill then."

"I just want her to know I would never steal from her. I could just tell her that much. I really don't want Ma Ray thinking I'm that low."

"I understand that. And for whatever reason, she hasn't said anything to you about it yet. Let me ask you this: is Ma Ray treating you any differently than before?"

"No. She still puts her purse in a place where I know. She doesn't act like she's mad at me or anything."

"Then let Ma Ray handle this the way she wants to. Apparently, she has a plan in mind or she would have said something already. Don't you think?"

"I don't know. I don't see what it would hurt by me walking in that house and telling her what you just said about stuff missing, and letting her know it wasn't me."

"So, are you saying you think it could have been Crystal?" He picked up his bag.

"Crystal? Steal something from Ma Ray? Are you out of your mind? No, I don't think it could have been Crystal, either. And I don't think Ma Ray thinks it was Crystal. If she thinks it could be either of us, then I'm definitely the one she suspects."

"Are you *that* bad?" Andre said, almost with a tease in his voice.

"What do *you* think?"

"I'll tell you what I think. I think you're a wonderfully intelligent and beautiful young woman who has potential she's not using in the best way possible," Andre said.

"Is that right?"

"Yes. But then again, who cares what I think? In your eyes, I'm just some country hick who doesn't know diddly-squat."

"I never said you were a hick," Sahara said with a laugh.

"Oh, okay. So country still stands?"

"Hey, I don't make the rules. I just call them like I see them," Sahara said as she began to walk toward the house.

"Listen, at the conference next weekend, they're having a fashion show. I was thinking you'd be great as one of the models. I wanted to ask you earlier, but you don't seem to like talking to me very much. Would you be interested in modeling at the youth conference on Saturday during that segment?"

"Yes," Sahara said. "I would *love* that!" She paused a second. "Wait a minute, what are they going to be modeling? Because I'm not down with flour or croker sack dresses. I can make *anything* look good. But I don't want any evidence out there that I *ever* had bad taste when it comes to clothing or anything *else* for that matter."

"Is that why you can't stand to be around me?"

"What?"

"Is that why you don't care to talk to me, even in general conversation? You think I'm in bad taste?"

"I just don't like you, that's all. It has nothing to do with how you look. Because quite frankly, I think you should put your name in for the modeling gig yourself. Regardless of what I think about you personally, with the right stylist, dressing you all crisp, you could be drippin'."

"Dripping?" He laughed. "I bet you think that I'm so backward that I don't know what you just said."

"You're saying that you *do?*"

He smiled. "Crisp means new or current, basically used in reference to clothing. And dripping—"

"It's not dripping, Mister Proper English man; the correct pronunciation is drippin'. You need to drop the *g*."

"Okay, then, drippin'." He grinned. "Drippin' means very cool, one who stands out, or more to the point, totally *awesome*."

"Check out Mister L7"—Sahara made an L7 with her hands and fingers, effectively creating a nice square—"who apparently really isn't as square as I thought."

"So, are you and I cool? I mean, can we at least be a little more civil toward each other?"

"As long as you don't crowd me or try to make things out to be more than they are, we can be civil toward each other."

"And may I tell the folks over at the conference that you'll be a model?"

"Yes, you may. As long as they don't dress me like an old fogey, a hick, or a hillbilly, I'm down. I'm just not going to wear something that makes me look stupid."

"I will tell them *just* that." Andre grinned, then looked away. "But you'll actually be modeling your own clothes . . . oh, I'm sorry, I meant to say threads. So, however you end up looking— in the end—is *entirely* on you. You'll be modeling your own out- fit."

"Oh," Sahara said. "Well, that will work. That will *definitely* work!"

Chapter 30

And thou shalt command the priests that bear the ark of the covenant, saying, When ye are come to the brink of the water of Jordan, ye shall stand still in Jordan.

—Joshua 3:8

Almost a week had passed, and for Sahara, things felt rather quiet for a change. She really loved the swing Andre had put up. She was shocked at how much that swing truthfully affected her. Ma Ray had even gone out, after Andre finished, and tried it for herself. Sahara and Crystal both laughed seeing Ma Ray acting just like them. She was yelling, "Whee!" as she pumped her legs and made herself swing higher. *Who would have thought something as simple as two chains and a leather strap for a seat, suspended in the air from an old oak tree resembling an old man, would be the cause of so much joy?*

Junebug hadn't tried contacting Sahara again. He had given her his home and cell phone numbers in case she ever wanted to "get at" him. She definitely wasn't expecting him to try that Bible study trick again. It had made Sahara laugh, although if anyone should have been upset about Ma Ray crashing like that, it should have been her.

Sahara was the rebellious one. Sahara was the one that did what she wanted no matter what anyone said. Sahara was the one who had tried drugs. She hadn't cared for it, though. But when you're trying to be "in," you're supposed to act like you like it, or something similar to it. That was also how she'd felt about her sexual encounter.

All the hype the other girls were making about how great it was . . . totally blown out of proportion. Sadly, it hadn't been that great to her. She'd felt cheated and cheapened after it was over. She'd felt used. And that was when she learned the real deal behind the peer pressure from other girls to do it. Turns out, it wasn't this fantasy world the girls who'd done it portrayed it to be. There was nothing *magical* or *spiritual* about it at all. Not for her, anyway. Sahara didn't feel special after the deed was done. Actually, she'd felt like some used-up, disposable thing that didn't have its same value anymore. She was no longer different, no longer the girl with something other girls no longer possessed. And the guy she'd given her heart and virginity to? Turns out, he hadn't really cared all that much about her after all. It was a game to him. Like the Wild West, when gunslingers shot someone, then scratched a notch on their belts to keep a running count.

It didn't mean a thing to him. And it was too late for her to go back, now that it had been done. So she did what all the other girls who had discovered that they'd merely been bamboozled, hoodwinked, sold a bill of goods: She pretended like it was the greatest thing that had ever happened to her. And everybody should only be so lucky as to experience it. *Lies, all lies.*

That's where she was beginning to see she'd been wrong. Just because *you're* miserable doesn't mean you have the right to trick other people into joining you. The only thing was: no one except her would admit the truth. She, like all the other girls who had been bamboozled, had discovered it wasn't all *that* special. Not the way Ma Ray had described and told her God had intended it to be. The holy way—between a loving husband and his loving wife. Ma Ray, as well as her mother, had the "talk" with her years ago. But of course, older people are *supposed* to tell you stuff like that. You expect that from them. Sahara figured that their whole objective was to keep young people from having fun. *They were anti-fun and anti-happiness— miserable people who now refused to sit back and watch a bunch of young folks enjoying a life that they no longer could.*

But Sahara now finally knew the truth. *Andre.* Andre was a different kind of guy. He would be the guy she, and all of her friends, would be making fun of in her normal world. He hung around his grandmother—one strike against him. He went to church and seemed to like it—another strike. He loved the Lord—a huge strike, especially for a guy. He was athletic—not a strike in itself, but if he didn't use that to his advantage, why have it? He did well in school, a straight-A-plus student—double strike, unless one had to do well to play sports or to get a scholarship. But a guy who did well for the sake of doing well or to show how smart he really is—not what most guys she knew went for.

But Andre had paid attention enough to see the oak tree there, near her favorite spot. He'd observed enough to realize its flexed arm should be holding a swing. And he'd moved on it, doing something that he knew would benefit her, in spite of how horrible she'd been to him. And he'd done all of this from his heart, taking his own time to do it.

Spiritually, she felt she was at the edge of the water. It was like those people in the Bible, on more than one occasion, who came to a body of water that was impossible to get across. In one of the recants, it had been the Red Sea. In another, it was the Jordan River. At the Jordan, God told Joshua to tell them to stand still in the Jordan. People would likely be surprised at how much she actually read the Bible to even know this.

Nevertheless, her life really *was* a hot mess. She had to acknowledge *that* herself. And as she sat quietly on the swing, she couldn't help but feel like God was telling her that she really needed to stand still, even as she had her own Jordan before her to cross.

Chapter 31

And Joshua said, Hereby ye shall know that the living God is among you, and that he will without fail drive out from before you the Canaanites, and the Hittites, and the Hivites, and the Perizzites, and the Girgashites, and the Amorites, and the Jebusites.

—Joshua 3:10

"Are you sure you don't want to go to the store with us?" Ma Ray asked Sahara as she stood in the doorway of the front door.

"I'm sure."

"I can't believe you would turn down the chance to buy a new outfit," Ma Ray said.

"Me either," said Crystal. "Clothes are what you live for."

"That's just your opinion of me," Sahara said to Crystal. "I really don't care about buying something new to wear to some youth conference. What I have already is fine."

"Great," Crystal said. "Then that means Ma Ray can buy me *two* outfits."

"Is that right?" Ma Ray said to Crystal with a grin. She turned to Sahara and tilted her head down slightly. "Well, you be good. We'll be back in a few hours."

Sahara smiled as they left. "Finally," she said. "Some *real* peace and quiet around here." She went to the kitchen to make a sandwich. For some reason she wanted a fried bologna sandwich. She couldn't help but laugh since she didn't really think she liked bologna sandwiches that much. But Ma Ray had a way of making it so good, she decided to try her hand at making one. Just as she was pressing the top bread down on the sandwich with her hand, she heard a hard knock at the front door. She left her sandwich and went to see who was there.

She cracked open the screen door. "Junebug, what are you doing here?"

"I came by to see you," he said.

"To see me? I thought you were scared of Ma Ray."

"Nah, I'm not really *scared* of her. I just try not to give her cause to hate on me. Besides, Ma Ray is not here. I saw her leave a little while ago," Junebug said. "So, you going to keep me out here all day or what?" He pulled the door open and stepped in.

"We're not supposed to let anyone in the house when an adult's not here."

"Is that right?" He scanned her body from her pulled-back hair to her wine-colored, polished toenails. "Well, aren't *you* an adult?"

"Not technically," Sahara said.

"You're seventeen. That's an adult in my book."

"Well, it doesn't count in Ma Ray's book. So you need to go back on the other side of the door."

He laughed, then sucked his teeth. "Okay, let's look at it a different way. I'm an adult. Right? I'm in the house. So that should make it all right for me to be in here, since that means an adult is *in* the house."

"Junebug, you know good and well that's not going to fly with Ma Ray. Now, you've told me that she's already gotten in your grill in the past. She was quite civil to you last Wednesday when you came here acting like you were going to some Bible study."

He smiled. "That's was good, wasn't it?"

Sahara laughed. "Oh, yeah. That was *real* good. So good that Ma Ray invited herself along."

"Man, old folks are *too* funny. I couldn't believe it when she came in with that purple hat on her head, purple and black feathers dangling around, talking about how she was ready to go. Old people don't have a clue."

"That's my grandmother you're talking about," Sahara said. "And she has more of a clue and more class than you *ever* will."

"Hey, I'm sorry. My bad. I didn't mean to talk about your relative. I know it's not cool to talk about folks' mamas *or* grandmamas." He primped his lips and kissed the air a few times. "You and I cool?"

"I guess. But you still need to get up out of here before Ma Ray comes back."

"Chillax. If your grandmother went to the store, she'll be there a minute. We have a good hour or two before she could make it back, even if she only went to town, bought a gallon of milk, and turned right back around. And I've *yet* to meet a woman who can ever go shopping, whether it's for groceries or clothes, and only stay in the store a good minute before she walks out. My mother will go to just get milk and come back with four or five bags, at least, every single time. That's the way the stores make things. It's psychological. They set things up to keep you there longer than you ever mean to stay." He went over and closed the door and stepped back closer to Sahara.

Sahara took a step back. "Stop, now. I'm serious. You really *do* need to leave."

"You don't really want me to go."

"Yes, I do."

He smiled, then ticked his head. "Nah, you're just trying to give yourself what you need to exonerate yourself, should you have to. You'll be able to say you told me to leave and I didn't. Fine. I'm down with you using me in that way. But you know you're bored out of your skull, and your body is probably screaming for some fun and excitement." He primped his mouth again. "I know females like you."

"Junebug, look. I've gotten in so much trouble that if I get caught doing one more thing, I know it's not going to turn out good for me. I don't need the trouble now."

"Girl, trouble is your middle name." He softly stroked her face with the back of his hand.

"Stop that," Sahara said, trying not to show her uneasiness. "I'm trying to tell you what's going on."

"And I'm trying to tell *you* that I know you want to have some fun. I'm here to help you get there. We could go up to your room. That way, if your grandmother comes back, we would hear her. And if I need to hide like before, I can do that, then sneak out just like I did the last time." He walked up on her and tried to kiss her on the neck.

"Stop it, I said! Now, I told you: I'm in trouble already. I don't need any more added on right now. That little marijuana joint you gave me the other day—"

"Mary Jane. How was she? Did you enjoy her? You know that I have a whole bag on me right now. Other stuff, too, if you'd prefer. We could *really* go to another place."

"I didn't enjoy *her*, because I didn't smoke *it*," Sahara said. "In fact, Ma Ray saw it and put her foot down when it fell out of my pocket."

"She put her foot down?" Junebug said.

"Yes. And by that, I mean she *literally* put her foot down. She stepped on it."

"You weren't able to salvage it? You know it would have still worked."

Sahara released an audible sigh. "You're missing the point."

"Well, I know your grandmother probably didn't know what it was."

Sahara shook her head, rubbed her face with her hand, then clapped her hands with each word that she spoke. "Why . . . would . . . she . . . *not* know what it was?"

"Because"—he held the *s* and pushed his face close to her face—"she's probably never *seen* one before. She likely thought it was an old-fashioned cigarette or something. You know that's the way they used to roll tobacco for cigarettes back in her day. They would buy the paper, put the tobacco in it, just like we do our stuff, roll it, lick it, and smoke away." He smirked. "No filter, no nothing. Just God's pure, naturale plants."

"You have got to go," Sahara said as she walked over to the door and held it open.

"Not until I get what I came for."

"There's nothing here for you," Sahara said, her hands raised up.

He walked over to her and stepped to her again. "Oh, I beg the differ."

She pushed him off of her. "Leave, please."

"Why are you acting like this? You know you want to get with me. I felt it that very first day when we were outside. You're just one of those girls who likes to tease . . . to play hard to get. Okay, if you want to know that I really want you, we'll skip the games. I *really* want you. Now you tell me what you want from me, and we can get this party started." He dipped his head in a dancelike manner. "But I know your kind. I know the signals when they're being sent out. And I can tell you that you want me, just as much as I want you." He licked the tip of his index finger, touched her on her bare shoulder, and made a sizzling sound. He grinned.

Sahara began to pray silently. She really didn't know what to do at this point. Junebug was tall and muscular. She knew she was no match for him *or* his strength. Just then, a car pulled up.

"Who is that?" Junebug asked, stepping back so as not to be seen.

"That's Ms. Tootsie's car," Sahara said, looking out.

"You talking about telephone, telegram, tell-a-Tootsie?" He stepped back some more. "Is she coming in?"

Sahara could tell he was not a fan of Ms. Tootsie's. "I'm sure she'll be here in a minute. You've got to get out of here. If she finds you here, we're *both* going to be in a lot of trouble."

"Just get rid of her. Tell her Ma Ray's not here."

"Ms. Tootsie's not going anywhere. She'll just stay and wait on Ma Ray to come back. They do a lot of canning and stuff together. You need to leave, and do it so she doesn't see you." Sahara looked out again. "She's coming! Quick, go out the back door!"

"Dog!" Junebug said. "Ain't this the devil?!" Junebug started to leave. He stopped and turned around. "Just so you know: we're not finished." He then blew her a kiss.

Sahara listened to be sure he'd left. She heard the back door open and close. She released a sigh, then stepped out on the front porch and smiled. "I'm so glad to see you," she said.

Andre looked behind him. "Say what? Who are you talking to?"

Sahara smiled. "Stop acting. I'm glad to see you."

"You're glad to see *me?* Okay, where are the cameras?" He looked high and low, pretending to search for a hidden camera.

She waved him off. "You're so silly. Ma Ray's not here."

"Yeah, I know."

"You know?" Sahara said with a puzzled look.

"Yeah. She called and asked me to come get you and bring you to Claudine's Boutique. She said she found something she thought you'd love. Asked if I wouldn't mind coming by the house to get you and bring you there."

"Are you serious?"

"Serious as a heart attack."

"Wow," Sahara said. She looked up at the sky. "Wow, God. Thank You." She began to nod. "You're *good!*"

"Are you talking to God?" Andre asked.

"Yeah. I was just thanking Him."

"And to think: Ma Ray said you'd likely give me a hard time." He looked up. "Thank You, God. You really *are* good!" Andre said.

Sahara looked back at the screen door, then back to Andre. "I need to get my purse," she said. "Then we can go."

She went back inside, ran upstairs, got her purse, and locked the front door on her way out.

Chapter 32

And it came to pass, when Joshua was by Jericho,
that he lifted up his eyes and looked, and, behold,
there stood a man over against him with his sword
drawn in his hand: and Joshua went unto him, and
said unto him, Art thou for us, or for our adversaries?
—Joshua 5:13

After fumbling around in her purse for a few minutes, Ma Ray finally found the key to the front door and unlocked it. She kept the car keys separate from her house keys since she didn't like having them on the same ring. She'd let Sahara drive back from the store, and on the back road home she'd allowed Crystal (who had her learner's permit) to drive the rest of the way home.

The girls were excited because they'd each found two fabulous outfits. Sahara had expressed total surprise in the outfit Ma Ray had picked out for her, then gotten Andre to come and get her so she could see it before she purchased it.

"I started to just buy it, and if you didn't like it, then return it," Ma Ray said. "But they didn't have that many of them, and I wanted to be sure that it was the right size. Just in case you *did* like it, I didn't want your size to be gone."

"Ma Ray, I'm so glad you sent for me," Sahara said as she rubbed her hands over the sunflower-colored pants outfit. "I love this! I can't believe you have such great taste. It's like you really know what I like when it comes to clothes like this. But I can't believe you actually paid this much for it," she said, gazing at the price tag still attached.

"Well, I thought it was beautiful. And I thought you'd look beautiful in it. What's the point of having money if we can't exchange it for things that make ourselves and the ones we love happy? In my eyes, that's *really* all money is good for. We sure can't take any of it with us when we leave this place."

"Yeah, but for what it cost, I never could have gotten Mama to buy it. Not for me, not in a million years," Sahara said.

"Well, I'm just glad everything worked out. And I'm glad you didn't give poor Andre a hard time when he came to get you. I started to call you and let you know, but I figured you might not answer the phone," Ma Ray said. "Besides, the art of surprise works every time."

"It was funny, though," Crystal said. "Ma Ray kept saying she had a funny feeling in her spirit. She kept saying it like something was bothering her. The next thing I knew, she was asking the lady in the shop if she could use the phone. She called over to Ms. Tootsie's house and asked for Andre."

Sahara pressed her hand up to her nose and mouth and shook her head.

"What's wrong?" Ma Ray asked Sahara. "Why are you looking like that?"

Sahara took her hand down. "Oh, nothing. I was just thinking about God, and how maybe God really *does* hear us."

"You had doubts that He doesn't?" Ma Ray said.

"Sometimes. I've just seen too many people pray and believe for stuff that never seems to happen."

"Oh, God hears us, now. I don't doubt that for a second," Ma Ray said. "We may not always get what we thought it was going to be like, but God hears us always. And He will show up in ways we never expect."

"Sort of like Andre coming over when he did," Sahara said.

Ma Ray tilted her head slightly. "Now, I don't know if we can say God was answering a prayer just because Andre showed up at the house today."

"You never know," Sahara said. "And I'm not talking about those outfits, either."

Sahara and Crystal went upstairs. Ma Ray sat down in the living room to catch her breath. She pulled off her shoes and began to rub her foot. That's when she happened to notice that her Swarovski crystal Maxi Swan was gone. It was easy to notice that it wasn't there, since it was one of the larger swan crystals. That's what she'd learned from Freda, who was as honest as the day is long. Freda's father had given Freda a smaller Swarovski swan. The one Boaz had given Ma Ray was around six inches tall, six inches wide, and cost around five thousand dollars.

When Ma Ray had learned that bit of information from Freda, she'd demanded that Boaz take it back. But of course, he wouldn't. He'd told Ma Ray to keep it and pass it down as a family heirloom, after she was gone, if she liked. But in the meantime, she could enjoy it. So she'd put it in the living room. Everyone who saw it was impressed. Most folks had seen the smaller versions, but few had seen one that size. It gave her great joy to say that her son had given it to her as a gift. *What a special child he is.*

Now, the swan wasn't there. She was praying it hadn't been broken or whoever had broken it was just too afraid to tell her. With her shoes still off, she went to the kitchen to take her medicine. While in there, she looked in the trashcan to see if there was any evidence of broken crystal. She didn't see anything. After taking her two pills, she set the glass on the counter, went back, and retrieved her shoes and purse, then went to her bedroom.

There was a tap on Ma Ray's bedroom door as she slipped her silk muumuu on. "Come in," she said as she tugged it down and straightened it.

"Ma Ray?" Crystal said.

"Yes, baby. Come on. I'm decent."

Crystal smiled and twirled into the room as she showed off the blue jean outfit Ma Ray had bought her. The skirt with beads and rhinestones flared out as she did her spins.

"My, my. Isn't that the prettiest thing," Ma Ray said.

"I love it," Crystal said. "I wanted you to see it with my shoes and everything."

"It's beautiful"—Ma Ray kissed Crystal—"just like you."

"Ah, Ma Ray. You're the only one who really thinks I'm beautiful."

"What?" Ma Ray said. "I am *not* the only one. I may just be the only one who can't hold it in. But you're a beautiful young woman, yes, you are." Ma Ray sat down on the edge of her bed. "Come . . . sit for a minute. I need to ask you something."

Crystal sat down next to Ma Ray.

"Would you, by any chance, know what may have become of my crystal swan?"

"You mean the one on the coffee table in the living room?" Crystal asked.

"Yeah. That one."

"It was there when we left to go to the store today."

"Are you sure?"

"Oh, yeah. I went over and looked at it. You see, the sun was flooding in, you know, like it does when you have the drapes opened. The rays were hitting it in such a way, it was making all these beautiful rainbows—colors spraying everywhere. I picked up the swan to look at it. It's just something how the sun rays can hit something like that and have all those beautiful colors—yellow, blue, purple, green—shooting all out from it."

"It *is* something, isn't it? But you're *certain* you saw it before we left? You're sure?"

"Positive. Maybe Sahara moved it. Do you want me to go ask her?"

Ma Ray forced a half of a smile. "No. I'll check with her later."

Crystal stood up, leaned down, hugged, then kissed Ma Ray on the cheek. "Thank you, Ma Ray, for this beautiful outfit." She struck a vogue pose. "I love you so much."

"I love you, too, baby."

After Crystal left, Ma Ray lifted her head up. "God, You're

going to have to help me down here on this one. I need You to
guide me, because I don't want to make a misstep. Please order
my steps. Help me get through to both my granddaughters.
Help me to say the right thing and to do the right thing. Please,
Lord. I need You. And as always, I thank You, kind sir. I thank
You. . . ."

Chapter 33

*And he said, Nay; but as captain of the host of the
Lord am I now come. And Joshua fell on his face to
the earth, and did worship, and said unto him, What
saith my lord unto his servant?*

—Joshua 5:14

Ma Ray spent time in prayer before making her way upstairs to Sahara's room. The door was open. She tapped on it. Sahara was dancing with the peach outfit she'd bought, held up against her body as she looked at her reflection in the mirror.

"Ma Ray," Sahara said, letting the outfit down slightly.

"That's a gorgeous outfit," Ma Ray said, sitting down on the bed.

"I know. I can't wait to wear it. In fact, Andre asked me about being in the modeling show they're having at the youth conference. I'm going to model this. It is *so* pretty." She hugged it gently before laying it carefully on the vanity chair.

"So, you're getting excited about the youth conference?" Ma Ray said.

"Kind of. It's something to do. I'm not sure that I won't be ready to leave before it's over. But hey, it's something to pass the time, right?"

"Sahara, I have something to ask you. Would you know what may have happened to my crystal swan?"

"The last I saw, it was downstairs in the living room on the coffee table." Sahara began to frown. "Is it not there now?"

"No, it's not."

"Did you check with Crystal?" Sahara asked. "Maybe she moved it."

"I did. She said she saw it earlier today but she didn't move it," Ma Ray said.

Sahara went and kneeled down by Ma Ray. "I didn't take it, Ma Ray. I didn't."

"Baby, I didn't say that you did. I'm just trying to find out what happened to it. I thought maybe someone broke it and whoever did just didn't want me to know about it."

"I saw it. I'm sure I saw it. I don't have a clue what may have happened to it after that. If Crystal didn't move it, and I didn't do it, I don't know what could have happened to it."

Ma Ray grabbed Sahara lightly by her chin and lifted her head slightly. "It's all right."

"No, it's not all right." Sahara stood up. "You think I took it!" She raised her voice somewhat.

"Now, I never said that," Ma Ray said, looking up at Sahara who, now, greatly towered over her.

"Yeah, but you're *thinking* it. You said something to Ms. Tootsie about stuff that's missing. But I want you to know that I didn't take your watch, or your money, or your crystal swan, or anything else you may find gone." Sahara's voice was still slightly elevated.

"Calm down. If you say you didn't take those things, then I believe you. But since we're talking, may I ask you something?" Ma Ray took Sahara by the hand and gently pulled her down next to her.

"Sure."

"Those drugs you had—"

"It was not drugs. It was *one* joint. One little joint," Sahara said.

"Okay. That joint—"

"Somebody gave it to me. I didn't buy it. I didn't take your money or things trying to get drugs. Ma Ray, you have to believe me. Someone gave me that joint, and I didn't smoke it, even though I could have."

"Sahara, could you tell me who gave it to you?"

"Ma Ray, I can't. Because if I tell you that, you'll just ask me more questions. And the honest truth is: the answers won't make a difference. I'd like to just drop it. But I don't want you thinking that me or Crystal are stealing from you. We wouldn't take anything from you. Not ever! You've been too good to us for us to ever do anything like that to you." Sahara began to cry.

Ma Ray hugged Sahara. "It's okay. It's okay. But you know what bothers me the most about what's been happening lately?"

Sahara pulled back and wiped her eyes with her hand. "What?"

"Why you accepted that drug . . . that joint in the first place. Why you brought it in the house. Why are you playing with fire the way you keep doing? You're on the edge, Sahara, and it's not going to take much to push you over completely. Now, I didn't just fall off of a turnip truck. Before you were even a twinkle in your parents' eyes, I've lived a life myself. And I want you to know that my life wasn't always pretty or sanitized. I've seen things. I know things. Don't let these wrinkles and this gray hair fool you."

Sahara stood up. "Why does everything have to be drama? I had a joint. People smoke marijuana now for medicinal purposes like glaucoma and to ease cancer treatments. And I *didn't* smoke it. In fact, I tore it up and threw it in the trash right in front of you. And even though you're not saying it, you really think I stole those things in order to get some drugs." Sahara wiped a few more tears from her eyes. "You're not going to say it, because you love me. But you're not sure that I *didn't* take it."

"I told you that it's okay. You say you didn't take the things, then you didn't take them. You say you're not doing drugs here at my house, I believe *that*."

"So if you don't think I did it, and if Crystal didn't do it, then who do you believe took your things?" Sahara asked.

Ma Ray smiled. "I don't know. But what I *do* know is that the truth will find its way to the light. It always does. Like a moth to the flame, it doesn't matter how long or what route it takes, the truth will always find its way to the light."

Chapter 34

And the captain of the Lord's host said unto Joshua,
Loose thy shoe from off thy foot; for the place
whereon thou standest is holy. And Joshua did so.
                                        —Joshua 5:15

After talking with Sahara, Ma Ray went downstairs to her bedroom. She began to pace back and forth as she prayed.

"Lord, it's me. It's me, oh, Lord. I'm at a crossroad right now. I have these granddaughters of mine here, and Lord, I'm going to be honest with You. I need Your help in knowing what You want me to do at this point. Lord, I know they have their things to deal with as young people. I know they are under a lot of pressure. I don't want to add to their problems by doing the wrong thing. I realize they look at me and merely see an old woman who doesn't understand. You, of all persons, know me. You know everything there is about me. You know my risings and my fallings. You know my ups and my downs. Lord, I need You to guide me. Show me what to do now. Show me what to do to get through to them.

"Especially Sahara. Lord, that child is hurting something fierce. She's in so much pain, I can feel it when I come near her. And it breaks my heart. It absolutely breaks my heart, Lord." Ma Ray began to cry. "Please, Lord. I'm begging You for divine guidance. Because I realize that if I make the wrong move, I could push her over, completely the wrong way. I know that the Bible tells us if we train up a child in the way he should go, when he's old, he will not depart from it. I used to wonder about that scripture.

Because Lord, You know how I brought up my own children. And honestly, there were times when they both seemed to have departed from what they'd been taught." Ma Ray got a tissue and wiped her eyes and her nose.

"But, Lord, You showed me that even though they may stray, that which has been put in them will always find a way to rise up again. Lenora is proving that with her life. She was a little out there herself, and You brought, or maybe I should say that You're *bringing* her back. Lord, I know Lenora still has stuff she's dealing with, trying to get things right with You. But she's trying, Lord. We're *all* trying. And You know I'm not trying to judge anyone down here. You know that. All I'm doing right now is searching to find a way to help save these precious gifts You've placed in our stewardship. I think I'm making some headway with Crystal. And I thank You for sending Aaron her way to help me in that effort. He's a good-hearted young man . . . a Godly focused young man.

"But Sahara . . . I don't know how to reach her. Lord, I really *don't* know what has happened to my things. And to be honest with You, I really don't care about the stuff per se. But it's what this missing stuff is representing right now that has me concerned. I know Lenora has said she believes both these children have or are doing drugs. Personally, I can't say—only You know *that* for sure. I can't say if Sahara is in need of money to fund a drug habit or not. Maybe that's what's going on here. What I *do* know is that *You* know, and that You have all the answers. I'm just asking You to direct me to do the right thing by them. Lord, whatever You want me to do. Whatever You would have me to do to get through to them of the dangers in the path they're taking, tell me and I will do that. Take my life and use my life to help someone else. That's why we're here on this earth. We're here to be a blessing to You, as well as to others. This is *all* about You, Lord. All about You."

Ma Ray suddenly felt a peace wash over her. And a flood of tears began to stream down her face. She took off her slippers and, before she knew anything, she was on bended knees, crying and praising God.

Chapter 35

So the ark of the Lord compassed the city, going about it once: and they came into the camp, and lodged in the camp.

—Joshua 6:11

Sahara paced back and forth liked a caged lion. She would flop down on her bed, then just as quickly jump back up and pace some more. So much was going through her head right now. It looked like when she was trying to do the right thing, something came along that just wouldn't let her. She was really trying to straighten up her life. At first she was giving Ma Ray a hard time because she didn't want to be here. But seeing how much Ma Ray loved them in *spite* of how she and Crystal were acting . . . Agape love. That's what Crystal said they had talked about at Bible study that night—agape . . . unconditional love. No condition to the love. Love for love's sake.

You can't do enough to earn it, and you can't do enough wrong stuff to lose it. Yes, love chastises you when you need to be chastised. But if one didn't love you, she wouldn't care enough to want for you the very best, even when, wrongly, you believe you know what's best.

Sahara stopped pacing, looked in the drawer of her nightstand, found the business card with the phone number, picked up the phone, and dialed. It went straight to voice mail without ever ringing. "This is Sahara. Give me a call as soon as you get this message." She hung up and began to pace some more. *That was the cell phone number. Cell phone receptions are the pits out here. Who knows when he may get that message,* she thought.

She picked up the phone and dialed the other number on the card. "Hi, yes. May I please speak with Junebug?"

"Hold on," said the person who answered the phone.

A few minutes later, Junebug picked up. "Hello," he said in his deep voice.

"Junebug, this is Sahara."

"Hey. What a pleasant surprise. To what do I owe this pleasure?"

"I need to see you," Sahara said.

"Okay. When do you want to do this?"

"Now."

"Right now?"

"Yes."

"You want me to come by and knock on the door or what?"

"No, I'll meet you up the road from here, near the fence, going toward your place."

"Can you give me about thirty minutes? I need to shower and shave," Junebug said.

"Fine. I'll be out there waiting. Up the road toward your way," she said. When she hung up, she began biting her thumbnail. "What is wrong with you, Sahara?" she said out loud. "What is wrong with you?" She placed her hands over her ears and pressed hard as she shook her head. "Shut up. Leave me alone! Leave . . . me . . . alone!"

Chapter 36

And Joshua rose early in the morning, and the priests took up the ark of the Lord.

—Joshua 6:12

Ma Ray had lain down and taken a nap after such a long day. Shopping always seemed to tire her out. Shopping with teenage girls was doubly tiring. It was dark outside when she woke, so that meant it had to be after eight now. She went into the kitchen and found a note from Crystal saying she'd gone to Bible study with Aaron. She'd come to tell her they were leaving, but Ma Ray was asleep and she didn't want to wake her. Ma Ray went up to Sahara's room. Sahara wasn't there. *Sahara must have gone, too,* she thought. Ma Ray smiled.

Crystal got home around nine-thirty. "Ma Ray, I hope you don't mind, but we went and got a hamburger and French fries after Bible study was over," Crystal said as she kissed Ma Ray on the cheek.

"No, that's fine. I suppose you girls are tired of *real* food and just need to have your fix of junk food every now and then."

Crystal laughed. "I guess you could say that."

Ma Ray looked at the door. "So where's Sahara? Is she still outside?"

"I don't know," Crystal said, bewildered. "I don't know where Sahara is."

"Sahara didn't go to Bible study with you?"

"No, ma'am. I suppose she must be in her room asleep. The

door was closed when I got ready to leave. I knocked on her door because you were asleep and I wanted to let someone know I was leaving, but she didn't answer."

"I looked in her room a little while ago. She's not there. I figured she'd gone with you all," Ma Ray said with a disturbed look.

"Sahara didn't go with us," Crystal said. "Maybe she went with Junebug. You know they were trying to go to Bible study last week. Maybe they tried again tonight."

"Maybe so. But she could have left a note, or told you, or *something*. That's not right. Will you try her cell phone for me?"

"I'll try. But I doubt she has it on her. Our phones have *yet* to work out here. We don't even bother charging them up anymore. But I'll see. It's possible where she is the call might go through." Crystal then went and dialed Sahara's number. "Nope. It goes straight to voice mail, and her mailbox is full. Most times when it does that, it means it can't locate a signal." Crystal hugged Ma Ray. "I'm sure she's fine. She'll be home any minute now."

"Yeah, I'm sure she is. I just wish I knew for sure where she went so at least I'd have some idea which direction to look in, should I need to."

"Sahara will be fine. She used to do stuff like this all the time at home. She probably didn't even think that you'd be worried. She's so used to just getting up and going when and where she pleases. Believe me, Ma Ray, Sahara can take care of herself. So don't worry *too* much about her, okay?"

Ma Ray nodded. But she couldn't help but think about the last conversation she and Sahara had. It was about the things that had gone missing and about drugs. She'd told Sahara that she believed her. She hadn't accused her or done anything to push her over the edge. *So what happened between their talk and now?*

Ma Ray stayed up waiting on Sahara to come home. She sat in the den on the couch to ensure she would see her no matter which door she might come in. At two o'clock, Ma Ray was past being worried. She was starting to question whether she should have, at least, called Lenora to let her know what was going on. Her mind began to race all over the place. *What if Sahara has actually been kidnapped? What if something bad has happened to her, and she is lying in some hospital with no one knowing who to contact?*

Ma Ray began to pray out loud. She sang a few of the old hymns that people rarely sang anymore. Hymns like "Amazing Grace" and "I Heard the Voice of Jesus Say." For some reason she began singing "Jesus Loves Me." As she sang, she thought of the words she was saying. "Little ones to Him belong, they are weak . . . "

At four a.m., she heard the key being placed in the lock. Then the front door was opened quietly and slowly, and closed just the same. Sahara had her sandals in her hands as she tiptoed into the house, past the living room, past the den, headed toward the stairs.

"Where have you been?" Ma Ray asked.

Sahara jumped and turned. "Ma Ray! You scared me." She placed her hand over her heart. "What are you doing still up?"

"Waiting on you," Ma Ray said, walking toward her.

Sahara let out a sigh and a short laugh. "You're not going to believe what happened."

"Try me."

"I decided to get out. I wasn't planning on staying long. I started walking down the road. I saw these girls close to my age. Their car had broken down. Of course, you know cell phones can't get much of a reception out here. I told them they were welcome to use our phone to call someone. You know, with you having a reliable landline and all. Well, it just so happens that someone pulled up with these all days—"

"Excuse me," Ma Ray said. "All days?"

"Yeah. Sorry. All days are twenty-four-inch rims. You know, those things that the rubber on tires wrap around."

"I know what rims are."

Sahara smiled nervously. "Sorry. Of course you know what rims are. Anyway, it turns out the girls just needed a jump. They got it and asked if I wanted to hang out with them. They were going to this place where this cool rapper was performing along with some spoken word artists. Well, I was going to ask you if I could go, but . . . "

"But . . . ?"

"Well, Ma Ray, I knew you would say no. And I'm seventeen years old. I'm old enough to go out without having to ask. I'm tired of you treating me like a baby. And honestly, I was a little upset with you because, even though you say you don't think I've been stealing from you, I believe that you do think I'm responsible."

Ma Ray shrugged. "I can't possibly think you're *too* responsible for anything much. You weren't *responsible* enough to feel you should let someone know what's going on when you *supposedly* just went off to some rap concert with a bunch of strangers, no less. According to you, of course. And you didn't think it was a good idea to let someone know what you were doing. If what you just told me is the truth, do you have any *idea* how dangerous what you just did is? Don't you watch or read the news?"

Sahara laughed. "Oh, Ma Ray. Nothing's going to happen to me."

"That's exactly what the last person who turned up missing or dead most likely thought. You young folks don't get it, do you? You think you're invincible. Well, you're not. Stuff happens to young folks just like it happens to middle-age folks and old folks. You don't get an exemption for doing crazy stuff just because you're too young to know better. That's why God gave you us. He wants us to look out for you, to guide you in the right direction and *toward* the right decisions. You need to thank God that you stepped back in this house unharmed."

"Sure. Thank You, God," Sahara said, looking upward.

"Now you're trying to be funny," Ma Ray said.

"I'm not. You said I should thank God. And you're right. What I did was stupid, and I'm blessed that things turned out okay. Although, I'm telling you, Ma Ray, I was really never in any danger."

"So, did you have sex while you were out?"

"What?"

"You're not deaf; you heard the question," Ma Ray said. "Did you have sex?"

Sahara started chuckling. "Ewww! That's gross, Ma Ray. I'm not *about* to have a conversation with you about sex. No specifics like *that,* anyway. Double ewww."

"Sahara, you're playing a dangerous game with your life. You're playing Russian roulette. You *have* to change! You *have* to stop and really think about what you're doing. This is your life we're talking about. You get one. One! And every decision you make affects your life now and even later, down the road. I'm telling you. You'd better hear me."

"Ma Ray, I don't mean to be disrespectful, but I *really* don't feel like hearing a lecture *or* a pep talk right now. I went out. I had a good time. I'm back here safely, unharmed. Hey—no harm, no foul. Now, if you want to punish me for going somewhere without your permission, then fine—punish me. Do what you have to do. I'm already going to be punished having to go to this boring youth conference on Friday and Saturday. We can consider that punishment enough. But for now, I'm tired—I'm sure you are, too—and I'm going to bed. So good night." Sahara walked up the steps and refused to look back.

Chapter 37

*And the second day they compassed the city once,
and returned into the camp: so they did six days.*
—Joshua 6:14

"Ma Ray," Tootsie said as soon as Ma Ray answered the phone, "these young folks need us. My pastor said we have to step up and help him get some real talk across to them."

"I hear you, Tootsie, and I agree with both you *and* your pastor," Ma Ray said.

"Then if you agree, we need you to get on board with what they're asking us to do," Tootsie said.

"Tootsie, nobody has asked me to do anything. I don't even go to your church."

"I understand that, but this is not about groups, it's about the Kingdom. This is Kingdom work, and we need all hands on deck. For this youth conference coming up, my pastor is sending out an S.O.S.—Saving Other Saints—for every willing and skillful, sanctified laborer to grab a rake, a pick, a shovel, a hoe . . . whatever you have that you can use, and to come help. We got some cleaning up to do. Pastor Weldon is sending out the distress signal for anyone who can help to come help."

"Tootsie, those young folks don't want us at their conference, and you and I *both* know that. This is *their* thing."

"It might be *their* thing, but they can't just do what they want to do. Pastor Weldon says our youth are in trouble and we have to step up and do our part to help save them. It's time that we throw out the lifeline and send out those little boats. . . . What do they call those little boats that be on those big ships?"

"Boats. Rafts."

"Yeah . . . rafts. We need to get some rafts out there and help pull our drowning children in and back safely on the Rock. And we know *that* Rock is Jesus!"

Ma Ray laughed. "Tootsie, you know you can get wound up."

"Of course I can. Who wouldn't get wound up when you're talking about Jesus? You and I know what Jesus has done for us. He saved me. I was sinking deep in sin, do you hear me? Sinking! God took time out to send His Son to save me. Then your husband, God rest His sweet soul, took time out to bless me and my family by sharing with us what Jesus *truly* did for somebody like little ole me.

"You know what God did in your own life. I know what He did in mine. It's high time you tell it, Ma Ray. Can't nobody tell your story like you can tell your story. It's time we get off the cruise ship, get into the little boats . . . the rafts, and go rescue as many of these precious, drowning youths as we can. Drugs, sex, bullying, gangs, huffing, puffing, texting, sexting: you name it, these precious ones are having to deal with it. We can't sit on the sidelines any longer. We can't let any more of our children get snatched up by the devil while we sit in our comfy little homes, on our comfy little chairs, waiting on the Lord to make a way or to call us home to glory. We just can't!"

"Fine, Tootsie. Whatever you need of me, I'm willing to do."

"Good! I'll let Pastor Weldon know," Tootsie said. "That young preacher *knows* he's a powerful man of God. Most of these young folks, including these preachers these days, seem to be trying to push us old folks out of the way and over to the side. But Pastor Weldon says God has need of us. We are the salt of the earth that has not lost our flavor. We are seasoned salt who not only have flavor but favor! And Pastor Weldon, for one, will not allow us to retire. Not on the Lord, and not in doing the Lord's work."

"I've never said I was retired," Ma Ray said. "As long as I have breath in me, I want to be used in the service of the Lord."

"Well, from what Pastor Weldon told me, he's planning to have a session with us older folks talking to the younger folks. He's calling the session, Let Me Rap to You. I couldn't help but laugh. Young folks think they came up with the word rap. They don't have a clue. That's what Jacob, the man who eventually became my husband, said to me when he was trying to talk to me. 'Hey, girl. Let me rap to you.' That man's rap was so strong, I couldn't help *but* to end up marrying him."

"Whatever is needed of me, just let him know I'm more than willing to do it. If Pastor Weldon needs me to march around the city and keep my mouth closed, I'll march around the city and hold my tongue. If he wants me to shout unto the Lord when he gives the command to shout, I'll shout with all that I have. We'll bring down the walls that are separating us from God's promises. Then we're going to go into that land, and take what God has already given us, and take *back* what the enemy has stolen from us. Sign me up. I got my war shoes on, and I'm ready for battle," Ma Ray said.

Tootsie laughed. "Listen at *you*. You're a bit radical, don't you think?"

"Hey, whatever it takes to do what God has called, I'm ready, willing, and able," Ma Ray said. "I'm not sure how the young folks will receive us, but it's not about us."

"You got that right! Well, I can tell you that Pastor Weldon put me over this part of the program. All I need is for you to bring something to the table that will get these young folks' attention in a big way. They need to hear some truth. As my grandson Andre likes to say—Real Talk. It's time out for us trying to hide things God has delivered us from. It time out for us trying to uphold some image of us being perfect all of our lives. These young folks need some *real talk*. They need to know there really is nothing new under the sun. They need to hear some truth and some straight talk. And Ma Ray, I believe you can bring it, if you'll keep your thoughts on the end goal here. Sometimes, Ma Ray, we have to show our scars, to let others know that we've been in battle before and we came out victorious, anyway. Our scars may show that we've been battered, but our present lives prove it was God who brought us through."

Ma Ray was quiet for a second. "I don't know about showing our scars, Tootsie. I mean, that's in the past. It's over and done with."

"Ma Ray," Tootsie said, "if it saves one life . . . one soul, then there is a purpose in what you've come through. It shows others that if God did it for you, He will do it for them as well. God is no respecter of persons. These are *our* children. They're *all* our children. This is war, Ma Ray. The enemy got my daughter; I'm not going to let him take any more of our children. Not when it's in our power to stop him. And God has given us everything we need to do what He's called us to do. Everything!"

Ma Ray sighed. "You're right, Tootsie. I'm fired up and ready to go! I'll pray on what God will have me to say."

"Well, whatever you talk on, it needs to last no more than twenty minutes. There will be three of us during this session. I'm going to tell the truth about my alcohol and drug abuse problems. A woman named Jessie Mae Wooten is going to speak on the dangers of hooking up with the wrong crowd."

"Jessie Mae Wooten? Is she that woman that went to prison for killing someone?" Ma Ray asked.

"Yep. That's her. Hopefully, she can keep someone from experiencing what happened to her. She thought she was being cool by hanging out with the 'in' crowd. And when that murder went down, she found herself smack-dab 'in,' all right. In the middle of being charged with pulling the trigger as though she had, even though she didn't. She thought she was hanging out and having fun and found herself incarcerated for fifteen years. She's a good Christian woman now, but she lost a lot of her life, rotting away in that prison cell. Jessie Mae Wooten has a powerful testimony."

"So," Ma Ray said, "do you know how you plan to talk about yours?"

"Not right this minute. But you can believe I'm going to pray about what God will have me do. And I'll bring it just like you and Jessie Mae had better bring it. Just make sure whatever you plan on talking about is not boring or sounds like some old person trying to tell young folks what to do. Young folks hate that. They tune out when we do that."

"I *know* you're not trying to tell *me* what to do," Ma Ray said with a short laugh.

"Yeah, well, we all know you, Ray. You're so prim and proper most of the time. The last thing we need is for us old people to be up there looking down our noses at the young folks, like we ain't never done a wrong thing. We have to let them see that we were young once upon a time. Truth be told, I still feel like I'm seventeen on the inside. My mind ain't aging a lick. It's this old body that's trying to betray me," Tootsie said.

"What you talking about," Ma Ray said, agreeing. "When I look in the mirror sometimes, I say, 'Who is that old woman staring back at me?' My body is quick to remind me, though, that although my mind is telling me I can still do some stuff, it *ain't gonna happen.* And I'd *better* go sit my *old self down* somewhere."

"You mean like when you think about doing a fifty-yard dash and you discover you're doing good just to stand up without wobbling?" Tootsie said, chuckling.

"Precisely. If we could only get young folks to understand. We are *definitely* not the enemy."

"Well, turnabout is fair play. We didn't want to hear none of this junk when we were coming up," Tootsie said. "Now, we're on the other end."

"I know. Do you have any idea how many times I've wished I could go back and have a little chat with the young me? I would tell that child to not be in a hurry to grow up. To enjoy every minute of life while she can instead of wishing her days and years away. And to let her mother and father love on her, for as much and as long as she can, while she can. That's what I'd tell the teenage Rayna Armstrong. Oh, and to make some better decisions."

"Girl, if I could go back in time . . . I would tell myself to put more of my money in the bank instead of trying to buy everything I saw. 'Cause nothing ever seems as great as when you thought you first wanted it. I have dresses right now that I bought, and they still have tags on them, hanging in my closet. I can't even fit in some of them anymore."

"Sounds to me like maybe you should be telling your *old* self to tell your old self a few words of wisdom."

"Okay, I can tell it's time for me to get off this phone now. Anyway, we're on program to do this Saturday, at eleven that morning. All Pastor Weldon asks is that we *bring it.*" She giggled. "That's how he talks, you know. He said, 'Mama Tootsie, whatever you all decide to do, I need you to bring it, and to bring it hard.' He's a good pastor. And I'm just thankful that my grandsons are being so touched and blessed by this man of God."

"It sounds like you're being touched and blessed a lot yourself," Ma Ray said.

"If you can bring the Word of God, you have my attention. Well, I'm getting off of this tele-phone here. I need to work on my presentation. 'Cause I know you're going to try to show off with yours."

"Oh, Tootsie, now that's not a Christian thing to say to your fellow sister in the Lord."

"Yeah, well, I know you. And you're not going to have me looking bad because you brought it while I was trying to be nice. I'll talk to you later," Tootsie said.

Ma Ray looked up. "God, direct my path. Let me know what *You* want me to do for this event. Let me decrease while You increase. It's not about me. I know this. It's for Your glory. I want You to get the glory through whatever I do. Whatever You direct me to do, I'll do. Please, just use me, Lord, in Your service. In Jesus' name I pray. Amen."

Chapter 38

And it came to pass on the seventh day, that they rose early about the dawning of the day, and compassed the city after the same manner seven times: only on that day they compassed the city seven times.

—Joshua 6:15

Sahara and Crystal were getting ready to go to the youth conference on Friday morning. Andre and Aaron were coming to pick them up to keep Ma Ray from having to take them and drop them off. Sahara had countered that idea, volunteering to drive them. But Ma Ray told her she didn't care to be at the house without her transportation at her disposal.

"You just don't trust me," Sahara said. "What do you think? That I'll not go to the conference? Or that I'll go but then sneak off and go somewhere else? You have two cars here. You could let me drive one of them. I'll happily drive the deuce and a quarter. Ma Ray, I've apologized for the other night. I promise you: I'll drive your car straight to the church and straight back home after it's over. Crystal will be with me. She's gung ho about this conference. If I were to sneak out or anything, you know she'd tell it."

Ma Ray cut her eyes at Sahara and merely smiled.

"Ma Ray, are you listening to me?" Sahara said. "There's no reason for the Woods twins to come and get us. People may get the wrong idea. You know if we arrive with them, people will think we're their dates or something. And I don't want anybody thinking I'm with Andre. Ms. Tootsie is letting them drive themselves. Why won't you let me?"

Ma Ray smiled again. "You need to hurry and finish getting ready. They'll be here in about twenty minutes. You know how they don't believe in being late for church."

"Ma Ray, why aren't you listening to me?" Sahara said, stomping her foot a few times. "Now you're just making me not even want to go to this stupid conference."

"Sahara, don't start with me. My patience can only be worn so thin."

Crystal started laughing. "You sounded just like Mama when you said that. Mama says that to us all the time."

"I guess that means she must have gotten it from me. And we know what they say: The apple doesn't fall far from the tree. That's also a great lesson regarding the people you choose to hang around. Before you know anything, you're doing some of the same things they're doing without you even realizing it."

"Ma Ray, please. I'm begging you. Please let me drive your deuce and a quarter to the conference. Please." Sahara gave Ma Ray her best puppy-dog look.

"Okay, so now you're begging me to drive the car you usually act like you don't want to be seen dead riding in?" Ma Ray said with a chuckle. "Sahara, please finish getting ready. You're not driving the car, either car, and that's final."

Sahara stomped off.

"And stop that stomping!" Ma Ray said, hollering behind her.

Crystal stood there grinning.

"What are *you* so happy about?" Ma Ray asked.

"Nothing."

"Nothing, huh?" Ma Ray smiled back equally as devious. "You just make sure you behave yourself with Aaron, Missy. I see how the two of you are with each other."

"Ma Ray! Stop *that!*"

"What? Rock, paper, scissors and the winner gets a peck."

"You're not supposed to be talking like that," Crystal said, her eyes bucked.

"Oh, but it's okay for your know-nothing friends to tell you stuff that have to do with *that*." Ma Ray slightly mocked Crystal.

She grabbed Crystal gently by her shoulders and turned her squarely in front of her. "You see this face?"

"Yes, ma'am."

"You see these wrinkles and these sags?" Ma Ray said, pointing at her own face.

"Yes, ma'am."

"Well, I want you to know that I earned every one of them. This came from years of living. That means I know a thing or two. If you really want to know something and you want to know the truth, *and* you want to know the truth from someone who has your best interest at heart, then you come to *this* face or your mother's face and you talk to us about it. Your little friends, and even Sahara, don't know jack! Not really. They're merely experimenting, doing trial and error, just like you. We older folks already have what people call 'bought sense.' Already paid for. That means: there's no reason for you to go out and purchase some sense again. Just come to us and get what we have for free. Save your money, your time, and your experience. Use your experience on some good stuff and skip the bad. Believe me, all that's yellow and shines ain't gold. Sometimes, it's simply fool's gold."

"Right," Crystal said, sounding more like she was merely humoring Ma Ray.

"Oh, you're just trying to patronize me now. All right. If you mess around and get your wagon stuck in a ditch after this, don't come hunting for me," Ma Ray said.

Crystal started laughing. "You're so funny, Ma Ray. You don't have to worry about *my* wagon getting stuck in a ditch, because I don't *have* a wagon."

"All right, Little Miss Smarty-Pants. But seriously, though—wagon or no wagon—if you ever find yourself in trouble, just know that I'm here for you."

When Sahara and Crystal returned from the youth conference later that evening, Sahara stopped by the kitchen where Ma Ray was busy cooking.

"Thanks a lot!" Sahara said to Ma Ray in a slightly nasty tone.

"You're welcome," Ma Ray said, cheerily. "Supper is almost ready."

"I didn't really *mean* thank you," Sahara said.

"Really now." Ma Ray began to put homemade rolls onto a greased pan.

"That was a day, all right. And just like I told you, some of the people there thought I was with Andre. It was like, just because some of those emos saw me getting out of the car with Andre, they were making an effort to try and take him from me."

"Emos? What are emos?" Ma Ray asked as she put the pan in the preheated oven.

"Emo is short for emotional. You know, people who are suicidal, depressed, or dealing with emotional stuff. Emos."

"Oh." Ma Ray sang the word. "That terminology could apply to a *bunch* of folks I know. Emo. I'll have to remember that one and use it. Tootsie is always trying to throw out some newfangled word to show how hip she is. Wait until I throw this one on her."

"Ma Ray, can we please stay on topic?" Sahara said. "I'm trying to tell you that because you made me ride to church with Andre, now those girls are stepping up their game, as though they could *really* take him from me."

"Why do you care? You don't want him, anyway. Let them step it up. Although I *do* feel sorry for poor Andre. He's such a nice young man. But I'm sure he knows how to handle a gang of little women."

"None of them could take him from me," Sahara said, defiantly.

"I know," Ma Ray said.

"Would you please stop trying to use reverse psychology on me," Sahara said. "I'm not interested in Andre, and I'm not going to fight to keep him. If any of those girls want him, they are welcome to have him. Most of them are a hot mess, anyway. And if he's interested in them, it only shows how shallow he *really* is and that he has no taste. And I *definitely* am not interested in a guy who has *no* taste."

"Absolutely," Ma Ray said. She stopped and smiled at Sahara.

"Well, tomorrow you won't have to worry about riding to church with Andre."

"Really!" Sahara's eyes lit up. "I won't?"

"Nope." Ma Ray tapped her on the nose. "Tomorrow, I'll be driving you and Crystal to church."

"*You're* driving us?"

"Yes, I am. I was asked to be one of the morning speakers." She hunched her eyebrows up a few times like Groucho Marx. "How about *those* apples?"

Sahara's smile instantly left. "What? You're speaking *and* you're taking us?"

"Yes, I am. So that's one more thing you can thank me for." Ma Ray checked on the rolls. "Now, go wash up and tell Crystal to get off the phone and come on down for supper."

Sahara turned in a slight huff to leave.

"Oh, and Sahara, try not to stomp when you go upstairs. I have a sour cream pound cake in the bottom oven and, even though it doesn't happen like it used to when I was growing up, I don't want to take any chances with my cake possibly falling."

Sahara turned back around, squinted her eyes, and shook her head. "You're doing this to punish me, aren't you?"

"Child, please. Trust me when I say this: the world, and the people in it, truly . . . *truly* does *not* revolve around you!"

Chapter 39

And it came to pass at the seventh time, when the priests blew with the trumpets, Joshua said unto the people, Shout; for the Lord hath given you the city.
—Joshua 6:16

Sahara dragged into the eleven o'clock session. She was not looking forward to this one *at all.* She would never let Ma Ray know this, but all of the other sessions from Friday until this point had been really quite wonderful. She'd had a lot of fun, despite her objections and her having set herself from the start that she was not going to.

Crystal had been right about the church and the pastor. Pastor Weldon was really in tune with *all* the people he was the undershepherd over. That's how he referred to himself: an undershepherd under Christ. The young people loved him just as much as the older crowd. He was funny. He kept your attention. And he had, so far, orchestrated an event that had been both informative and entertaining. Sahara was already starting to rethink things in her life. She wasn't completely ready to do a 180-degree turn just yet, but a 45- or 90-degree change was positively probable.

Now they were set to hear from the senior citizens, or the seasoned-salt folks, as was printed on the agenda. The pastor came up first to set the atmosphere as to why he wanted and requested this session. He prayed for the speakers and for the young people to have ears to hear. Some of the young people snickered; Sahara understood why. They *had* ears, they could hear fine, so *why pray for people who have ears to hear?* That never made sense to her.

The first person that spoke was okay. She did a one-woman show demonstrating how going along to get along can get you more time than you may want, in places you don't want to be. Her name was Jessie Mae Wooten. They soon heard how she'd spent time in prison because she'd hooked up with the wrong crowd that ended up killing a man while trying to rob him. She wasn't the one who pulled the trigger, but her being there was just the same as though she had. Sahara never really considered herself as a follower. So even though she heard what Ms. Wooten was trying to say, she didn't feel the friends in her life were a problem. She would just need to be sure she didn't get framed, along with people who could be doing the wrong thing. *Lesson received. Check.*

Then Ms. Tootsie got up, coming with real talk on the dangers and pitfalls of alcohol and drugs. She told how she started drinking at the age of twelve. After she couldn't get the same feelings she'd gotten with drinking, she stepped up to soft drugs, then the hard drugs. Eventually, she met someone who told her how much God loved her. It was rough, but she was finally able to get clean.

"Unfortunately, one of my daughters ended up walking in the exact same path as I," Tootsie said. "I can't even begin to tell you how bad I felt when I learned my daughter was doing the things I'd done myself. I felt like it was all my fault. I'd started this curse, looking for my own pleasure, to ease my own pain. And somehow, I passed the curse on to someone I love dearly. I watched my daughter literally ruin her life. And there was nothing much I could say or do to get through to her. It's hard to get people to listen to you when *you've* done things equal to it. Mostly because they think you're just trying to keep them from having fun after you've had it. Like it's fun to be so wasted that you wake up in places you don't even know how you got there. To wonder what you've done, and with *whom,* that may come back and bite you big-time later."

Some in the audience lowered their heads.

"Oh, some of you have been there or you know someone who has?" Tootsie said. "Honestly, that breaks my heart. You know why it breaks my heart? It means some of you have been in pain to the degree that you were trying to self-medicate and make the pain go away. Some of you are hurting so bad that you don't want to be conscious as you go through life. That's just wrong. None of you should be in that place. None of you should be throwing your life away like that. I know what you're thinking. I'm an old lady who's had her fun. I don't have the problems nor have I experienced your problems." Tootsie nodded.

"Okay, let's see now. My daddy used to beat my mother so bad that she couldn't get up and walk for days. Then he would beat her again *because* she hadn't gotten up and cooked and cleaned in days, *because* she'd been beaten so bad that she couldn't get up. I couldn't go to school much because me and my siblings were needed to help out on the sharecropping farm during that time. People made fun of us because we didn't have anything, and everybody in the community knew what kind of a father we had. At fifteen, I met this fellow who showed me a lot of attention. We drank, did lots of drugs together. A few days after I turned eighteen, he overdosed. Right in front of me . . . dead. Just like that, he was gone. I don't know if you've ever been with someone who died right in front of you, but suffice it to say, it affected me hard. It caused me to see where I was headed myself. That it wasn't a game; this was real life. And except for Jesus, nobody gets out of here alive."

A girl sitting directly in front of Sahara began to cry. She cried so hard, Tootsie stopped talking for a minute and went over and hugged her. Tootsie held on to her as she continued to speak. "Young folks, there's a better way. You don't need alcohol or drugs to make it. You're better than that. You're stronger than that. You've already shown how strong you are just by making it to this point in life. Now, let that other junk go. That's the devil's way of trying to steal from you, trying to kill you, trying to destroy you. Can't you see it? Please, I'm begging you. If you're doing these things, make up in your mind that you're going to change your life today." Tootsie walked back to the front.

"We're going to have a time today where you can talk to somebody and take steps to get help," Tootsie continued. "This is not about taking away your fun. This is about you realizing how valuable you are and having the *right* kind of fun. It's about seeing the truth, which is: Satan wants to take you out. Satan doesn't want you to experience the abundant life Jesus gave His life for you to have. And I'm not talking about life after you leave this place. I'm talking about life *while* you're here on earth. You want to get high, then get high on Jesus. You need a drink, take a drink from the Living Water. You know: there's nothing like getting drunk on the Holy Spirit. He's a sweet, sweet Spirit."

Everybody clapped when Tootsie finished. What she said hit Sahara harder than she cared to admit. She wasn't *heavy* into drugs by any means. She'd tried marijuana, but she'd also learned that marijuana really wasn't her thing. Maybe there had been times when she'd gone along to appear cool, which the more she thought about it now, the more she was able to see how foolish that was. She was smarter than most of the people she hung out with. But she was acting dumber by letting them make a fool out of her. They were showing *their* strength. Not her. But after this day, she would definitely make a change and not, as Ms. Tootsie had said in her talk, "go along just to get along." This was her life, and she had to take it back . . . completely. Completely. Not a piece of it—all of it.

"We're taking the city," Pastor Weldon was saying. "We're taking the city!" He was hyped. "After we march, we're going to shout the walls down, and we're going into God's Promised Land!"

Chapter 40

*And the city shall be accursed, even it, and all that
are therein, to the Lord: only Rahab the harlot shall
live, she and all that are with her in the house, because she hid the messengers that we sent.*

—Joshua 6:17

"My name is Rayna Towers, but everybody calls me Ma
Ray. I'm the mother of two grown children, the grandmother of six grandchildren. I prayed about what God would
have me tell all of you here today. The funny thing about God
is, sometimes, He will have you to do the uncommon thing to
reach those He loves the most. I know when you young folk
look at folks like me, Ms. Tootsie, and Ms. Jessie Mae Wooten"—
Ma Ray nodded at the other women—"all you see is what we've
become. You think that what you see now is who we always
were. Well, God has instructed me to let you know that where
we are is not where we started from. God told me I had to bring
you a true ray of hope. To let you know that you may be going
through a terrible storm, but God will always give you a ray of
hope.

"A ray of hope can be a powerful thing. I don't know if
you've ever seen sunlight peeking through a crack. But that
one small ray can affect its surroundings. A ray can bring light
to a dark place. When you look in the mirror, what you see now
is what we *used* to see. By that I mean, we were once young and
vibrant, and we thought we knew everything, much like many
of you do now." Ma Ray pointed her finger and made a sweep-
ing motion. "Like you, we were beautiful—"

"Handsome," Aaron said as he did his head and neck like a rooster scratching while strutting. "Guys are handsome."

"Excuse me, young men. I definitely mean no disrespect to any of you young men present today. So, as I speak, please adjust the girlie references accordingly," Ma Ray said with a smile. "Let me say this before I continue. I really didn't want to tell this today. I didn't. In fact, I've kept this a secret for most of my adult life. My own children certainly don't know it. And I will be completely honest with you: I argued with God something fierce about me having to come before you and reveal this at this time. But you know what? This *truly* is a testament to just how much God loves you. He loves you so much, He's impressed upon me to tell this, so that I might be able to help at least one"—she held up her index finger—"of you. Of course, I'm hoping for more than one because, believe me, this is not an easy thing for me to share with anyone. If you know me, you know it's not. But if this helps at least one, then it will be *more* than worth it.

"This is made even more difficult for me because I'll be sharing this for the first time in front of my two lovely granddaughters." Ma Ray briefly glanced at Sahara and Crystal. "I imagine this won't be easy for them to hear, either." Ma Ray again looked over toward Crystal and Sahara and swallowed hard. She could already see the plea making its way on Sahara's face for her not to do or say anything to embarrass her.

Ma Ray took a deep breath, released it, then smiled. "I want to talk with y'all about sex outside of marriage and all this other stuff you teenagers and young adults are so gung ho to engage in. And if the shoe happens to fit, any of you older folks here, too."

"Oh, no," Jessie Mae Wooten said, standing and waving her hand in the air. "I don't know if that's something that ought to be discussed in a place like a church. Not by us Christians."

Pastor Weldon stood and directed his comments to Jessie Mae Wooten. "Ms. Wooten, if the church doesn't address this with our youth, then where and from whom do you think they're going to go to learn it? At least learn it God's way?"

Jessie Mae Wooten nodded slowly. "You right, Pastor. I'm sorry. Go on and testify, Ms. Ray." She sat back down.

Ma Ray continued. "I know what it is to be young and to feel like you can conquer the world. To my young women, I especially know, as a young woman myself with curves in all the right places, the power you feel in garnering young men's attention. I can only imagine, as a young man, the effect of seeing us in all of our glory has on you. It can be quite intoxicating. But to my young women and my young men, let me tell you this: your body is the temple of the Lord. I don't know if you truly understand what that means."

"It's where God chooses to dwell," Andre said. "Instead of the church building, God actually dwells inside of those who have invited Jesus into their hearts and lives."

"Absolutely correct," Ma Ray said. "And when you're doing things that are displeasing to God . . . that offend God, especially after you've invited Him to come and live . . . to dwell, to set up residence inside of you, I want you to remember that God is there with you, having to be present and to witness *whatever* it is that you're doing at the time. Sex outside of marriage is wrong. It's a sin. Period. It doesn't matter how you try to fix it up, dress it up, put perfume on it—it's wrong. And every time you're doing what you do, God is right there with you." Ma Ray took a swallow of the water she'd been given. "At age eighteen, I became a prostitute—"

Sahara jumped to her feet. "Stop it, Ma Ray. Stop it! What are you doing?"

Ma Ray looked at her. "Sahara—"

"You're just doing this to get my attention," Sahara said. "Okay, Ma Ray. I get what you're trying to say. But you don't have to go to this extreme to prove your point. I'm sorry for the way I've acted. I promise you, I'll do better. But you don't have to get up here, saying stuff like this, stuff that's *not* true, just to punish me or to get my attention."

"Sahara, this isn't all *just* about you. This is to help someone here to understand that sex before marriage and outside of marriage is wrong. It's not cool, it's not hip, and it's not even safe, most of the time. You young people who are having sex are putting yourself at a risk you don't even realize. I read, just the other day, where the CDC is saying that herpes, which is simplex virus type 2—a lifelong incurable disease—is *twice* as high among women than men and more than *three* times higher among black people than whites. And the most affected group of all is black women. I believe it said forty-eight percent. And most folks who have the herpes virus don't even have a clue that they have it. Some just think that they merely have a yeast infection when that's not at all what it is. Then there's HIV/ AIDS. Lord have mercy, it's killing folks, and Satan is taking out our young, middle-age, *and* older folks, using the oldest trick in the book: sex outside of God's best for you. Fornication and adultery, that's what we're talking about here."

Keisha raised her hand. "Ms. Ray, for some of us, it's too late to go back."

Ma Ray began to shake her head. "No, baby. With God, it's never too late to do the right thing. God can fix things, He can fix things. God is a God of another chance. I'm telling you, He's God of another chance."

"So, what is God's best?" eighteen-year old Marvin asked.

"God's best is for you to save yourself for that one special person He has created *just* for you. You see the problem is: we act like we have to do something that we really don't. We need to get our bodies under the control of the Holy Spirit. I'm talking about submitting to the direction of the Holy Spirit residing inside of you, who will let you know when you're headed in the wrong direction. The Holy Spirit will rein you in and tell you to pump your brakes."

Everybody laughed.

"Ma Ray, what do you know about 'pumping your brakes'?" Marvin asked.

"I have a car," Ma Ray said with a laugh. "Actually, I've been brushing up on my teen terminology. You know there is a language class for senior citizens and saints on young folks' talk."

"There is not," a teenage girl said. "Is there?"

"I'm just kidding. But I do try to keep up, so y'all can't get *too* much over my head. Me and Ms. Tootsie there"—she pointed at Tootsie—"find new terms and share them with each other. In fact, I learned a new one just yesterday: emo."

"Ah," Pastor Weldon said. "You are *quite* the bomb, Ma Ray."

"Now, Pastor, that one's a little over my head. Although from the tone of your voice, it sounds like it's a *good* thing," Ma Ray said.

"Absolutely," Pastor Weldon said. "It means you're dynamite . . . explosive."

"So, to conclude my presentation," Ma Ray said, "I just want you to know that the greatest gift you could ever give your husband or wife on your wedding night is yourself—untouched and undefiled. I would love for all of you to pledge today, truly with your heart, that you'll protect that precious gift with everything you have within you, until that time."

"What if it's too late to be able to do that?" Allison asked. "What if someone would like to be able to do that, but they've already messed up?"

"Ah, then there's something you can do today called revirgin. You can vow to start from this day forward to protect your special gift. Vow that you'll keep your precious gift, to be given only on your wedding night, and thereafter to your spouse, and only to your spouse."

"It's not easy for us," Allison said. "Back in the old days, y'all could do stuff like that. Folks during your day got married at thirteen, fourteen, fifteen, and sixteen. From all I've heard and read, you were considered an old maid if you turned twenty and weren't married yet. What you—and I don't mean you in particular, Ms. Ray, but I mean all the church folks who believe we're supposed to remain virgins until we're married—don't understand is how much pressure we teenagers are under. And it's not always somebody else pressuring us. Sometimes it's our hormones and the feelings we get that are difficult to keep under control. To have to keep ourselves until we've graduated college is hard, almost impossible really. I would be twenty-two. When you're young, time moves slow."

"I know it's hard," Ma Ray said. "But if you could just think about how awesome it would be to hold on to your precious jewel, determined not to cast your pearls before the swine. If you can just hold on to the thought of a wedding night where you can present your husband or wife, whichever is the case, with something that no one else has ever had before—my goodness! What generally happens, though, is your friends will tell you how great their premature experience was, make it sound like it was the best thing that ever happened to them. And truthfully, some of the places people lose their virginity in is neither romantic nor sexy at all. Forgive me, I don't mean to be graphic."

"Well, you're telling the truth," Allison said. "You're just telling it like it is."

"You sure are." More teens nodded and chimed in.

Ma Ray swallowed, then smiled. "Well"—she clapped one time—"my time is up. I hope I've said something to make you look at this in a different way. You are *worth* the wait. If someone doesn't want to wait for you or they try to convince you that you're so special you *have* to do this, whether it's to prove that you love them or them to prove that they love you, then they don't really love you the way you deserve to be loved. Yes, it's hard. Yes, you're dealing with hormones. I'll let you in on a little secret: many adults don't have this under control, either. Sad, but true. That's why we all need the Holy Spirit.

"So, it's not just a teen or YA problem. But all of us must realize that when we're going against what God has said, after we have asked Him to come into our hearts and our lives, that what we do, He is right there seeing everything when we do it. Now, do you really want God there watching as you blatantly disobey Him? Because He's there. You don't get to ask Him to leave while you satisfy your flesh, then come back when you're done. He sees everything. God is the One we *really* should care about. Amen?"

"Amen," the teen group said in unison as they clapped and stood to their feet.

Pastor Weldon came up and asked them to show some love for all three of the seasoned-salt women. They waved and bowed to standing applause like rock stars.

Chapter 41

But all the silver, and gold, and vessels of brass and iron, are consecrated unto the Lord: they shall come into the treasury of the Lord.

—Joshua 6:19

"I can't believe you did that! That was cruel, Ma Ray," Sahara said. "I'm ready to go. There's no way I can stay here with people who think you were actually a prostitute. A prostitute, Ma Ray? You actually thought you could pull off something that far-fetched?"

"Stop, Sahara," Ma Ray said. "I didn't make up anything. If anything, I didn't tell as much as I'd planned to because of how you started acting."

"I was acting that way because you were only saying that to get back at me. Okay, I get it. If I embarrass you, you'll do something even bigger to embarrass me. I get it. The only problem with *your* little stunt is that you have to live in this community with these people. Now they're going to believe you were once actually a 304."

"Whoa. What's a 304?" Ma Ray asked. Sahara didn't answer her, so Ma Ray turned to Crystal. "Crystal, what's a 304?"

"Why ask me? I wasn't the one who brought it up," Crystal said, then walked away.

Ma Ray turned back to Sahara. "Sahara, what's a 304?"

"It's a term that means a prostitute, someone who's promiscuous. . . . If you were to look at a digital instrument upside down, 304 spells *h-o-e*."

"Goodness gracious! What will you young folks think of next?" Ma Ray said.

"Can we go home now?" Sahara said. "Please, Ma Ray. Let's just go."

"No. According to you, it's *my* reputation that has just taken a hit. Besides, after lunch, aren't you're supposed to model?"

Sahara vigorously shook her head. "I'm not modeling now. Everybody will be pointing at me while whispering stuff about you and your teenage life."

"Oh, yes, you are modeling, too," Ma Ray said with her hand on her hip. "If some of the things you've done in your own life hasn't shamed you, then that little information I just revealed about myself should only be a drop in the ocean of life."

"See, that's what I mean. You were just trying to make a point. You went to the extreme to show how horribly embarrassing my past actions have been to you and my mother," Sahara said.

"Go eat your lunch. I'll be anxiously waiting to see you show us how great you are on the runway this afternoon."

"I'm not doing it, Ma Ray. I want to go home. Now."

"We're not going home. So act right." Ma Ray then started to walk away.

"Ms. Ray," Allison said as she stepped up to her. "I just want to thank you for what you did today," she said. "That was *so* dope . . . I mean, cool . . . I mean, great. We generally see people like you as though you were this sweet *old* person all of your life."

"Okay." Ma Ray sang the word as she nodded and smiled.

"I'm sorry, that's not the way I meant for it to come out," Allison said.

Ma Ray touched her hand. "I was only joking with you. It's okay. And call me Ma Ray." She smiled. "You should have seen me when I was your age. I thought age twenty-three was old. Fifty meant you had one foot on a banana peel and the other foot in the grave. But at age seventy-five, I'm still kicking, just not as high. I see how much age really is just a number."

Sixteen-year-old Allison laughed. "But you really gave us something to think about. When we're giving our bodies away without the spiritual bond God intended to be linked with it in marriage, we're all pretty much prostituting. Some of us are exchanging ours for money whether we think of it in terms of that or not. Some, for what we feel is to get some needed attention. Some, to stand in a prestige place with our peers or others. But to share what is the symbol of true love, something that was worth protecting and waiting to give to that special someone, oh, what I wouldn't give for that. I see now that when you do it God's way, it's like a dream."

Ma Ray patted Allison on her hand. "Well, it's like I said earlier, you can begin again. Just don't keep making the same mistake and coming back trying to start over again just because you can. Go to God. Tell Him what you really desire. Pray for strength and guidance, and expect the best God has for you. True love is not cheap. But believe me: it really is worth its weight in gold."

Allison hugged Ma Ray. "Thank you. Thank you for caring so much about us that you would come and be raw with us, to lay it out like it really is. I wish more adults would treat us like we're intelligent and can handle the truth. Instead, most of them keep quiet, acting all holy. They let us find out in the streets what we should be finding out at home and at church. And it's like you said in your talk, it becomes the blind leading the blind, and we both end up in the ditch." Allison turned to leave. She stopped. "Ma Ray?"

"Yes."

"Would you mind if I got your phone number and called you sometimes? I don't mean to impose, but having someone like you to talk with would really help me."

Ma Ray smiled. "I would be honored." Ma Ray took out her pen and tore off a sheet of paper from the tablet that was in her folder. She wrote down her phone number and handed it to Allison. "Anytime you feel like you need to talk or if you have a question, you just call me."

Allison took the paper with the number, hugged Ma Ray

again, and scurried away. She stopped at Sahara, who had hung close by, and said, "You are *so* blessed to have a grandmother like Ma Ray! So blessed! She is a *true* Ray of Hope."

Sahara looked over at Ma Ray. Ma Ray smiled, then winked as she nodded one time.

Chapter 42

The fashion show was wonderful. Sahara got a standing, whooping ovation. But of course, she was the most professional with her walk. She was born to be a model, and Ma Ray knew that much. People came up and told Sahara how good she was, encouraged her, telling her she really should pursue a modeling career.

The purity ceremony followed the final session. It started at five o'clock and was open to parents and friends of the teens who wished to attend. The fellowship hall had been transformed into this beautiful room of white. The youth who made the purity vow received a ring during the ceremony. The pastor and his wife performed the service. Each person who went forth was asked to make a vow to remain pure from this day forward until their day of marriage. The ring that was placed on their finger was to symbolize their vow to the Lord to keep themselves until the one they joined in holy matrimony replaced that ring during their wedding ceremony.

The pastor emphasized the ring that would be placed during their wedding ceremony because he knew the various tricks people try to use to circumvent this covenant they were making today. Some would get a friendship ring and feel that constituted a valid replacement ring. Some might act like an engage-

ment ring was enough. Pastor Weldon made sure they understood it had to be a wedding ring during a legal wedding ceremony. No crazy stuff like a bootleg ceremony between two people
who would try to say they were married in God's sight without a
legal ceremony having taken place.

Ma Ray cried a little as she witnessed her granddaughters re-
ceiving their rings.

Sahara was quiet on the ride home. Ma Ray understood they
were both probably tired. A reception, with a live band, had followed the purity ceremony. But Crystal, on the other hand, was
a little chatterbox. She had truly been touched by the youth
conference in a profound way. She talked about her dreams
and plans for the future. How she was going to change how
she'd approach her life from how she'd done it in the past.

When they got in the house, it was a little after eight. Ma Ray
went straight to her room. This had been a long day for her.
She could feel this one in her bones. As she sat down in her
rocking chair, she rubbed her legs to try to relieve the throb-
bing.

"Ma Ray, may I come in?" Sahara said as she peeked her head
inside.

Ma Ray smiled when she looked into Sahara's eyes. "Sure.
Long day, huh?"

"Yeah," Sahara said, kneeling on the floor beside Ma Ray.
"Your legs hurt?"

"A little. But nothing my old friend Ben can't help make feel
a little better."

"Your friend Ben?"

Ma Ray laughed. "Sorry, I forget you young folk don't always
get it. Ben is short for Bengay. That's the stuff we old folks use
to ease the aches and soreness in places like our limbs and
back."

"I wanted to come in and apologize," Sahara said as she held
Ma Ray's left leg in the air and began to massage it.

Ma Ray waved her off. "Already water under the bridge."

"You were really great today. I didn't realize until later how
much you touched so many people. All I saw was that you were

my grandmother, whom I adore, and there you were up there telling people you were once a prostitute. I get what you were doing now. But at the time, all I could think about was how what you were doing was impacting me."

"That's natural. Definitely what we as parents sometimes do when you children do contrary things. We look at our children and think about how they're impacting our reputations or our standing with others. With our little children, we're busy making sure they look just right and are presentable for the world, lest it reflect badly on us as a parent. We forget that when that child stands all bright eyes before us, all they care about is our love." Ma Ray slowly lowered her foot back to the floor. "There's a light in young people's eyes that rivals the sun shining at the peak of the day. Then we adults say or do something that causes the light to duck behind a cloud and, sometimes, set before time."

Sahara laughed.

"What's so funny?" Ma Ray asked.

"You do that a lot."

"Do what?"

"Say a bunch of stuff that sounds really great but is so like Shakespeare, you completely lose me," Sahara said.

Ma Ray nodded. "Okay, let me try that again. We parents should be caring about what you children are feeling and not so much about how the world is judging us through you. Children mess up sometimes. Instead of us adults flipping out, we need to help you up, find out if you're hurt, then help you move in the right direction." Ma Ray tilted her head. "Was that better?"

"Better," Sahara said. "You want me to rub your other leg?"

"Nah. I'd rather you and I talk."

Sahara completely sat down on the floor, Indian style.

"You can sit on my bed if you like," Ma Ray said, looking over at the bed.

"I like it right here. It's something special about sitting at your feet. I never thought about how special it was until today. Today, I saw *me* in you, if that makes any sense. I saw a teenage woman dressed in an old person's suit. I heard my and my friends' words coming out of *your* mouth."

"Wow, now that's something I wasn't expecting to hear you say."

"You were willing to push the envelope today just to fit in. You said some things to shock us, so you could get our attention. And it worked. Some people believed you about being a prostitute. That's because they don't know how straight up you really are."

"But what I said was the truth," Ma Ray said.

Sahara shook her head. "Ma Ray, you don't have to keep this up just to impress me. I'm telling you, I'm impressed. You were using a metaphor about being a prostitute. And then you used the word emo. That was off the scales for some of those folks there."

Ma Ray got up out of the rocking chair.

"Where are you going?" Sahara asked as she sat up straighter.

"Stay right there. I have something I want you to see." Ma Ray went to her closet. It took her about five minutes. She came back carrying a large hatbox. She sat down in the rocking chair and opened the box. Inside, there was a scrapbook and a few old, yellowed clips of newspapers. Ma Ray set the box on the floor and opened the scrapbook.

"I want to show you something," she said to Sahara. Sahara kneeled so she could see better. Ma Ray turned the scrapbook more toward Sahara. "See her? Well, that's me."

Sahara bucked her eyes. "That's *you?* In *that* thing? That's *you,* Ma Ray? *You?*"

"That's me. And that's me." Ma Ray pointed to other pictures, mostly with her posing all foxy with lots of men.

"Wow, you were a party girl for sure. And you were hot—hotter than me, even."

"You sound disappointed," Ma Ray said.

"No, I just thought I had it going on. But I can see from these photos, you would easily give me a run for my money."

"In more ways than you think," Ma Ray said. "I was fine as wine *way* before my time. And my onion, as the men like to refer to women's derrière, has caused a great many men to cry like a baby."

"Ma Ray, I'll tell you like I tell Mama sometimes. TMI! TMI!"

"And that means?"

"Too much information. And in this case it's ETMI: *Entirely* Too Much Information!"

"Boy, I'm gonna have fun with Tootsie next week. TMI and ETMI."

Sahara took the scrapbook and sat back down on the floor. She turned to the other pages. "There are so many photos of you in here."

"And none of them I'm really proud about now," Ma Ray said.

Sahara looked at Ma Ray. "Then why did you keep them?"

"I'm not sure. I think at the time I kept them so in my old age I could revisit a time 'back when.' Back when I was hot. Back when I was beautiful. Back when I was fine as wine and had a twirl in my swirl. Back when men were knocking down doors to get to me. Back when I had a steel-tight memory. Like you young folks now, I saw folks age when I was young as well. I know what the outcome will be if you keep living. I suppose, I thought there might come a day when I might wish to stroll down memory lane and I'd need a little help with that stroll." Ma Ray took the scrapbook from Sahara and closed it. "The thing is: My latter days have been so much greater than my former, so much that I've not given this book or that life another thought."

"So, why now?" Sahara asked.

"Because I'm running a risk of possibly losing you, my granddaughter, to the world. And I refuse to go down without a fight. The devil has come into our camp to take what doesn't belong to him, and I'm going back into his camp and taking back what's ours. Sahara, if you have to see me in a different light than what you've known before, then so be it. If I can get you to understand that what you're doing is nothing new or grand, then all of this is worth it." Ma Ray gave Sahara a weak smile. She picked the hatbox up off the floor, reached into it, and pulled out the news clippings. Ma Ray handed Sahara the yellowed, brittle papers. "Take these and read them."

"They've almost disintegrated."

"After you, I hope I won't have a need for them ever again," Ma Ray said. "Go on over to the bed and read them. Take your time; I have all the time in the world."

Sahara went over to the bed and sat down with four news clippings. She handled them carefully, ensuring they didn't fall apart in her hands.

Chapter 43

And the young men that were spies went in, and brought out Rahab, and her father, and her mother, and her brethren, and all that she had; and they brought out all her kindred, and left them without the camp of Israel.

—Joshua 6:23

Ma Ray put the scrapbook back in the hatbox. She closed her eyes as Sahara read. Every now and then, she would hear Sahara read something out loud—as though speaking it into the air would change what her eyes were reporting.

"'Rayna Armstrong . . . a known prostitute in a community filled with drugs, sex, and corruption . . . Detective Salmon Towers . . . one of a few Coloreds on the police force . . . partner, Beau Azra . . . raided . . . shoot-out . . . isolated community . . .'" Sahara looked over at Ma Ray. "Salmon was Granddaddy," Sahara said. "You were the Rayna Armstrong they were writing about. Beau Azra? That's Uncle Boaz's name."

Ma Ray nodded. "Yes, your uncle Boaz was named after your granddaddy's partner and friend, Beau Azra. That man lost his life saving your granddaddy."

Sahara continued reading, again speaking various words and sentences out loud. "'The prostitute, identified as Rayna Armstrong, was credited with helping save these two upstanding detectives before the raid went down. Dealers killed . . . some taken into custody . . . the biggest operation in this city's history. No charges filed against Armstrong because of her prior cooperation in this operation.'" Sahara looked at the rest of the articles. Getting up, she came over to Ma Ray and held one of the articles out to her. "Is this what the neighborhood looked like after it was over?"

Ma Ray looked at the photo in the article. "That was my street. And that's *nothing* compared to what it *actually* looked like in person." Ma Ray began to rock the chair. "Some houses were pretty much demolished. That was a scary day that day. Lots of gunfire . . . shouting . . . yelling. The people who write those articles don't always capture the human side of the story. All they care about is details and creating sensationalism."

Sahara sat down at Ma Ray's feet again. "So you were really a prostitute?"

"Yes, I was." Ma Ray looked into her granddaughter's eyes. "Not something I'm proud of, but it was my life once."

"It's so hard to believe that. You were married to a preacher. You played the piano for the church. You're a prayer warrior. You're nothing like the person described in those articles. I've seen you shout and dance in church, even if you don't dance so well."

"I beg your pardon," Ma Ray said with a laugh. "I still got some pep in my step."

"You know what I mean, Ma Ray. You dance with such a joy and love for the Lord. I can't imagine you being this person in those photos"—she nodded at the scrapbook—"or the person they were writing about in those articles."

"Detective Salmon Towers, who everybody called Sal, showed up at my house, my place of business if I give full disclosure here, with Detective Beau Azra. The two of them were looking for someplace to hide. You see, back in my day, a lot of the illegal activities took place in *our* communities, meaning the black community. There were shootings and illegal things going on twenty-four seven."

"Sounds like *today*, in some of our communities still."

"That is the sad part of this story. That in some cases, nothing has really changed. In fact, in some places, it seems to have gotten worse. This shouldn't be. This is America. We put a man on the moon. I don't understand how the most powerful country in the world can have this kind of stuff . . . war zones, in some cases, going on in places where decent folks are merely just trying to survive." Ma Ray shook her head. "That's why we have to keep praying but keep on both ourselves and our elected officials to care enough to clean up our *own* communities. But I don't want to get on *that* soapbox tonight. I'm going to stick with the discussion at hand."

"Wow, I'm having a hard time wrapping my head around this. Ma Ray . . . Rayna Armstrong, written about in the newspapers."

Ma Ray went back to her story. "Detectives Sal and Beau showed up, almost in a panic, at my door claiming they were being pursued. They said they needed a safe place to hide. Well, you can imagine I wasn't falling for *that* cockamamy tale, a good-looking, light-skinned black man in the mix or not. I knew how tricky the authorities could be. You never knew what crooked cops were up to. Most folks knew what was going on at my little house. I figured it was a setup, and I wasn't *about* to fall into that trap. But there was something about the look in Sal's light green eyes that convinced me they truly were in danger. They needed my help. So, I let them in. And I hid them."

"You hid them?"

"Yeah. In my attic. And I'm not talking about some fancy room attic. I'm talking a crawl space. It wasn't five minutes after I hid them that folks were almost beating down my door. Two were policemen; one of them was the drug king in the community. They asked me where the two officers were that had come to my house. I acted like I didn't know what they were talking about. They said folks told them they'd seen the officers at my door."

"Were you scared?"

"Scared? Who? You talking about Rayna Armstrong?" Ma Ray laughed. "Baby girl, I was absolutely terrified! We're talking about two policemen and a guy that could make me *literally* disappear without a trace. Not that anybody other than my family would have cared enough to look for me or try to find out what happened. But still . . . "

Sahara put her hand up to her mouth. "I can't believe this.

I've never heard anything about this *ever*. This is like a gangster movie, only my own grandmother is the star of this story line. So Mama doesn't know about this? Uncle Boaz, either?"

Ma Ray pressed her lips tightly together, then shook her head. "No. After this was over and my life became transformed, I buried this and never felt a need or a reason to bring it up. I mean, who would? No one wants to brag about a past life like mine. God changes things, you walk into a new life . . . a new beginning, and you leave that old stuff behind you."

"Well, you certainly left *yours* behind, almost without a trace." Sahara readjusted her body. "Like the three Hebrew boys that were thrown into the fiery furnace, and when they came out, there wasn't even the smell of smoke on them. Okay, so, you had two rogue policemen and a drug kingpin at your door, and two detectives hiding in your crawl space attic. You were scared, then what?"

Ma Ray pulled back and tilted her head slightly at Sahara. "Calm down, this is not a movie I'm recanting. This was my actual life. And as scared as I was, I realized it was *my life*. That's why I knew I had to not show fear and not lose my cool. Back then, there weren't the kind of laws to protect you like there are now. No warrant necessary to come in. All of them could have busted in my house without presenting anything to do it and done whatever they wanted, and there wasn't a thing I could have done about it."

"Wow, this is something!"

"So, I used my charm and other assets to distract them, all the while trying to convince them there's no way I would *ever* let 'The Man' in my place. Not to hide. Back then everybody in our community called police *The Man*. I did acknowledge the officers had come to my door. But I told them I'd sent them on their merry little way, just like I was about to send *them* on *theirs*. Lawrence—that was the drug king—wasn't buying my act. The policemen could tell I really didn't care for people with badges, so they thought I was likely telling the truth. My daddy, bless his heart, lived a few houses down the street from me. Somebody must have told him the police were at my house. He got there as soon as he could and acted like we were this religious group of people who didn't tolerate men coming inside and being alone with a single woman."

"I've heard of a religion like that. Men who aren't the father, brother, or husband of the woman aren't allowed to *ever* be alone with her," Sahara said. "It defiles the woman and is a *huge* problem in their religion."

"Yeah, I suppose that's what my daddy was going for. Anyway, it worked. One of the policemen asked me if I knew which direction the two officers may have gone. I pointed them in a direction. It really didn't matter which way I pointed, since I was sending them on a wild-goose chase either way."

"And all this time, I thought you were pure boring," Sahara said, laughing.

Ma Ray chuckled. "I guess, for the most part, I am. Even back then, it wasn't a great life. It sounds interesting as I'm telling it now. But the truth is, Sahara, I wasn't fulfilled. I had those men wanting to be with me, paying money to be with me, and I was so very empty on the inside. None of that fulfilled me. I didn't feel loved. Even though a monetary value was placed on what I did, I didn't feel as though I really was valuable. Think about it: men paid money for my time and service, and I didn't feel valued. That's a sorry indictment. Now, you—"

"I somehow knew this would come back to me," Sahara said. "But the difference in where you're trying to go with this is: I am *not* a 304 or a pro. I don't sell my body or any service like that, Ma Ray. I don't do that."

"You're not a pro in the sense of slapping a monetary price on your body for sex, but if you're doing what I've been told you're doing—"

"Mama always exaggerates," Sahara said. "Mama wants me to tell her things, and when I won't open up to her, she jumps to all kinds of overly dramatic conclusions. Let her tell it, I'm having sex with everybody and his brother. Well, I'm not. I'm not. She thinks I'm doing drugs. Now, I will admit I've tried it, but it's really not my thing, so I don't do it. When I try to tell Mama that, she still wants to feel like she's some kind of victim, so she blows everything way out of proportion. I suppose it works; she was able to pawn us off on you for the summer."

"Whoa, whoa, whoa. Hold your horses. I'm not going to let you say those things about your mother—"

"See, that's exactly why I don't like to talk. I try to say what I think and what I feel, and people like you, Edmond, my mother act like I'm wrong to speak my mind."

"That's not what I was going to say. It's fine with me if you want to express what you feel. I was just going to say that I'm not going to let you say those things about your mother without me challenging it," Ma Ray said. "Your mother loves you. She was just at her wit's end, and she needed my mother wit. She didn't *pawn* you *or* your sister off on me. That's an insult to me."

"I'm sorry, Ma Ray. I didn't mean to insult you. But you have to admit, you know we came here because Mama was talking about sending us off to some boot camp or something. I know you love us. That's why you put yourself up to save us."

Ma Ray ticked her head a few times. "I see you and your sister's potentials, and I'm highly upset that both of you are throwing your life away. And for what? To be popular with a bunch of knuckleheads? That's not a strong person. Any dummy can follow a knucklehead. It takes a strong person to chart their own course and not allow those who are *less* than them to derail them."

"I know, Ma Ray. I've gotten that since I've been here with you. I've messed up. . . . I keep messing up. I want to do right, but then I don't know what happens. Something takes over, and before I know anything, I've done something I wish I hadn't and can't take back. You come to a place of wondering, What's the use? What difference does it make? Then someone like you comes along and challenges me to examine my life and my motives and to get myself together."

"Well, then, I'm doing my job. As someone who loves you dearly, I'm doing my job. And if you don't get that, then that makes *you* a knucklehead." Ma Ray tapped Sahara's head softly with her knuckles.

Sahara released a girlish laugh.

Chapter 44

*And Joshua saved Rahab the harlot alive, and her
father's household, and all that she had; and she
dwelleth in Israel even unto this day; because she
hid the messengers, which Joshua sent to spy out
Jericho.*

—Joshua 6:25

Sahara stood and hugged Ma Ray. "So, tell me. How did you
and Granddaddy end up together? You know I *love* a good
romance story." Sahara sat back down.

"I don't know how much of a romance story this really is, but
it does have its moments. After the thugs left and it was safe for
the officers I'd hidden to come out of the attic, Sal and I talked
for a few minutes. My life was *tore* up from the *floor* up. Still, I
could see there was something different about him. So I told
him I knew they were planning to come in and take this place
down, and that it would be soon. I knew God was in his life and
that God was going to be with him and give them the victory.
People in the community talked about two officers that couldn't
be bought. That's why Lawrence wanted them taken out completely. Those thugs were running scared.

"So, I got Detective Salmon Towers to promise me that, since
I'd shown them kindness, he would return the favor. I asked
him to ensure me and my family be spared during whatever was
scheduled to go down in our community in the end."

"Wow," Sahara said. "My grandmother—Eliot Ness and The
Untouchables."

"Child, what do you know about Eliot Ness and The Untouchables?"

"Ma Ray, we have cable. They show the classic shows on the cable channels."

"Anyway, I had these red curtains in the front of my little house—"

"Like you do here," Sahara said. "Only these are drapes."

"Yeah, like I do here. I hadn't thought about that. I guess that means I like red hanging at my windows." Ma Ray smiled. "Sal told me to twist the curtains to look like a rope. That way they would know not to touch my house. But I had to have my entire family inside the house if I wanted them to be saved. I did what he said. No less than two weeks later, everything went down. And, I mean everything went *down*. The only house pretty much that remained untouched and was left standing was mine."

"A shoot-out at the O.K. Corral."

Ma Ray cut her eyes at Sahara. "Little girl, you're a mess. The O.K. Corral? But it *was* pretty intense that day, pretty intense. You talking about some praying folks up in my house, we were down on our knees praying *that* day. When it was all over, these news reporter folks came knocking on my door. They wanted to know why my house was not caught in the cross fire. The rest of the community said I had to be a traitor or a snitch. That's how the news folks ended up writing so much stuff about me and my life. Some folks in the neighborhood couldn't wait to tell how I was a prostitute and all. That's how people are. They *love* to bring others down if they can."

"Haters," Sahara said. "We call folks like those haters."

"Okay. Haters. Well, even after giving my life to the Lord, I've found some church folks can be haters as well," Ma Ray said. "Anyway, Sal came to check on us after everything was over. About a week after that, he and I went out for a cup of coffee. He then asked me out on a *real* date."

"In spite of him knowing what you were?"

"In spite of him knowing everything by that time," Ma Ray said. "We dated a few months, and he asked me to marry him. We married. Sometime later, his partner and friend, Beau Azra, was shot and killed in the line of duty. A few years following that, I got pregnant despite being told I would never be able to conceive. That's why I had my children so late in life. Well, late for back then. Thirty-five is fashionable to have a first child now. Sal decided to leave the police force. We had our son. We named him Beau Azra in honor of Sal's fallen partner. Around this time, Sal was called to preach. Two years after Boaz was born, your mother arrived on the scene. Ten years later, we moved here to the country so Sal could pastor a church out this way. We were practically starting over. Two years ago, Sal died. But after everything that's happened, I'm still standing for the Lord."

"When you were speaking today, you talked about a ray of hope. You said we may be going through a storm, but that God will always give us a ray of hope. Well, Ma Ray, you're giving me my own personal ray of hope right here, right now, aren't you?"

"Yes. The hardest thing for me to do today was to put myself completely out there. But God was letting me know that the most important thing any of us can ever do is to impact someone else's life with our own. Sahara, you need to get it together." Ma Ray nodded at her. "It's time for you to put away childish things and get it together."

Sahara began to wipe tears from her eyes. She nodded back as she did so. Sahara looked at Ma Ray and forced a broken smile. "I know," she said. "I know."

Chapter 45

But the children of Israel committed a trespass in the accursed thing: for Achan, the son of Carmi, the son of Zabdi, the son of Zerah, of the tribe of Judah, took of the accursed thing: and the anger of the Lord was kindled against the children of Israel.

—Joshua 7:1

Sahara's journey was far from being complete. But Ma Ray had put herself out there for her, to help save her from the path she was going down. A path that even *she* knew would only lead to destruction. Sahara prayed with Ma Ray that night. Made up in her mind she was going to walk the Godly way. She would give up her conning ways. She cried with Ma Ray as she promised she would change. She repented and committed to turn in a different direction. Sahara was smart. She vowed to work hard to make As in school from here on out. She would be true to the vow she'd made to keep herself until the one who would cherish her as his wife . . . love her as Christ loves the church, came to her. She fully understood now how *truly much* she was worth the wait. And if a guy tried to convince her otherwise, she would examine his words against the unadulterated Word of God.

"Ma Ray," Sahara said, snuggled safely in Ma Ray's arms after she'd cried until she was pretty much spent. "I want to come clean with you about some things. I just don't feel right with these things over my head. Not now. I need to get all of this out of me. I refuse to allow the devil to *have* or *hold* anything over my head at this point."

Ma Ray continued to embrace her. "I'm here."

"Can we keep this between ourselves?"

"If that's what you want," Ma Ray said.

"It is." Sahara sat up straight, arched her back a bit, took a deep breath, smiled, then began. "The other night, when I told you that I'd gone to a rap concert with these girls I'd met. Well, that wasn't true." She paused, then continued. "I really went somewhere with Junebug."

Ma Ray's demeanor remained unchanged as she nodded.

"I'm sorry I lied to you. But Ma Ray, I couldn't take being cooped up in this place any longer. I was literally going crazy!"

Ma Ray shrugged. "But there's more," Ma Ray said, her hands folded in her lap.

"How do you know?"

"With lies, there's always more."

With those stinging words, Sahara nodded. "He wanted to have sex."

"So, did you?"

"Ma Ray, I'm not a virgin. I've not been one for about a year now. I'm sorry to disappoint you."

"Yes, I *am* disappointed. But I can assure you that God is even more disappointed with you."

"See, that's what I mean. I didn't think what I was doing was doing anything against *God*. In fact, I didn't think about God at all. I just saw it as being something that I felt I wanted. The truth is: I wanted to belong. I wanted to feel like someone wanted me . . . that someone cared about me. I wanted somebody's eyes to light up when I walked into a room. I wanted to feel loved. How could God not understand that?"

Ma Ray got off the bed and sat back in her rocking chair. "I know you think I don't understand, but I do. The truth is: you already belonged. You were already wanted. And you were most definitely already loved. God loved you before you even knew who you were. Then there's your family who loves you greatly, the chief among them, me."

"But it's not the same, Ma Ray. You know this. I know that God loves me. I know that you love me, and Mama, and Daddy, and Edmond, Uncle Boaz, Aunt Ruth . . . there are a host of people who love me. I know that. But sometimes, on another level, we all want more than family's love. Sometimes we *need* more, to feel like we really matter."

Ma Ray began to rock a little. "Really now?"

Sahara let her body sag. "Yes. It gets lonely sometimes. And when you're not doing what others are doing, you become an outcast. You feel so isolated. Sometimes, you just want to know that you look good other than to mere family. Maybe that's wrong, but who wants to feel ugly and unwanted?"

Ma Ray stopped the chair. "So having sex, throwing caution to the wind, makes you feel loved, makes you feel beautiful, makes you feel wanted? Really, Sahara?"

"It did. But I see it differently now. And I want to live for the Lord, I really do. But I need to know how to keep myself. I mean, I heard what they said at the youth conference. But words are easier said than done. It's the action behind the words that can cag us, sometimes . . . trip us up."

Ma Ray smiled. "I told you, I really do understand everything that you're saying. But I want you to think about how much Jesus loves you. How He gave His life for you. How He wants the best for you. When you give in to the devil's fool's gold, what you're going to end up with is the fake and not the real thing. Love yourself enough to want God's best for you. Don't settle. That's all I know to tell you. That when you give in to the wrong thing, you disappoint our Heavenly Father. That may not always matter during the heat of the moment. But if you think about how you're cutting yourself off from God's best when you take less, that should be enough to *always* give you pause. Love you, Sahara. Love yourself enough not to settle for less than God's very best."

"I understand," Sahara said. "And I know you probably think you're just wasting your breath. But I hear you. And it's res-onating. It is. It's resonating down in my spirit."

Ma Ray got up and hugged Sahara. "How about we pray?"

"Okay," Sahara said.

"You want to lead it?"

Sahara smiled. "Yeah. I'd like to."

Ma Ray smiled. Sahara and Ma Ray held hands as Sahara began. "Heavenly Father, I just want to say thank You. Thank You for loving me enough to give me people who love me. Thank You for my grandmother, Ma Ray. My Ray of Hope. Thank You for her loving us so much that she would be *this* transparent with me, despite its cost to her. Thank You for loving me so much that You gave Your Son, Jesus. That He gave His life, so that I might not just have life, but life *more* abundantly. Lord, I want to live for You. Please forgive me of my sins. I want You to be Lord of my life. Right now. Come into my heart. No more games. No more excuses. No more time wasted not walking in my divine destiny. Bless my mother, my stepfather, my father, my sisters, and my little big-headed brother. Help me to forgive those who have hurt me. And forgive me for those who *I've* hurt. Bless my aunt and uncle, my cousins, and my friends. Lord, I even ask that You bless my enemies. These and other blessings I ask in Jesus' name. Amen."

"Amen," Ma Ray said as tears rolled down her face. She grabbed Sahara and hugged her hard. "Amen."

Chapter 46

Israel hath sinned, and they have also transgressed my covenant which I commanded them: for they have even taken of the accursed thing, and have also stolen, and dissembled also, and they have put it even among their own stuff.

—Joshua 7:11

Three weeks after the youth conference, Sahara was doing well. She was attending Wednesday night Bible study with Aaron, Crystal, and Andre. She and Crystal got Ma Ray to let them attend Sunday services at that church as well. Ma Ray let Sahara drive the Cadillac there. Sahara even found herself being halfway decent to Andre. She could see how focused he was. Andre had dreams. He had a plan for his life. And in all of his planning, she saw how he always put God first in everything he was doing. That's what he told her had caused him to be successful in all that he'd put his hands to so far in life.

"I put God first, and the rest just comes along with the Lord. It works," Andre said. "Whenever I get off track, I know it's the devil trying to get me to say the wrong thing so he can cause me to *do* the wrong thing. I pray a *lot*. And I study God's Word."

Lenora and Edmond were having a big party for their tenth wedding anniversary. Sahara and Crystal were looking forward to going home for that weekend. Ma Ray was coming to the party as well as Boaz, Ruth, Owen, and Freda, who were both home from college. It was going to be a lot of fun celebrating with family and friends.

Lenora came and got Sahara and Crystal from Ma Ray's on Friday afternoon after she got off from work. The party was set for Saturday at seven p.m. Sahara and Crystal were going to help in getting things set up.

Sahara and Crystal talked to Lenora in great lengths after they arrived home.

"I can tell such a difference in both of you," Lenora said, sheer glee in her eyes. "It's so wonderful to have my girls back again. You both seem so happy, so content . . . so much more mature. Maybe *I* should go stay with Ma for six weeks."

"Not happy, Mother," Crystal said. "We have joy."

"Ooh, listen to you. Joy, huh?" Lenora said, smiling.

"Yes, joy," Crystal said. "You see, happiness is based on outside happenings. When things are going well, you're happy. When they're not, then you aren't. Joy is not dependent on your circumstances. You can have joy even in the midst of a storm."

"The joy of the Lord is our strength," Sahara added. "That's what the Bible says."

"Okay, where are my real daughters?" Lenora teased. "Wow. Wow. But seriously, I've missed you both *so* much." She hugged them. "It's so good to be together again."

"We missed you, too, Mother," Crystal said. "But we've had a great time at Ma Ray's."

When Sahara got more settled, she logged onto the Internet. She had tons of e-mails in her in-box to go through, a lot of them spam, of course. She let a few friends know that she was back in town.

Dollar was the first to call on her cell phone. "Hey, so you're finally back?"

"Yeah."

"So, when can I see you?"

"I don't know," Sahara said.

"What do you mean, you don't know?" He let out a short laugh. "Shawty, I told you I was missing you. Now that you're back, we need to hook up."

"I don't think that's such a good idea," Sahara said.

"Not a good idea? Please. You're supposed to be my girl. I've been missing you, missed loving on you. Let's hook up," Dollar said. "Seriously, we need to talk."

"I'm not going to be here for long. We just came back for the weekend for my folks' wedding anniversary celebration."

"Apparently, you're not hearing me. I said we *need* to hook up so we can talk. I have something important we need to discuss."

"Okay. I'm listening."

"I can't tell you this over the phone. Quit playing now. You know I don't like playing games. Now, I said I have something we need to conversate about. Quite frankly, I really don't have time for your attention-for-attention's-sake little act today. Not today."

Sahara took a few seconds before she responded. "I'm not trying to get attention. Listen, Dollar, things have changed between us."

"Oh, girl, you don't even know the *half* of it."

"If you have something you want to say, you can tell me now," Sahara said.

"A'ight. You want to be like that. So be it. How about this: you probably need to go and get yourself checked . . . tested, that is, more to the point," Dollar said.

"Checked? Tested? For what?"

"Hey, I'm not positive, but it looks like you may have given me something," Dollar said. "Or I may have given you something. Who knows?"

"I may have given *you* something? And exactly where would I have picked up *something* to give to you? Huh, Dollar?"

He laughed. "Hey, all I know is that I got a call telling me I needed to get tested for HIV/AIDS. This chick had the nerve to name me in her list of folks who had been exposed to her. Can you believe this mess? That's what makes me mad about y'all."

"Y'all?! What do you mean 'y'all'?" Sahara felt the tears begin to sting her eyes. "I was with you. You were the first guy I was ever with. And now you're telling me I may have contracted AIDS from you?"

"Hey, it's like I said. I got a call myself. It was a blow to me. They've tested me—"

"And?"

"And, I'm still waiting for a final verdict. But the people there asked me to list all the people I'd been with in the past year or so. So, of course, I had to give up your name."

Sahara was really crying now. "No. No." She shook her head. "This can*not* be happening to me," she said. "Not me. It can't! Not now."

"Happening to *you?* How do you think *I* feel? I'm having the time of my life; I'm at the *height* of my popularity, and now I have to chill, or at least take extra protection, because I *might* be considered lethal. All because of some girls who can't keep their legs closed and don't have a problem with giving it up to any and every body who comes along?"

"Oh, now you weren't saying that when you were trying to tell me how much you loved and wanted me—how you *had* to have me. That's not what you were saying then, Dollar."

"Listen, I'm not trying to have drama with you. Not today. The people at the clinic suggested it would be best if this news came directly from me, but they said they would be contacting you to ensure that you knew. So, I've told you. What you do from here is entirely on you," Dollar said.

"What am I supposed to do? I can't tell my mother something like this! What am I supposed to do, Dollar? Huh?"

"Not my problem. I have my own troubles to deal with. But if you want the name of the person at the clinic I dealt with, I can give you that. You can call her and ask *her* what you need to do. But the way it generally works is: you go get tested, they'll ask you for all the names of the people you've been with, and you wait to learn your fate. If it turns out you're positive, the people at the clinic say it's not the death sentence it used to be. They have meds now. From what they told me, you can take a cocktail of drugs that won't cure you, but at least they could extend your life while some genius comes up with a cure."

"I can't tell my mother this. What have you done to me? What have you done to my life?"

"I didn't force you to do anything," Dollar said. "You were hot and heavy to be with me. You were the one wanting to be part of the list of those I've loved. I still love you, but right now, we have to put some things on hold. If it turns out you're clean, we can go back to where we were. If it turns out I'm clean and you're not, then you need to find the person who did you in and handle your business from there."

"If it turns out that I have *this,* then it couldn't have come from anybody *but* you."

"Sahara, I'm not trying to say anything bad about you. But let me drop this 411 on you, okay? If you gave it up to *me,* I'm sure I wasn't the only one smashing you. Girls like you tend to be like that. You'll give it to anyone who acts like they're remotely interested in loving you. Now, that's not a bad thing. It's kind of sad when you really think about it. Girls . . . women who think so little of themselves that they'll actually trade sex for love."

"Dollar, stop it! You said you cared about me. You said you loved me. You said you could see yourself marrying me someday. . . ."

Dollar laughed. "And you fell for *that?* See what I mean? Too easy. It's like taking candy from a baby or a Nintendo DS from a chump."

"I'm getting off the phone now," Sahara said, crying even more.

"Yeah, okay. I was finished, anyway. But if you find out things are good with you, hit me back so we can pick up where we left off. I told you, I've missed you. I meant that."

"In your dreams!" Sahara said. She clicked off her cell phone and began to cry hard. "God, what is this? What is going on? I give my life to You completely, and now this happens?" she said. "I don't understand. It's not fair! I don't understand! I finally decide to get myself together and to start living right, and now this? Oh, God, my mother is going to freak! This is not fair! It's just not *fair!*"

Chapter 47

Now Joshua was old and stricken in years; and the Lord said unto him, Thou art old and stricken in years, and there remaineth yet very much land to be possessed.

—Joshua 13:1

Sahara didn't talk to anyone after her talk with Dollar. Ma Ray came in on Saturday morning and instantly sensed that something was wrong. She tried to find out what was going on, what had taken away the laughter and joy Sahara had had when she'd left her home.

"Did something happen when you got here?" Ma Ray asked Sahara when she walked into Sahara's bedroom and caught her crying.

"Not exactly," Sahara said.

"Sahara, you promised you would be truthful with me. If something has happened, I wish you'd tell me. How can anyone help you if you won't let anyone know what's going on?"

Sahara got up and grabbed hold of Ma Ray. She hugged her tight. "Oh, Ma Ray. It's not fair! It's just not fair! Something that happened in my past is threatening my present and my future. I confessed my sins. I gave my life to the Lord. It's not fair that I have to deal with this now! Not now. Not at this point in my life. It's just not fair!"

"What are you dealing with?" Ma Ray asked as she stepped back from Sahara a little to get a better look at her face. "Pull yourself together so you can tell me what's going on. Come on, now. Get it together. Whatever it is, it can't be *this* bad, can it?"

Sahara walked away toward the desk with her computer. "Oh, it's bad, Ma Ray. It's *really* bad."

"Well, no matter what it is, I know we're going to get through it. What did I tell you about our God?" Ma Ray said.

Sahara looked at Ma Ray as though she wasn't getting it. "But God is likely allowing this. He's punishing me for what I've done. Other people do this stuff all the time. Grown folks, especially Christians who act all high and mighty . . . like they're better than other folks, they're doing it. Married folks, cheating on their spouses, a lot of them even we children know about, they're doing it. Preachers, for goodness' sake! Preachers are doing it as well. In fact, you can hardly read anything these days without reading or hearing about some preacher having done the exact same thing. And preachers are supposed to be above this; they're supposed to be the example for the rest of us."

Sahara was losing control now. "At least, that's what I thought. So if they can do it and get away with it, then of course, we young folks think it must be okay. It has to be. If those God is supposed to be talking to are doing it, and they don't appear to have a problem in doing it, then it *must* be okay. Right?"

"Doing what? Sahara, please tell me what you're talking about. You need to calm down, take a deep breath, and tell me what's going on so we can fix it."

Sahara tried to get herself under control. After a few minutes of heaving and sniffling, she became calm enough to talk. "I may have AIDS, Ma Ray. AIDS," Sahara said.

"What?"

"This guy I used to date . . . well, he called me last night and told me that I needed to get tested. Not for an STD, not for herpes, not for VD, but AIDS, Ma Ray. AIDS! I'm seventeen years old, and I, of all people, am not pregnant, which was the most I ever worried about. But I may have contracted AIDS." She began to cry again. "What am I going to do?" She fell into Ma Ray's arms.

Ma Ray held her. "First off, we're going to pray," Ma Ray said.

Sahara jerked up and looked at Ma Ray like she was crazy. "Pray? Pray? How can we pray? God is not going to answer my prayer. I was the one wrong. I went against what God said. Sex outside of marriage is wrong. Fornication is wrong. And had I heeded to His Word and His way, none of this would be happening to me right now. So how can I possibly go to God and petition Him for His help now? I'm getting what I deserve!"

Ma Ray braced Sahara. "You walk boldly before His throne and you ask Him for mercy. Because Satan is trying to convince you not to go to the One who has the power to help you, the power to change things, the power to make things right, the power to heal you, the power to grant you mercy—withholding the punishment that you deserve. Satan is trying to convince you that you can't go to God, because Satan *knows* all about God's power. Don't let that crafty devil deceive you. Besides being a thief, the devil is a liar and a deceiver. Satan will tell you that God is mad at you, that you have no right to go to Him. But if you can't go to God, then where and who else is there for you to go? Who?"

"But, Ma Ray, I'm a sinner—"

"Actually you *were* a sinner. You are no longer in the perpetual state of sin. You've relocated to the great state of grace. That now makes you a sinner who has been saved by grace. You've been made and are being made righteous, through the righteousness of Jesus Christ, through the shedding of His blood. Do you understand this?"

"I understand that I wish I could go back and do things over again," Sahara said as she walked away from Ma Ray. "I would choose a different path. I promise you that I would if I could. I would make a different decision. If I could just go back in time and choose again, I would choose differently."

"But you can't go back. None of us can. So that means you have to begin where you are, and where you are right now . . . right this minute, is under God's grace and His mercy. And I don't know if you've heard this before, but every day, God gives us brand-new mercy. You don't have to live off yesterday's mercy or even what's *left* of yesterday's mercy. God gives you and me, and all the saints, new mercy daily."

"I hear you, Ma Ray. But what do I do? What if it turns out that I have AIDS?"

"Stop it. Stop speaking these things. Life and death is in the power of the tongue, and you must speak life. That's all I want to hear out of you from here on out—life words. The scripture says by Jesus' stripes, you're healed. So whose report are you going to believe? God's or Satan's? Choose, and then stick with it. Speak life."

"Of course, I want to believe God. But what if God is mad at me? What if God is making an example of me? What if God says, 'Forget you. Just like you forgot Me.'"

"Stop, Sahara." Ma Ray walked over and hugged Sahara. "Here's what we're going to do. We're going to pray. Then you're going to tell your mother what's going on—"

Sahara broke away from Ma Ray's embrace and walked again over to the window. "I can't tell my mother, Ma Ray. She's not like you. She's going to hit the ceiling. She's going to blame me for having lived the way I have. I know she loves me, but she's going to go off about this. I can't tell her." Sahara ran over and grabbed Ma Ray. "You could tell her for me. Or better yet, you can take me to get tested, and she'll never have to know anything. That way, should the report come back that I'm fine, she'll not have had to go through anything. Please, Ma Ray. This will work."

Ma Ray shook her head. "That's not right, baby girl. That's not how it should be done. You have to step up to the plate. That's your mother, and she deserves to know what's going on with her own child. It's not right for me to plot against her. And you shouldn't want to plot, either. I'll be here for you—you know that. But God has instructed you to honor your mother and your father. It's not right for you to do something like this behind your mother's back. And I won't participate or allow you to disrespect your mother in this way. I won't. She's your mother, Sahara. Besides, honestly, we can use all the prayers we can get for this situation."

Sahara broke away as she shook her head slowly.

"Come here," Ma Ray said, beckoning her back to her arms.

Sahara continued to shake her head.

"Come here."

Sahara came back.

Ma Ray wrapped her arms completely around Sahara. "I'm an old woman now. My time is not as long as it's been. I've run a good race. I'm not saying it's over yet, but I'm just letting you know. Somebody is going to have to pick up the mantle in my place after I'm gone. I need you to step up, Sahara, and be all that God is calling you to be. God has not given you a spirit of fear, so you don't need to be afraid. I just told you I'm old. Psalm 37:25 says, 'I have been young, and now am old; yet have I not seen the righteous forsaken, nor his seed begging bread.' Did you hear that?"

"I heard you, Ma Ray."

"No, you didn't. I said I've been young. I've had my ups and my downs. I've dealt with some things that could *have* and should *have* taken me out a long time ago. Yet, I'm still here. I'm old now. And in all of this time, dealing with what life has dealt me, I have never . . . never . . . *never*—in the end—seen the righteous forsaken—"

"Nor his seed begging bread," Lenora said.

Sahara turned around and looked toward the door. "Mama."

Lenora came in and hugged her daughter. "What's wrong, Sahara?"

"Mama," Sahara said again, then burst into tears.

Lenora turned to Ma Ray as she held Sahara. "What's going on, Ma?"

Ma Ray shook her head and started toward the door. "Sahara will tell you."

"Ma Ray, can we pray?" Sahara asked as she stretched her hand toward Ma Ray. "Before you leave, can we pray? Please."

"Oh. Now, you *know* me," Ma Ray said, walking back. "Ma Ray *never* passes up a good prayer meeting." She took Sahara's out-stretched hand and squeezed it. "Never."

Sahara took her mother's hand. "I'll lead it," Sahara said.

Lenora pulled back. "God is good," she said, looking up toward the ceiling with a smile. She looked over at Sahara, shook her head, and once again said, "God is good!"

Chapter 48

But cleave unto the Lord your God, as ye have done unto this day.

—Joshua 23:8

Boaz came to visit with Ma Ray the week following Lenora and Edmond's anniversary celebration.

"It's certainly been an interesting week, huh?" Boaz said as he and Ma Ray sat outside on the porch swing.

Ma Ray pushed off a little with her feet to make the swing go. "Well, that's an understatement if I've ever heard one."

"So . . . how are you feeling?"

"About what?"

"About the girls not being here anymore. About everything that's gone on this past week."

"It is what it is." Ma Ray looked over to the side and back. "I miss having Sahara and Crystal here. But it was the right time for them to be at home. They certainly brought a lot of life to this place, that's for sure. As for Lenora, I think she held up pretty well at the party. Nobody but me and Sahara probably had any idea how much her heart was breaking. But Lenora managed to hold it together. Better than I thought she would. At first, she wanted to cancel the party outright. I told her that wasn't going to change anything one iota. What was . . . was. You deal with things as they come. She and Edmond had spent all that money that they *didn't* have to rent a place, hire a caterer with all that food. Family and friends had made arrangements to be there. They might as well celebrate what they could."

"Honestly, Ma, Lenora generally brings so much drama, anyway; I didn't realize anything was different. Sure, she was crying at certain times during the party. But then, that's Lenora. I just thought she was happy about having made it ten years with Edmond," Boaz said. "Granted, she *has* had a hard time. As much as I mess with her, I know she's been through some difficult periods in her life. Some things I *have* felt she's brought on herself. But still, she's my sister. I love her. It hurts when I see that she's hurting."

"I know," Ma Ray said. "But the Bible has told us that in this life we're going to have trouble. Some of it is of our own making; some of it . . . is not. It rains on the just and the unjust. But I still know one thing. And that's after the rain, the sun always shines. So it is in our spiritual lives. After the rain, the Son, that's capital *S-o-n,* always shines."

Boaz smiled and nodded. "That's a fact, Ma. And God truly is faithful. Even when we're not so much. God is faithful."

"That's why when I turned my life over to the Lord, I held on to Him with all that I had," Ma Ray said. "I held fast to Him and my faith, that even to this day, I refuse to let go. I'm just glad that when the devil has tried his best to pluck me out of God's hand, God has held on tightly to me. God promised never to leave me nor forsake, and at seventy-five, I'm a living witness and here to tell you that God honors His every Word."

"Well, you know how I feel about God," Boaz said. "I've been sold out for a long time myself. Seeing God work in your and Daddy's life affected me back then, and it affects me today. But what I'm most thankful about is that I know the Lord for myself. I don't have to look at what He's done for others. I can look back over my *own* life and know who brought me over. I'm talking about things God has brought *me* through. Things that you don't even a clue about; stuff no one knows *but* me and the Lord."

"All of us have those," Ma Ray said.

"So, what do you think is going to happen with Sahara now?" Boaz asked.

"Well, the preliminary results came back negative, thank the Lord. The doctor said he thinks she may have dodged the bullet. They want to test her again in six months to be sure."

"But do you think Sahara gets it now? I mean *really* gets it? Do you think she's going to turn her life around?"

"Boaz, before she left here, going back to Lenora, she was already a changed person. Will she fall again in the future? Who can say for sure? Who can say about any of us? Temptation lies before all of us. You know that. From the pimp to the pulpit, we all have choices placed before us daily. Sometimes folks choose right; sometimes they choose wrong. Who can say with certainty on any of us? That's why we have to pray *constantly*."

"But I'm trying to live right, Ma," Boaz said.

"And even with that conviction, none of us can completely keep ourselves. That's why we need the Holy Spirit, gently telling us 'No,' 'Stop,' 'Not that,' " 'Not there,' 'Go another way.' Our biggest problem is not that we don't *know* the right thing to do. Our biggest problem is keeping our flesh under submission of our spirit. There's a war going on inside each of us. Even an old woman like myself has my days. The flesh pulling one way, the spirit pulling another."

Boaz chuckled. "Ma, what do you have to war against inside of your sweet, little, boring self?"

"Man, please. Some of these Christian folks can test you so badly. Do you know how often I want to tell somebody off? And some of my Christian siblings can make you want to cuss, not curse, cuss sometimes. Then there are those times when you know the right thing to do, like loving your enemies, but that war begins. Voices start jabbering, telling you how you don't have to take things from folks. How you need to tell them where they can get off and how fast they can do it, and be done with them. Boaz, you go to church. You're a deacon in the church. You know *exactly* what I'm talking about."

"Yeah, Ma, but that's not like fornicating, committing adul-

tery, killing, stealing . . . stuff like that," Boaz said. "You know . . .
the top ten commandments," he said slightly joking. "The normal ten commandments we also refer to."

"Well, sin is sin," Ma Ray said. "It doesn't make a difference
to God which one you're charged with. To God, sin is sin,
whether it's a sin of omission or commission. Whether it's done
in the flesh or done in the heart—sin is sin."

"Yeah." Boaz rubbed his head, shaking it as he crinkled his
nose a few times. "Well, thank God for mercy and thank God
for grace. That's all I can say. Thank God for grace."

Chapter 49

*One man of you shall chase a thousand: for the
Lord your God, he it is that fighteth for you, as he
hath promised you.*

—Joshua 23:10

Both Sahara and Crystal had wanted to come stay with Ma
Ray that particular weekend. Lenora didn't want them to;
she'd felt she'd imposed upon her mother enough already. But
with Ma Ray insisting, along with the girls, Lenora was triple-
teamed and outnumbered.

It had been a month since the anniversary party. School was
set to start in less than a week. This would be their last opportunity this summer to have some fun with Ma Ray before the serious business of school began.

Aaron must have known Crystal was coming. He'd arrived at
Ma Ray's house before Crystal got there. Of course, he tried to
play it off like he just *happened* to be stopping by to say hello to
Ma Ray.

"They should be here shortly," Ma Ray said, after he'd said
his greetings to her and told her he just came by to say hello to
her. "You're welcome to wait on the porch with me if you like?"

"What?" Aaron said, trying to look bewildered.

"Boy, don't play with me," Ma Ray said. "I know you're here
looking for Crystal."

He started laughing. "Ma Ray, you're all right. I'm glad you
and my grandma are friends. You've definitely made a difference in my life."

"Then my living has not been in vain."

An unfamiliar car pulled up in the driveway. Ma Ray looked. It was Sahara and Crystal.

"Your mother bought a new car?" Ma Ray said as soon as she realized it was them. She gave Sahara and Crystal a big hug.

"You're not going to believe this, but my *father* bought this car for me," Sahara said.

"Edmond bought you a car?" Ma Ray said. "Edmond?"

"No. My *father.*"

"You talking about Quinton? Your father, Quinton? Quinton Nichols? Bowlegged Quinton? Quinton bought you this car?"

Sahara grinned. "Yes, ma'am. My father, Quinton Nichols."

"I'm not trying to start nothing," Ma Ray said. "Lord knows I'm not trying to start anything. But you're telling me your father, Quinton Nichols, bought you this car?"

Sahara laughed. "Yes, ma'am. That's what I'm telling you."

Ma Ray looked up toward the sky as she slowly spun around a few times.

"Ma Ray, what are you doing?" Crystal asked as she began to look up as well.

"I'm looking for Jesus. He must be on His way back. He's supposed to come back on a cloud. That's how He left. And He said He was coming back the same way He left." Ma Ray looked at the girls and laughed. "If Quinton Nichols bought Sahara a new car, then I *know* this has to be a sign that Jesus is on His way back."

"Ma Ray, that's not nice," Sahara said.

Ma Ray spanked her hand with her own hand. "You're right. I'm wrong. Lord, forgive me. Forgive me, Lord." She looked at Sahara and Crystal. "Now you know I was just playing about your father buying that car. I think that was really great of him. And it's a little bitty cute thing, too. Perfect for you, Sahara. That's wonderful, really wonderful."

"Considering he hasn't paid child support in who knows how long," Sahara said. "That's what you *really* want to say, isn't it, Ma Ray?"

"Who me? Not me." She primped her mouth and shook her head.

"Well, you don't have to say it," Crystal said. "That was the first thing out of Mama's mouth when Daddy brought it over."

"It's not my business, and I'm keeping my nose out of it," Ma Ray said.

"Hi, Crystal," Aaron said with a smile. "I'll be happy to get your bag for you."

Crystal smiled back. "Hi, Aaron. Thank you," she said. She looked over at Sahara, who grinned and popped the trunk, using the key to the car. Crystal walked to the back of the car with Aaron, who got both their weekend bags and carried them.

"Such a gentleman," Ma Ray said as Aaron carried the bags.

They all went inside the house. Thirty minutes later, Tootsie called Ma Ray.

"Marva is in the hospital," Tootsie said, practically out of breath. "I want to go over and see her. Will you ride with me? I'll drive."

"What happened to Marva?"

"She had a slight heart attack. They're going to do bypass surgery on her. I want to get there before they do the surgery. I want to see her before they wheel her into surgery."

"Sure. I'll go with you," Ma Ray said.

"Thank you. I'll be there to pick you up in about fifteen minutes," Tootsie said.

"Well, I need to change into something more presentable," Ma Ray said. "I'll be ready when you get here." Ma Ray hung up and hurried to go change her clothes.

Sahara followed her to her bedroom. "Ma Ray, what's wrong?" Sahara asked.

"A good friend of Ms. Tootsie's had a slight heart attack. They're going to do open-heart surgery on her. Tootsie wants me to ride with her to the hospital to see her before they do."

"I hope her friend is going to be all right," Sahara said. "I'll say a prayer for her."

Ma Ray stopped and patted Sahara on the shoulder. "I appreciate that. The devil and his minions are busy. But the Bible tells us in Leviticus 26:7 and 8 that 'we shall chase our enemies, and they will fall before us by the sword. Five of us will chase a hundred, and a hundred of us shall put ten thousand to flight.' The devil may be busy, but our God is busier. Somewhere else in the Bible it tells us that one can put a thousand of those demons to flight, and two can put ten thousand. Let's send some demons packing and on their way."

Ma Ray put on her pink hat to match the soft pink dress she was wearing. She grabbed her matching purse and headed outside to wait on Tootsie, who pulled up just as she stepped out on the front porch. Ma Ray looked up and said a quick prayer.

Chapter 50

*And ye have seen all that the Lord your God hath
done unto all these nations because of you; for the
Lord your God is he that hath fought for you.*
—Joshua 23:3

Aaron was still there with Crystal. Ma Ray had always told
them not to have anyone in the house when an adult wasn't
there. But Ma Ray had been there when Aaron came. She'd left
without telling him to leave. Crystal didn't know whether she
should put him out or if it was okay for him to stay. Crystal decided, to be on the safe side, it was best that they go sit outside
on the porch. At this point, she didn't even want the appear-
ance of disobeying Ma Ray in any way.

About an hour later, Andre came over. Crystal went inside
and got Sahara.

"Hi," Andre said when Sahara stepped out on the porch.

"Hi," Sahara said, walking closer to him.

Then there was nothing but silence between them for a good
two minutes.

"You're looking good as always," Andre said, finally breaking
the silence.

"So do you," Sahara said. "I mean, you look nice." She blushed.

"Grandma called about ten minutes ago. They're taking Ms.
Marva into the operating room. She and Ma Ray are going to
stay there until she comes out. They've called the prayer warriors, as they call their little prayer group. So they're down
there at the hospital, I'm sure, praying up a spiritual storm."

Sahara laughed. "That hospital had better be careful. With Ma Ray and Ms. Tootsie, along with the prayers of their prayer warriors, they'll have that hospital almost empty in no time with all the people being healed from their powerful prayers."

"Yeah. Grandma and Ma Ray are two praying folks, that's for sure," Andre said.

"Would you like to go out in the back?" Sahara said. "I mean to see how the swing you put up is faring?"

"Don't tell me it broke already," Andre said with a slight chuckle.

Sahara shook her head. "Oh, no. I didn't mean to imply anything like that. It's doing very well; at least the last time I checked it was. In fact, I've missed it since I've been back home. I've missed being out there completely."

"It definitely is a nice place to retreat to," Andre said. "Those tall weeds and wildflowers back in that natural area. Certainly, we can go out there if you like."

They walked through the house to go out the back door. Sahara turned to Andre. "Ma Ray doesn't like us having people in the house when she's not here. We're just taking a shortcut, so this doesn't really count."

"I understand perfectly. My grandmother is the same way. She doesn't like us having our friends in the house when she's not there, either. Must be an old folk thing."

They went outside. Sahara sat on the swing. Andre stood behind her and gave her a push off.

"Thanks," Sahara said, glancing back at him with a smile.

"No problem."

After a few pushes, he allowed her to swing on the inertia of his prior actions.

"Andre, I want to apologize to you," Sahara said.

"For what?"

"For the way I've acted toward you. You really are a nice person."

"Yeah, but I hear most females prefer a roughneck. They're not interested in the nice guys. I guess we're too boring, not exciting enough for their taste."

"Not all girls like bad boys," Sahara said, using her legs to pump higher.

"What about you?"

She leaned back as she pumped. "Maybe at one time, I used to. But I'm not the same person I used to be."

"Really now. What changed you?" Andre asked.

"Not what—Who. Who changed me? I can sum up the difference in my life in one word: Jesus. I finally learned for myself who Jesus was and is to me. I found someone who loves me unconditionally. Someone who loved me before I even loved Him. Someone who loved me enough that He actually gave His life for me."

"Oooh, sounds like you and I are in love with the same person. Because I love the Lord, and I'm not ashamed to admit it. I've never been ashamed. I gave my life to Him when I was eight years old, and I meant it. My relationship with Him has only grown and gotten stronger each year after that. And through His strength, I've been able to do some amazing things. Through His strength, I've been able to overcome things that should have taken me out. Having a mother who was, and truthfully still is, so on crack that she doesn't know who *she* is, let alone who me and Aaron are. But that's okay. God has been a mother for us. And we have been so blessed to have Grandma, a God-fearing, Holy Ghost–filled woman, in our lives to lead and guide us in the right direction."

"That's a great testimony, Andre," Sahara said. "Almost makes me jealous."

"Jealous?" Andre said, pushing her a little when he noticed the swing was starting to slow down.

"Yes, jealous. To have what you have for as long as you've had it. And to think: all those times, I thought I was having fun, when really I wasn't. I was making some bad . . . foolish decisions really. Thinking I was something when I was so far off the mark that I didn't have a clue and wasn't in a position to even *buy* a clue."

Andre laughed. "You certainly have a way of saying things."

"Yeah. I really like words. I love the syntax of words. I love metaphors, similes. I love synonyms, homonyms, antonyms, rhythmations, and alliterations. I love adverbs and adjectives, nouns and verbs. I love words . . . the way they roll off your tongue."

"Rhythmation? I'm sorry. I'm not familiar with that one."

"Oh. Actually, I made that word up. Rhythmation: the art of rhythm and rhyme."

"Okay. Well, you know God blessed man with something no other creature truly possesses, and that's the gift of speech. I know you're probably going to argue that parrots can talk. But really, they can't. They mimic. Man is the only creation that can truly speak. Dogs bark. Cats meow. Cows moo. Horses bray. But man, man can speak. Man has the power of the tongue. Life and death is in the power of the tongue. Humans can speak to a situation, and change begins to take place behind the power of spoken words."

"May I ask you something?" Sahara said, stilling the swing completely.

"Go for it."

"You don't have to answer this if you don't want to." Sahara took a deep breath, then released it. She looked up into Andre's gorgeous brown eyes and twisted her mouth a few times. "Are you a virgin?" she asked.

Andre laughed. "Isn't that what a guy normally asks the girl?"

"Generally, that usually *is* the case. At least, that's what I've experienced."

"So, why do you want to know?"

"Look, you don't have to answer that if you don't want to," Sahara said, refusing to turn away from his smiling stare.

"I don't have a problem with answering that. Yes. I'm a virgin." He held up the hand with his purity ring on it. "And I decided *long* before I put this ring on that I would remain a virgin until my wedding night. It is a gift I've vowed to give only to *my wife*—the gift of *me*. A gift no one else will taste or sample, a gift she, and she alone, will possess. Nobody else will ever be able to claim having had it before her, only the bride of my affection. Not my girlfriend, not my fiancée. It will be my wife, and only my wife. But that's just me. It may sound crazy to others. I may be called all kinds of names. . . . Oh, wait. What am I saying? I *have* and *am* being called all kinds of names right now. But the only voice I care about and what He has to say is God. The only name I care about being called is a child of God. I love God too much to compromise, if it's at all within my powers not to do so."

"Wow, that was powerful," Sahara said, nodding. "Impressive . . . truly inspiring." And before she knew anything, she was crying.

Andre squatted down before her. "What's wrong?" he asked. "What's the matter?"

Sahara stood up. "I have *completely* messed up my life. Hearing what you just said with such conviction and passion . . . Oh, what I wouldn't do to be able to say that. And the thought of the woman who is so special to you that you're willing to sacrifice and keep yourself for her and her alone . . . I'm talking about a guy . . . a handsome guy, at that, saying all of this. That's special, Andre. It really is." She wiped her eyes, then wiped the tears from her hand on her taupe Capri pants.

Andre stood up. "You're crying. I'm sorry if I said something that disturbs you."

"Oh, don't be sorry. You've nothing to be sorry about. You have shown me something in what you said. Honestly, I wish I'd met you earlier in my life. In fact, I wish you and I had had this conversation a few years back. Maybe I could be strong in the Lord the way you are. Maybe I could have had a relationship like you have with God."

"Well, you still can. You can have everything I just said. Just start now. Start from where you are. Put your hand in the hand of the man who is able to keep you from falling. Put your hand in the hand of the only wise God and magistrate, who has dominion over every name that exists on earth and galaxies beyond, and follow His lead."

Sahara nodded as she wiped her face with her hands some more. "Okay. I'll start now. And I'll start from here," she said, shaking her hands dry and forcing a smile.

Andre smiled back.

"I suppose we should go back now." Sahara looked down at her feet.

"Back?" Andre said.

Sahara looked up. "To the house. We should go back to the house. I trust your brother, but I don't trust him *that* much. Not alone with my sister. She really likes him."

Andre laughed. "Got'cha. Yeah. My brother really likes *her,* too."

Chapter 51

*Be ye therefore very courageous to keep and to do
all that is written in the book of the law of Moses,
that ye turn not aside therefrom to the right hand or
to the left.*

—Joshua 23:6

As Sahara walked a few steps behind Andre, she saw Junebug waving at her from the place where she usually went to get away. She figured he must have been there the whole time she was sitting on the swing talking to Andre.

"Go on," she said to Andre. "I'll catch up with you in a few minutes." She didn't mention anything about Junebug.

"Did you forget something?" Andre asked as he stopped and looked around. "I don't mind waiting for you."

"Oh, I'll just be a few minutes," she said. "You go on. That way if you need to jack up your brother before I get there, you can handle that, and keep me from having to go off on him like my mother or Ma Ray would."

"Okay. I'll see you in a few then?"

"Yeah. I'll just be a few minutes. Five tops."

Sahara stood and watched Andre walk toward the house. Sahara figured he wouldn't go through the back door because she wasn't accompanying him. Andre was respectful like that. She just hoped Crystal and Aaron were behaving themselves. When Andre was near the house, she turned and hurried through the natural area and past it.

"Junebug," she said when she was close enough for him to hear her without her having to raise her voice.

"Here," he said. He came up from the bank she normally went down and walked into the clearing near the natural area.

"What are you doing here?" Sahara said. "Were you there listening to us the whole time?"

"You mean that wuss . . . that little punk you were talking to? Yeah, I heard him. A virgin at his age. Don't tell *me* if he could get with a girl, he wouldn't have already."

"You still haven't told me what you're doing out here," Sahara said, refusing to go there with him about Andre.

"I was looking to talk to you. I saw your sister on the front porch, so I figured you were probably out here. I got a call yesterday talking about some HIV/AIDS test or some nonsense like that. They say you gave them my name and number? What's that all about?"

"They're just *now* calling you?"

"Yeah. They finally were able to catch up with me. I don't believe this." He shook his head. "They're saying you may have exposed me to AIDS?" He grabbed her arm hard and pulled her up to him. "Your little tramp self may have given me AIDS? AIDS?"

"Stop, you're hurting me!"

"Oh, I ain't near 'bout doing what I'd *like* to do to you right about now if this is true!"

Sahara tried to pull her arm loose, but his grip was firm. "I said you're hurting me!"

"I should have known not to bed with a hack-poodle like you. My mama always told us that if we lie down with dogs, we'll end up with fleas. Looks like I hit the motherlode with your stank self."

"I said let go of me!" Sahara shouted and jerked. She fell to the ground.

"I ought to slap that look off your face," he said, standing over her. "Done messed around and possibly given me some killa disease!"

"I was tested, and my test came back fine. But when you're being tested, they ask you for all the names of anyone you have sexually come in contact with. I gave them your name because I didn't want you to possibly be in danger and not know it. But I don't have AIDS. My results were negative. I'm fine."

"Yeah, well, you'd better pray that I don't have it," Junebug said. He reached down and yanked Sahara up off the ground. "Fooling with you has definitely *not* been worth it. And that chump cash and crap jewelry don't *begin* to make up for any of this."

"What cash and jewelry?" Sahara said as she fought to break loose from his grip.

He grabbed her around the waist and picked her up off the ground to manage her better. "The cash I took out of your grandmother's purse, that diamond watch with a chipped diamond that caused its value to be less, the diamond necklace out of her jewelry box, a man's ring, some other useless junk. The only things that were even worth taking, for real, were that collectible Joe Louis clock and that Swarovski crystal swan. Did you know that swan was worth a few grand? Who would have ever suspected that? I only took it because it was sitting there on the coffee table practically begging to be taken that day your little virgin boyfriend stopped by and interrupted our romantic time together." Junebug yanked her again and shook her. "Be still!

"Maybe I should go find the virgin boy and thank him. Looks like he was doing me a favor, keeping me from getting with you. But good old persistent me. I just don't know how to quit when I'm ahead. I just *had* to have you. And now look what else I may have gotten along with it—AIDS."

"I don't have AIDS! If you have it, you didn't get it from me. Now put me down or I'll scream," Sahara said.

"Scream then. Don't nobody care. That little weasel you were talking to earlier *might* come running back. I'll just end up kicking his little tail and sending him home crying to his mama. Oh, wait—that's right. He's one of those Woods twins. Their mama is too busy keeping folks like me in business to even care about her snotty-nose brats."

"Put her down!" Andre said to Junebug.

Junebug stopped and stepped over toward Andre, still holding Sahara in midair. "Excuse me, but are you talking to *me?*"

"I said put her down," Andre said.

"And if I don't, what are you going to do about it? Huh, VB?
Huh, Virgin Boy? What you gonna do?"

Andre didn't raise his voice. "Put . . . her . . . down."

"I'll tell you what," Junebug said. "How about we have a
prayer meeting? The three of us, right here, right now. You
care so much about God. And this one here"—he flailed Sahara around in front of Andre—"she's too busy giving folks
deadly *diseases.* I'm *sure* she wants to pray to God for *me* right
now. Don't you, sugar?" He puckered up and pretended to try
to kiss her.

"Man, why do you want to do something like this?" Andre
said. "She's a girl. You should be better than that. You're trying
to show how tough you are by picking on a girl?"

"Oh, oh, oh, listen to Mister Christian boy here. You want
her? Huh? You want her?" Junebug said. "Then here!" He slung
Sahara down hard to the ground.

Sahara cried out when she landed. Andre ran over and
helped her up. "Are you all right?" he asked.

She wanted to cry, but she nodded as she brushed away tiny
rocks and debris from her now-bruised body.

"Oh, she's all right. She's tough," Junebug said. "I don't know
that we can say the same about you, though, Virgin Boy. You
think you're bad? You think you're bad? Well, let's see how bad
you really are." Junebug pulled out a gun.

"Hey, hey—come on, now. Put that thing away," Andre said,
backing up with his hands slightly elevated. "There's no need
for you to go there."

"Oh, you're not so tough now. Where's all that mouth *now?*
Where's all that tough talk *now?* You're singing another tune all
of a sudden, now that I've introduced you to the equalizer."

Sahara stepped over and stood next to Andre. "Leave us alone,
Junebug! Nobody's trying to hurt you. Go on. Leave us alone.
This is private property, anyway."

Junebug started making a smacking sound. "You know, I have a better idea. Since the two of you seem so dedicated to each other . . . so dedicated to God, why don't you let *me* see the two of you kiss."

"Junebug, go on now. This is not funny anymore," Andre said.

"It was never funny for *me*. In fact, had you kept your nose out of what clearly wasn't your business, Sahara and I would have handled our business just fine. But since you decided you wanted to step up and be a man, be some kind of a hero, then I think it's time you know what it's like to be a *real* man. It's time you be initiated into the real men's club. So I want you . . . and Miss Sahara here . . . to have sex. Oh, forgive me. I keep forgetting. Women like being romanced. I meant to say: I want you and Miss Sahara to make love." He smiled at Sahara and bowed slightly. "Better?"

"That's not going to happen," Andre said.

Junebug started laughing. "Oh, that's right. Because you're going to keep your little virgin self until you can give your precious little stale gift to some woman called your wife. First of all, junior, you're not going to find a woman who's still a virgin to have an equal exchange of gifts. Trust me, there's no woman out there, not these days, anyway, talking about keeping herself. Not like your fool self is talking about keeping yourself for her. That's first off." He flicked the gun at Andre. "So that means *you* may be bringing a special gift to your honeymoon, but you're going to be coming to *that* party all by your lonesome. Secondly, I'm sure God could care less *what* you do behind closed doors. I heard that God invented sex. That's what a preacher said one time. He said sex was God's idea . . . that Satan is the one trying to hijack it and negatively stigmatize it."

"Look, Junebug, I'm not going to let you disrespect my God like that," Andre said.

"Boy, please! Where is your God now? Huh? You're out here staring down the barrel of this gun"—he held it steady at Andre's head—"and God ain't studying you. Did you hear what I said? God ain't *thinking* about you. Neither one of you. So, I'm going to do you *both* a favor. I'm going to play the angel and bless both of you. I'm going to help Virgin Boy here become a man today. And little Miss Sahara here, who says her AIDS test came back negative . . . says that she's clean, shouldn't mind smashing you at all, little homie.

"Now see what a great guy I truly am? The worst-case scenario, Christian boy, you can tell God that you didn't have any choice *but* to have sex. Tell Him that I held a gun to your head and made you do it. You know, the way people usually say that the devil made them do it. Well, instead of blaming the devil, you can blame me. In fact, what I'm doing for you right now, you can say that an angel made you do it. Because in spite of how upset I am with this one *here*"—he flicked the gun toward Sahara—"I'm gonna tell you: you're about to be in for a real treat, a *real* treat. She's good now. Trust me, Sahara is *good!*" He took his two fingers, kissed them, and blew a kiss her way.

Junebug stepped a little closer to them. "Now, I want you to go over to that weeded natural area over there and start shedding clothes, so we can commence to getting some *real* action up in this place." He smirked, winked, ticked his head, then grinned as he nodded.

Chapter 52

*But I would not hearken unto Balaam; therefore he
blessed you still: so I delivered you out of his hand.*
—Joshua 24:10

Andre pulled Sahara close to him and stepped back from Junebug. He put his mouth up close to her ear.

"Now, that's what I'm talking about," Junebug said. "There you go, Virgin Boy. I knew you wanted her. Go on, boy. Enjoy yourself on me!"

Andre whispered softly in Sahara's ear, "I'm going to jump him, and I want you to run as fast as you can toward the house. Get inside and lock all the doors. Then you call 9-1-1."

Sahara looked out of the side of her eyes at Junebug. He'd lowered the gun to his side. She pretended to kiss Andre on his ear. "I'm not going to let you do something like this. He has a gun. He'll shoot you."

"That's enough kissing on the ear," Junebug hollered from where he stood. "Y'all are just stalling. Sahara, you're the experienced one. You might need to show Virgin Boy there what to do next," Junebug said. "Move over closer to the weeds like I told you. This ain't no peep show for everybody to see."

"Sahara, please don't argue with me," Andre whispered. "When I push you, I want you to take off running as fast as your legs will carry you." Andre put his hands on her shoulders, turned her around quickly, and pushed. "Run!" he said; then he ran straight toward Junebug.

Sahara ran as fast as she could, glancing over her shoulder on occasion. So far, Andre appeared to be holding his own against Junebug. She ran even faster.

Sahara started yelling as she ran. Crystal and Aaron met her before she reached the back porch steps.

"What is it?" Aaron said. "Is it a snake?"

"No, it's Junebug!" Sahara said, practically out of breath now.

"It's a June bug?" Crystal asked with a quizzical look. "You're running and yelling like that because of a little old June bug? A green beetle? A June bug like those we used to tie a string around its hind leg and fly in circles like a toy plane?"

"No." Sahara panted, doubled over now. "Junebug. Junebug! The guy who lives up the road. He has a gun. Andre is down there wrestling with him now." She pointed to where they were. "We have to help him!" Sahara stood up straight.

Aaron took out running toward his brother.

"Aaron, come back here!" Crystal said. "Sahara told you he has a gun! Aaron!"

Sahara ran in the house, picked up the phone, and dialed for the police. Breathing hard, she then ran to the closet and took out Ma Ray's shotgun. She reached up on the top shelf and took down the box of shells.

"Sahara, are you out of your mind? You don't know how to use that thing," Crystal said, her eyes wide. "You could hurt somebody, including yourself. You don't know how to use a gun. The police will be here soon. Just wait until the police arrive."

"Crystal, if you've *ever* prayed, you need to pray right now. Pray that God helps me, because the police may not get here in time to help Andre! Pray, Crystal, pray. Pray like you've never prayed before. I need you to pray!"

Sahara also prayed. She prayed that she wouldn't hear Junebug's gun go off before help arrived. She prayed that if she was forced to use this gun, that God would help her not to accidentally hurt Andre, or herself, for that matter. She prayed that God would deliver them from this unfolding nightmare.

Sahara heard a car drive up. "Somebody's here!" Sahara said

to Crystal. "Go tell them what's going on. Hurry, Crystal! Hurry!" She continued to try to figure out how to load the shotgun.

Ma Ray rushed in. "Give me that thing!" Ma Ray yelled at Sahara as she practically snatched the shotgun out of Sahara's hand. "What do you call yourself doing?" Ma Ray took the shells and began to quickly load the shotgun as she spoke.

"I was trying to help Andre," Sahara said. "Junebug is out back! He has a gun. Junebug has lost his mind. Andre is wrestling with him now. But we have to hurry, Ma Ray! Andre is running out of time," Sahara said. "You have to hurry!"

Ma Ray started running toward the back door, the butt of the twelve-gauge shotgun securely tucked underneath her armpit. Sahara was right there alongside her every step of the way. When they were close enough, Sahara saw Junebug standing over Andre (who was now lying on the ground on his back), pointing the gun at his chest. Aaron stood helplessly, left only to watch. Sahara couldn't hear what Junebug was saying, but she could tell he was close to pulling the trigger by the agitation on his face.

"Andre!" Sahara yelled out. "Junebug!"

Junebug turned around and pointed the gun in their direction.

Ma Ray raised her shotgun and pulled back the hammer. Sahara was certain Junebug heard the metallic click.

"If you don't put that thing down," Ma Ray said in a voice Sahara had never heard her use before, "I promise you, you may not have met Jesus in your personal life as yet, but I will make *sure* you get a *personal* introduction from me, to speak with Jesus on *this* day, if you don't put that gun down *right . . . now!* Whether in your body or out, I cannot say—but one way or the other— you'll get to have a conversation with the Lord on *this* day!"

Junebug quickly directed his gun at Ma Ray. "Ma Ray, you need to put that shotgun down," Junebug said. "Wasn't nobody gonna hurt nobody. So lower that thing and go on now." He nodded his head at Ma Ray's gun.

"You put *yours* down," Ma Ray said. "I'm not playing with you,

Junebug! Now, I know your mama. She's a good woman, your mama is. Please don't do this to her. Your mama raised you better than this, Junebug. You know she did. You've gone and allowed Satan to mess with your mind. So just lay that gun down, real careful and *real* slow like, onto the ground right there, and we'll be all right. 'Cause I'm going to be honest with you at this point. You know, I'm an old woman. And we old people have our occasional bouts of uncontrollable shakes. Now . . . I don't want to start shaking, and we end up with an accident around here. I don't want to hurt anybody, and you of all people know this. You hear what I'm saying, Junebug? I don't want anyone to get hurt. So put your gun down, and we'll all be okay."

Junebug hesitated a minute before stretching his arms out to show Ma Ray that she didn't have to worry about him doing anything stupid. He slowly lowered his gun down to his side.

Just then, sirens were heard blaring. Tootsie had stayed in the front yard. She could now be seen frantically directing the police toward the backyard.

The police came with guns drawn and arrested Junebug without incident.

"You also might want to check him out for all of these robberies that have been taking place around here," Sahara said. "He was just bragging to me about some things he stole from my grandmother. I'm sure she's not the only person he's stolen from."

"Will do," one of the policemen said. "We've had Mr. Cornelius Sparks here under surveillance for quite some time now, quite some time. Drugs, number one on our list. Theft, number two."

The police took Junebug away in handcuffs. Tootsie was sitting on the back porch steps, rocking back and forth as she hummed a song.

Andre walked over to her. "Grandma," Andre said, "are you all right?"

She shook her head. "I can't take this," Tootsie said with her hand over her heart. "I can't take this." She stood up and quickly pulled Andre into her, hugging him tightly. She was crying hard now. "Thank You, Lord! Thank You for keeping my grandson safe! Both of my grandsons. Thank You, Jesus!" She rocked Andre from side to side as she hugged him.

Tootsie continued to thank God as she sobbed and held on to Andre as though she was holding on for dear life.

Chapter 53

*And the people said unto Joshua, The Lord our God
will we serve, and his voice will we obey.*
                                        —Joshua 24:24

Ma Ray hung up the phone after speaking to the police.
Tootsie, Andre, and Aaron were still at her house. Boaz
and Ruth, as well as Lenora, Edmond, and their children, came
over as soon as they heard what had transpired.

"Well," Ma Ray said to the adults sitting in the living room,
"they're holding Junebug without bail. At least for now. It appears that Junebug, along with his merry little bandits, have
been some busy little bees. They've officially now been linked
with the break-ins that were taking place around here as well as
nearby towns. Not counting those drugs he was peddling, even
to the middle schools. I just don't understand how the police
can have known thugs under their surveillance for over a year
and not do anything to take them off the streets. I just don't get
that."

"They don't want them to get off due to some technicality or
a lack of or insufficient evidence," Edmond said.

"I get that much," Ma Ray said. "But they know these people
are selling drugs in our communities, and they just watch them
as they keep stacking up more stuff against them. Meanwhile,
they're putting innocent folks' lives in jeopardy." Ma Ray shook
her head slowly. "That boy could have *killed* somebody today.
I'm not going to say he wasn't going to hurt anybody. All I know

is that when I looked in his eyes, right before he realized my gun was bigger than his, I believe he was contemplating pulling that trigger."

"Ma, you don't know that for sure," Lenora said, glancing over at Tootsie, who started to cry some more. "You can never know truthfully what another person is *really* thinking."

"Think and say what you like," Ma Ray said. She started out of the room. "I'm going to check on the kids. This has been a trying day for everybody. That's for sure." Ma Ray stopped at Tootsie, who was now leaning her head back with her eyes closed. "Tootsie, you all right?"

Tootsie opened her eyes, sat up, and slowly shook her head. "God is good. I'm just thanking God, right now, that all is well." Her voice shook as she spoke. "I thank God for you, Ma Ray. Because had it not been for you and your quick thinking and action . . . I just don't know."

Ma Ray leaned down and gave Tootsie a hug. She rubbed her back. "It's going to be all right. Now, don't you let this get to you, you hear? We don't need you getting sick." She released her. "Were you able to talk to Marva's family when you called?"

"Yeah," Tootsie said. "They say Marva appears to be coming along fine."

Ma Ray patted Tootsie's shoulder. "That's good news. God is good."

"All the time," Tootsie said. "Will you tell Andre and Aaron that I'm ready to go?" Tootsie said as she struggled to stand to her feet. "I'm really tired, really tired."

"Aaron can drive your car home for you," Ma Ray said. "You don't need to be trying to drive. Not now. Why, you're shaking like a leaf on a windy day."

Ma Ray walked into the den. Crystal and Aaron were sitting next to each other on the couch. Andre and Sahara were sitting in separate chairs near each other. Nia and Kyle were lying on the floor rug, coloring in their coloring books. No one was saying a word. The television wasn't even on.

Ma Ray went and hugged Crystal, then Aaron. She walked over to Andre. He stood up, and she gave him a long hug. Sahara just sat there swinging one leg. Ma Ray leaned down and hugged her. Sahara grabbed Ma Ray and almost wouldn't let go.

"Tootsie is ready to go home," Ma Ray said to Andre and Aaron when she was finally able to get Sahara to release her. "I spoke with the police. They say Junebug will be there, at least for a little while. His bail is set so high, you can pretty much say he didn't get bail. Don't know where his folks will get that kind of money to get him out anytime soon. I feel for his mother, though, I really do."

"I'm glad he can't get out anytime soon," Crystal said. "I can't believe what happened today. I've never been through anything like this before in my life. And I hope I never experience anything like this ever again."

"Amen to that," Aaron said as he stood up and stretched.

Ma Ray watched as Aaron tried hugging Crystal on the sly. She couldn't hold back her smile. She could see that boy was crazy about her granddaughter. And he was a nice young man. She didn't have a problem with Aaron liking Crystal.

Andre stood up. He went over, took Sahara's hand, and squeezed it. Sahara tried to smile. She continued to stare out into nothing, almost like a zombie.

Aaron and Andre left. Crystal went to see Aaron off. Ma Ray went outside as well, arm in arm with Tootsie. Ma Ray and Tootsie hugged. Tootsie was still shaking.

"You get some rest now, Tootsie, you hear?" Ma Ray said. "I'm going to check on you first thing in the morning. Okay?"

Tootsie merely nodded, then got in the car with Aaron driving.

Ma Ray went back inside, checking once again on Sahara. Kyle and Nia had left. Sahara was now sitting on the couch, still staring into nothingness.

"You want to talk?" Ma Ray asked Sahara.

Sahara shrugged.

"You don't have to now. But if you want to, I'm here. It's entirely up to you. I know you told the police everything already. That had to be difficult for you . . . having to recant every single detail of what happened with Junebug. They say they'd like to talk with you again later, maybe in a few days."

"Ma Ray, I'm just thankful that you happened to come back when you did. I don't know what I would have done if you hadn't. I wanted to be brave and help Andre, but I didn't know *what* I was doing. And I was scared! I was so scared. There's no way I could have held that shotgun and convinced Junebug that I was serious about using it. Not like you were able to do. What am I saying? I didn't even know how to load the thing."

"You really didn't need to be in that position. Honestly, I'd prefer that you never touch a gun, of any kind, ever again," Ma Ray said. "Ever."

"You and me both. I don't know how people do it. It's scary. Guns are terrifying."

Ma Ray hugged Sahara. "How do you think Andre is holding up? I mean, really."

Sahara sat up. "He's quiet. He didn't have much to say after things calmed down. I think he's probably in shock somewhat, like I am. But he's trying to be a man about it and get through it."

"I understand that," Ma Ray said. "From what you said, he was literally wrestling with someone who had a loaded gun in his hand. That would mess with anyone's mind."

Sahara twisted her mouth. "The other thing: Andre heard Junebug talking to me about me possibly having exposed him to the AIDS virus." She looked at Ma Ray and began to cry. "Oh, Ma Ray, Junebug was awful. He was so awful to me!" Sahara laid her head on Ma Ray's shoulder. Ma Ray caressed her face as she tried to quiet her. "Junebug was cruel, and there was no reason for him to have talked to or treated me the way that he did. No reason."

Ma Ray began to rock Sahara in her arms. "You don't have to do this again if you don't want to."

Sahara lifted her head up. "I hate thinking about what Junebug was trying to force me and Andre to do. It was horrible, Ma Ray! He was being uncivilized. He was barbaric. And I hope he *rots* in prison after he's convicted!"

"No, baby girl. You can't hold hate like that in your heart. It will only hurt you. Do you know what I want you to do? I want you to pray for Junebug. That's right. I want you to pray for him. Pray that he gives his life to Christ. Pray that his heart and life changes. Will you do that for me? Do that for *me*, but even more so, do it for you?"

"I don't know, Ma Ray. You weren't there when he called Andre all those names, then tried to force him, at gunpoint, to—"

"Shhh. Don't do this to yourself." Ma Ray pulled Sahara to her.

Sahara jerked back and looked at Ma Ray with a loving smile. "But, Ma Ray, Andre was truly wonderful. He's really a great guy. I don't know why I couldn't see how great he was earlier. And you know what? Whatever woman is fortunate enough to become his wife is going to be a blessed woman," Sahara said. "She really is."

"Well, you never know," Ma Ray said. "You may very well end up being that woman."

Sahara quickly shook her head. "I doubt that's ever going to happen—not me and him. Not after he heard those terrible things Junebug said about me."

Ma Ray patted Sahara's hand as she held it in hers. "Well, you never know."

"Oh, I know. You see, he told me about the special gift he plans to give his wife on their wedding night. And honestly, Ma Ray, I don't have anything that will *ever* be able to match his gift," Sahara said. "Not now."

Ma Ray patted her hand again, then squeezed it lovingly. "Baby, you never know."

"Oh, I know, Ma Ray. I've given *that* gift away already. You know? And I can't ever get it back. I messed up, and I don't have a way to go back and make it right. I can't get back my precious gift to give to him in return. Nothing like the gift he plans on giving his bride on their wedding night."

"Look at me," Ma Ray said, turning Sahara squarely toward her as she held both her hands in hers. "I don't care what your past has been. I ended up marrying the most amazing man, and if you'd looked at my resume at the time, which you have, I didn't look like the one who would have ended up with Sal, a detective who would later become a preacher. But you know what? I did. And it just lets you know that with God, all things are possible."

"But I'm not a virgin, Ma Ray. Do you understand what I'm trying to say? And I can *never* be a virgin again. So I can't give him that special something in exchange."

Ma Ray smiled. "Is that what this is all about?"

Sahara twisted her mouth again. She gently pulled her hands out of Ma Ray's and looked down at her now-opened palms. Tears began to fall into them. "I can't get mine back," Sahara said, almost in a whisper. "I can't."

"Well, I can't say what's going to happen for you and Andre. But what you *can* offer him, or whomever you end up marrying, is an even greater gift. And that's to keep yourself from here on out *until* your wedding night. So you can't give your very best gift. Then you give your *next* best. And what a gift in being able to say that you recognize how special what you have is now. And although you may have messed up early on in casting your pearls to the swine, from here on out, you know your value. And you're saving your pearls, protecting your pearls from here on out, for that special someone God has *just* for you. That you're worth it, and your husband-to-be is worth you keeping your pearls safe and sound, *just* for him."

Sahara cocked her head to one side and grinned. "You're something else. Do you know that? How did I end up so blessed to get you for a grandmother?"

Ma Ray laughed. She grabbed Sahara and squeezed her tight with a hugging sound effect to go along with it, then let go. "I suppose the same way I was blessed to have all of you in *my* life. I guess: we're just *blessed* like that!"

Chapter 54

*By faith the harlot Rahab perished not with them
that believed not, when she had received the spies
with peace.*

—Hebrews 11:31

Sahara was excited to hear Pastor Weldon preach again. Having been with Ma Ray for those six weeks had impacted her life. She was on the right track now, and she knew it. She had made up her mind that she wasn't going to let anything turn her around. The youth conference had also made a tremendous difference. She'd met other young people struggling with the same issues she struggled with. But many of them refused to give in to things that went against God's principles. That's the way she decided she was going to live the rest of her days on earth—uncompromisingly steadfast to the Lord, His Will, and His Way. That's one of the reasons she loved Pastor Weldon's preaching and teaching. He brought the Word of God where people live—right smack-dab in their real lives.

Pastor Weldon had even converted Ma Ray. Ma Ray hadn't officially left her church, but she regularly attended there now. "It's hard to leave somewhere you've been for ages," Ma Ray had said to both Crystal and Sahara when she told them she'd been going there, even after they'd gone back home. "But I know this is where God is leading me to be. So I believe a church membership change is coming."

"Today," Pastor Weldon began, "I'd like you to turn your Bibles to Hebrews, the eleventh chapter. While you're turning, many of you are familiar with these passages of scripture. This chapter is the one most refer to as the 'Hall of Faith.' We see that most of the scriptures begin with the intro words 'By faith.' In these passages, we are reminded of some things, men, and two women of God who did great things *by faith*. It begins with things happening in the book of Genesis and, in some ways, goes to Revelation. We find familiar names such as Abel, Enoch, Noah, Abraham, Isaac, Jacob, Sarah, Joseph the dreamer, and of course Moses. In fact, the scriptures in this chapter that refer to Moses and the children of Israel begin at verse twenty-three and continue down through verse twenty-nine. We see, 'By faith they passed through the Red Sea as by dry land: which the Egyptians assaying to do were drowned.' And then we make our way to verse thirty." Pastor Weldon started grinning and shaking his head.

"In verse thirty, we see the children of Israel finally reaching the Promised Land. In this verse, we see the obstacle that was keeping the children of Israel separated from God's promise to them literally falling to the ground without a single shot being fired. There was a great shout now, but not a *shot* or one stick of dynamite used. 'By faith the walls of Jericho fell down, after they were compassed about seven days.'

"What you have to understand about this wall is that it was so thick, and so wide, that chariots rode around on the top. This wall was so thick that houses were up on it. I know you're likely asking yourself, 'Why is Pastor Weldon telling us how wide the walls of Jericho were?' Well, it's because I want to talk to you today from the thirty-first verse." Pastor Weldon picked up his Bible and took one step forward.

"Hebrews 11:31 reads, 'By faith the harlot Rahab perished not with them that believed not, when she had received the spies with peace.' Today, I want to talk about a woman named Rahab. And I'd like to use as a title for this message: *Don't tell me what God can't do.*"

Pastor Weldon stepped backward and put the Bible down on the clear, Lucite lectern. "Now, I can hear some of you saying, 'What kind of a title is that?' I know you're saying that, because that was *exactly* what I said to God when He gave the title to me. Don't worry: I'm not going to be long today. But I want us to look at this woman named Rahab. We're *first* introduced to Rahab in the book of Joshua. Now, Joshua was the one whom the mantle was passed on to after Moses died and was not permitted to go into the Promised Land. Moses was allowed to go up to the mountaintop and *see* the Promised Land. But he was not permitted to go *into* the Promised Land. Joshua was the one who would lead the people into the land that God had promised. You see, sometimes, you may not be the one, per se, who gets *to* the Promised Land. But when your children or your children's children get there, it's just like *you* getting there. Now you see . . . some of you completely missed that." Pastor Weldon bounced and grinned.

"But Rahab was not one of the children of Israel. Rahab wasn't part of the Jewish clan. In fact, what you discover about Miss Rahab is that she already resides *in* Jericho, in a house, on the wall. See, I told you that knowing about this wall and its size was important to this message. The other thing about Rahab is that *she* is a harlot. Okay, a prostitute." He paused. "All right, let me break it down further for my young folk: a 304. Yes, I said *it,* up in here, in this church, with your holier-than-thou selves. But it's in the Bible. Rahab was a lady of the night. She was what some of you would call a '*good* sinner.' And by that I mean, some of you have your degrees of sin, and this is one that you put up there at the top when you're ranking levels of sins. Rahab's house was on the wall of Jericho. Now, my man Joshua sent *two* men to spy out the land. Two spies. Allow me to take a slight detour right here." Pastor Weldon stepped to the edge of the pulpit.

"Back when Moses sent out twelve spies before they ever reached this land, Joshua was one of the twelve that Moses sent. Ten of those spies came back in a panic, telling Moses that they were pretty much defeated, despite what God may have said on the subject. In fact, they told Moses that they were, and I quote, 'like grasshoppers,' unquote, in the eyes of the people there. In other words, the ten spies saw themselves defeated before they ever began. Am I stepping on anybody's toes right now? If I am, then instead of saying ouch, maybe you just need to shout hallelujah, pick your feet off the ground from where you are now, and come on up a little higher."

A host of the congregation stood and clapped as some shouted out, "Hallelujah!" "Go 'head, preacher." "You'd better preach this thing!"

One man yelled out, "I got on my steel-toe shoes. So go on and take care of business."

Everybody laughed.

"Did that man just say he has on his steel-toe shoes?" Pastor Weldon said as he laughed. "Well, praise the Lord for those who have come prepared today. Okay, back to the message. I told you about the ten who saw them as defeated. But there were two other spies, Caleb and Joshua, and those two had a totally *different* report. Those two saw what the other ten had seen with their natural eyes. But with their spiritual eyes, Caleb and Joshua saw what *God* saw. And what *they* saw was that, in their estimation, they were *well able* to take the land. Well able. And yet the children of Israel didn't do anything toward that end. We know this because of what I just told you earlier regarding Moses never physically going *into* the Promised Land.

"So here we have Joshua sending out two spies. You see, sometimes you only need two. The Bible says where two—"

"Or three!" the congregation yelled out, interrupting him.

"I see I have some Bible readers here," Pastor Weldon said. "The Bible tells us that God says, 'Where two or three are gathered together in my name, I'll be in the midst of them.' And we know about the power of at least two that touch and agree. So Joshua sent the two spies out. And in their course of doing their jobs, they somehow ended up at a prostitute's house. Stop. Stop." Pastor Weldon scratched his head, then shook it.

"What are these guys doing at a prostitute's house? Don't they know they should have searched out a saint? There had to be some good person *somewhere* around there. But these two jokers are at a sin house, a den of sin, essentially. And they're hiding from those who want nothing more than to snuff them out for good. But I submit to you today: you don't know *who* God can and *will* use to get His work done."

The congregation shouted.

"You see, people have looked at some of you and determined that you're not worth them even speaking to, because as far as *they're* concerned, you *ain't* nothing. Yes, I meant to say it like that. I'm well aware of how to speak good English, and I know I just violated a whole *host* of rules. But I'm going to say it again. As far as some folks are concerned, when it comes to you, you ain't nothing! But God—"

Shouts rang out through the audience as some even began to wail and cry out loud.

"But God," Pastor Weldon continued, "says differently. God says, 'I can use you, if you'll let Me.' Oh, man! Oh, man! I'm sorry, I just have to give God some praise right here, right now. Forgive me, but God has been too good to me! I know where God pulled me from, what He pulled me up out of. So, you can say what you want about me. You can sit here looking all prim and proper, too snooty to open your mouth, but as for me? I have to give God praise right now!" Pastor Weldon started dancing a quickstep jig.

Almost everybody was on their feet now shouting and giving God praises.

"Okay, okay, okay," Pastor Weldon said, calming the crowd after two minutes. "Got to move on; I've got to move on. Now, somebody was watching Rahab's house and let the king know that men of the children of Israel were there searching out the country. So the king sent word to Rahab for her to bring forth the men that had come to her, that had entered her house, because they were up to no good. They were spies. But Rahab had taken those two men and hidden them. Then she told those at her door, looking for them, that they *had* been there, but she didn't know where they were from. Then Miss Rahab said, 'When it was about the time of shutting the gate, when it was dark, and I really couldn't see, the men had left. And as far as which way they went, I don't have a clue. But if you hurry, I believe you can catch them.' Okay, that was Theodore T. Weldon's translation. But y'all are feeling me, right?"

People laughed. "Go on and teach that thing, Pastor!" someone yelled.

"I'm doing the best that I can," Pastor Weldon yelled back.

People laughed again.

"Okay, let me finish, let me finish," Pastor Weldon said. "Rahab had the spies hidden on the roof under stalks of flax. But Rahab was a smart woman. She'd told those two spies that she knew the Lord had given them the land . . . that the folks inside of the walls were terrified of them. You see, word had reached all of them of what God had done on behalf of the children of Israel. How God had dried up the waters of the Red Sea. I said, God dried it *up* when they came out of Egypt. They'd heard about what God did to the two kings of the Amorites who were utterly destroyed. But this is what Rahab said that let's you know she was a smart woman. She said, 'For the Lord your God, he is God in heaven above, and in earth beneath.' That's in the Bible. If you want to look at it for yourself, it's found in Joshua, 2:11, the last half of that scripture. She then got them to swear to her by the Lord that since she had shown *them* kindness, they would show *her* kindness, and her family, including in her father's house. That they would be saved and their lives delivered from death." Pastor Weldon thrust his fist into the air.

"My God, my God. I wish you could see what I saw when I read those passages of scripture. Rahab was essentially saying, 'Save us, and deliver us from death. I have heard about your God, and guess what? I believe *your* God. So I'm walking by faith on what I've heard, I'm showing that I believe, by acting like what I believe *is* so.' Church, faith comes by hearing and hearing by the Word of God. Rahab said, 'I believe your God is going to deliver this land into your hand. And *because* I believe *that,* I want to be on the right side. So, I'm going to *do* what I need to *do,* to *be* on the Lord's side.'"

The congregation exploded with shouts. Pastor Weldon paced a little, then stopped, and continued to speak.

Pastor Weldon glanced at his watch. "Sit down, sit down, sit down, I have to finish this. I told you I'm not going to keep you long today. Okay, so the spies said, 'Our life for yours, if you utter not this our business.' That's what those two spies promised Rahab. Can't you just hear Jesus saying to you, 'My life for yours.' Glory! God's Word is so rich! It's like an onion. I don't care how much you peel one layer away, there's always more underneath. With God's Word, you can go as deep as you're willing to go. Okay, okay, let me finish." He waved a few of them still standing to take their seats.

"The scripture says, Rahab 'let them down by a cord through the window: for her house was upon the town wall, and she dwelt upon the wall.' That's in Joshua 2:15. Because I know some of you didn't believe me when I told you that there were houses on the wall. I'm talking about the wall of Jericho. The wall that's going to fall flat real soon. The wall that held Rahab's house. You know, Rahab . . . the prostitute. She then told the spies to go to the mountain to keep those that were after them from running into them. She told them to hide there for three days until the pursuers returned. After that, the spies could go their way. You see, we know people were watching Rahab's house. That's how the king heard about the spies in the first place. Scholars say that Rahab's house was probably perched on Jericho's western wall from which escape directly to the mountain, most likely, could be accomplished without anyone seeing them. Rahab had sent the king's men *eastward* toward the Jordan River. Now, the question becomes: when the children of Israel come, how will they know not to destroy Rahab's house?" Pastor Weldon went over to his Bible.

"Joshua 2:18 says, 'Behold, when we come into the land, thou shalt bind this line of scarlet thread in the window which thou didst let us down by: and thou shalt bring thy father, and thy mother, and thy brethren, and all thy father's household, home unto thee.' The scarlet thread . . . the red that had come

streaming down to save them would be what would be seen
when it was time to save Rahab and her family. Like the blood
on the post during the first Passover that caused the death
angel to pass over the houses."

The congregation was on its feet at this point.

"The scarlet that covers our sin; the blood of Jesus that covers our sins, causing us to be saved," Pastor Weldon said. "People of God, because of the scarlet, because of the blood of
Jesus, whatever you've done, God doesn't see it anymore. All
God sees is the blood of Jesus, blotting out those sins. When
God looks at you, after you've received Jesus, all God sees is
Jesus. He doesn't see what you used to be. He sees a new creature in Christ. Whatever you've done in your past, after you
give your life to Christ, God wipes your slate clean. Okay, some
of you have messed up. Have you repented? Then after you re-
pent, God says we're starting over . . . we're starting anew. Is
there anybody here who wants to be made over, wants to become brand-new? Right here, somebody has been told that
God can't use you. To that I say: Don't tell me what God can't
do. Don't tell *me* what *God* can't do! You've been told there's
not a *ray* of hope for you—"

"Don't tell me what God can't do!" the congregation shouted
in unison. Some were giving high fives to those near them.

"Rahab, Rahab, Rahab." Pastor Weldon laughed as he said
her name. "Rahab wasn't one of the children of Israel. She didn't
grow up knowing about the One true and living God. She was
doing what we consider to be one of the worst things you can
do when it comes to our gradation of sin. Rahab wasn't in the
bloodline of the Israelites. But guess what? When you turn to
the genealogy of Jesus Christ as recorded in Matthew, chapter
one, you'll see all these great names we're all familiar with.
Names of men we can tell their stories without even having to
read it to do it.

"Abraham, Isaac, Jacob—all the 'who begat whom' coming
from Joseph's side. I'm talking about Joseph, the husband of
Mary the mother of Jesus. And as you march through the genealogy, you run up on verse five and you find, of all things,

'And Salmon begat Boaz of Rachab' or as we're used to seeing it spelled in the book of Joshua, *R-a-h-a-b,* Rahab. 'And Boaz begat Obed of Ruth; and Obed begat Jesse.' To really get your attention, peep over at verse six for a second, and you'll see, 'And Jesse begat David the king.' I don't even have to go any further. Because most of you can take it from there."

Pastor Weldon took his towel and wiped the sweat off his face. "Some of you have been beat down. Some of you have made some bad decisions in the past. Some of you can't walk in God's best right now because you won't let go of where you've come from. Rahab had all the reasons in the world to be down on herself. She didn't even have what some of you have right now. She'd heard of God, but by acting like what she'd heard was true, Rahab walked into a whole nother realm of God. She stepped up to another level. Her past—gone. Your past—gone. God says it's the past now. God has some new things for you. New blessings. New mercy. New grace. It's time to let go of the old stuff that's trying to hold you back. It's time for you to break loose . . . to walk in God's best. If you have to press to do it, then press. And when the devil tries to convince you that God can't use you because of who you *were* or where you've *been,* I want you to stand up straight, pull your shoulders back, plant your feet flat and firm, and I want you say it loud, and say it proud: 'Don't . . . tell . . . me . . . what . . . God . . . can't . . . do!' "

Chapter 55

Likewise also was not Rahab the harlot justified by works, when she had received the messengers, and had sent them out another way?

—James 2:25

"That was a good message today, wasn't it?" Andre said to Sahara when he saw her standing outside the church building waiting on Ma Ray.

Sahara smiled. "It really was. It's funny. I'd never heard of the name Rahab, let alone the story of Rahab. That was eye-opening and a wonderful message. Pastor Weldon has certainly been a blessing in my life. That's one thing I'm really going to miss."

"What?"

"Being able to go to church here," Sahara said.

"Why can't you come here?" Andre asked.

"You know I'm back living at home with my family now. And I'm more determined to be a different person than I was in my past. I'm starting anew, and I have a new attitude. I plan to buckle down and try to redeem all the time I've lost in my schoolwork. I'm shooting for straight As from here on out," Sahara said. "Don't tell me what God can't do!" She smiled.

"And I believe you're going to do it, too," Andre said. "But still, why can't you attend church here?"

"This church is forty-five minutes away from where I live," Sahara said.

"And?"

"And, that's too far to go to church."

Andre pulled back a little. "How far is too far to get your blessing?"

"What?"

"How far is too far to be blessed? If you know you're going to be fed the Word of God, and that you're going to be fed well, isn't it worth it to go where the best food is? I mean, why do people go to a church because it's close, especially when they know they're suffering from spiritual malnutrition. In my opinion, there's no such thing as *too far* when you're going for the best."

Sahara smiled. "You know, Andre, you really are wise beyond your years. It's just no one I know travels this far to go to church. It's not something a lot of people do."

"Well, it's not like it used to be in the old days when people had to walk to church. I understand people attending churches in their community. But we have cars, trucks, SUVs now. We'll drive to the mall we feel has the best selection of stuff. We'll drive to the grocery store we feel has the best selection of food. We'll drive to another city to catch a plane because we feel we get the best deal for our bucks. But when it comes to the things of God, we act like anything will do. We'll sit and eat stuff we know is not benefiting us, just because it's convenient. Junk food." Andre shrugged. "I'm fortunate enough that the church I'm being blessed by is close to me. But if it wasn't, and I knew there was one where I was going to be blessed, *nothing* would keep me from getting to it. Nothing. This is our spirit and our souls we're talking about. They need to eat well."

"You know, I really may need to talk to my mother about this. I do have a car now. I could drive here on Sundays myself," Sahara said. "So"—Sahara looked down at her sandaled feet—"how are you doing?" She looked back up at him. "I mean, really."

"I'm okay," Andre said. "I'm not going to say I wasn't shaken up about what happened. In the moment, I didn't think about it. But after it was over and I really thought about it, and I realized just how much the Lord had protected me in my doing something so stupid, I fell down on my face, and I just laid before the Lord and thanked Him."

"I know. I did the same thing. Coming here today, hearing that powerful Word from Pastor Weldon, and then him *specifically* calling our families up to the altar to have a special prayer over us, that was overwhelming. I just broke down in praise."

"Yeah, that prayer meant a lot to my grandmother. She's *still* shaking like a scared puppy. I've tried to make her think it really was no big deal—that I wasn't in real danger—but it's going to take her a minute to get over what went down. If I'm honest, it's going to take *me* a few minutes to get over it as well."

"Well, I just want to thank you for what you did for me," Sahara said, tearing up. "That was beyond anything I ever expected from anyone ever. For someone to actually put his life on the line for me . . . "

"Hey"—Andre smiled and touched her hand—"it's okay. God had us in His hands, angels all around us. Nevertheless, whatever happened or happens—as far as I'm concerned—God is still Lord of my life. If something had gone down wrong . . . hey, to be absent from the body meant I would be present with the Lord. If I live it's Christ; if I die it's gain."

"Please don't talk like that. If you'd gotten killed because of me, I would never have forgiven myself. I'm just glad God had His angels surrounding us. After this experience, I will never be the same. I'm completely sold out for Jesus now. And it's not based out of fear; it's based out of love." Sahara nodded. "But I appreciate you so much. You've taught me a lot, you really have. Just watching you walk the life out, not running your mouth like so many folks I know do. I'm talking about truly walking the Godly life; you've absolutely raised the bar for me." She blushed a little.

"Sahara, there's something I'm being led to do. Do you mind?" Andre said.

"No."

Andre took his purity ring off his finger. "I want you to have this," he said.

Sahara started shaking her head. "No, I can't take that. Thank you, but I can't take your ring. That ring is a symbol of true purity for you."

He took her right hand and slipped his too-big ring onto her finger. "I want you to have this because God wants you to know that even though you think you haven't lived up to where you should have, your past has been erased. God spoke to my heart as I sat there listening to Pastor Weldon today. God wants you to know that my ring symbolized to you someone who has not ever given his gift to anyone. God said for me to take my ring and to give it to you as a symbol of how Jesus took His life that was spotless and exchanged it for our messed-up ones." Andre let out a sigh. "This is not coming out the way God spoke it to my heart."

"You're doing just fine, Andre."

"Jesus lived a perfect life. Yet, He died on the cross in our place. In other words, Jesus gave His perfect life to us while He took on our sins. In doing that, God sees us as the righteous. With this ring, God wants you to know that He sees you as though you'd never done what you did. So, what you've done in your past, God is looking at you now as though you're pure. He has purified you with the blood of the Lamb. God told me to tell you to stop beating yourself up about how bad you've messed up and for you to start living the abundant life He has set before you." Andre took a deep breath and released it.

Sahara began to cry. "Oh, Andre. Thank you *so* much for this." She looked at the ring on her hand. "Thank you for hearing God and for being obedient. I'm going to put this ring on a chain, and every time my thoughts try to go back, I'm going to look at this ring and I'm going to think about how much God *truly* loves me. I'm going to step into the place God has called me, just like you do. I'm not going to try to be *like* you, as much as I'm going to be like you *trying* to be *like* Jesus. I want people to look at me the way they look at you, and for them to see Jesus in me, the way I, and others, see *Jesus* in you."

Andre nodded. He wiped his eyes a few times. "Umph. Something must have gotten in my eyes," he said.

Sahara started laughing. "Yeah. Something must have gotten in both of our eyes." She wiped her own tears.

Andre held out his arms and gave her a big hug. "It's going to be all right. None of us knows for sure where God is leading us. But we just need to be sure wherever we're headed that we're following Him."

"Hey, you two," Ma Ray said as she walked up to Sahara and Andre. She hugged them. "I was wondering where you were," she said to Sahara.

"Oh, just basking in the love of God. Basking in the ray of hope," Sahara said.

"Well, I can't think of any better place to be than that," Ma Ray said. "I was just in there spreading my own Ray of Hope. I was telling Pastor Weldon, well done." She released a short laugh. "Get it? Weldon . . . well done. That man knows he's a blessing!"

"That's cute, Ma Ray," Sahara said. "A little corny, but cute. So you told Pastor Wel-don, well . . . done."

"Yeah, well, you know me. I do have my moments," Ma Ray said with a wink.

Sahara nodded. "Well, all I can say behind all that I've been blessed to hear today is: don't tell me what God can't do!"

Ma Ray raised her hand up and gave Sahara a high five. Sahara then turned to Andre and gave him one. Andre high-fived Ma Ray.

Sahara put her arm around Ma Ray's waist, and they literally skipped to the car while singing "Little Sally Walker," a children's rhyme they both were more than familiar with. Crystal joined in with them when they reached the car. Sahara couldn't contain her laughter as Ma Ray began to literally shake it to the east, then shake it to the west; then she shook it to the one that she loved the best, pointing her finger upward, as she lifted her head to the sky.

RAY OF HOPE

Vanessa Davis Griggs

The following questions are intended
to enhance your group's
discussion of this book.

Discussion Questions

1. Was Ma Ray wrong to have pulled out a gun those times when she did it?

2. Did Lenora do the right thing by sending her grand-daughters to stay with her seventy-five-year-old mother? Why or why not?

3. Do you feel Boaz was unfair to Lenora? Was he justified to feel as he did?

4. Do you believe Sahara and Crystal were as bad as Lenora and Edmond made them out to be? Explain.

5. What do you believe was going on with Crystal that was causing her to act out as she was doing? What about Sahara? Did you see a change in them? If so, at what point?

6. What did you think of Andre and Aaron?

7. Tootsie was a character for sure. Discuss her relationship with the other characters in the novel.

8. Many times people do things they don't really want to do. Discuss Sahara and the mistakes she made along the way. What did you think was going on with her and the guys as well as girls she allowed into her inner circle?

9. Was Boaz wrong to be proud of his family, or more to the point: should he have tamped down his comments to make Lenora feel better?

10. What do you believe causes one sibling to feel like another sibling is more loved by a parent? Do you believe parents really love their children equally? Please discuss.

11. In your opinion, do you feel grandparents are easier on their grandchildren than they were raising their own children? Why or why not?

12. Why do you think young people believe adults are the enemy when it comes to their advice? What appears to be the disconnect? Discuss.

13. Ma Ray told Sahara about her past. Was Ma Ray right to do that, or should she have left that secret buried? Why are older people reluctant to disclose things that could possibly help a younger person? Should they disclose, or find another way when possible? Discuss.

14. Sahara had a real health scare. Do you believe Ma Ray and Lenora handled this the correct way? Why do you believe it's so difficult for people to see the dangers they are exposing themselves to when making certain decisions?

15. Discuss the scene where Junebug confronts Sahara. Do you feel Andre did the right thing by voluntarily placing himself in harm's way? Why or why not?

16. Was Andre's desire to keep himself until marriage a realistic one? Do you feel there is a different standard for males than females when it comes to virginity and sexual encounters? Discuss.

17. What did you think of the exchange, at the end of the book, between Andre and Sahara following Pastor Weldon's sermon? Discuss.

Don't miss Michelle Stimpson's

Last Temptation

Available now wherever books are sold

Here's an excerpt from *Last Temptation*. . . .

Chapter 1

Quinn's proposal was not a big surprise. Actually, it was one of those "it's about time" moments. We'd been dating exclusively for almost eighteen months, and those karats were long overdue, in my book. I believe in taking my time, but my body doesn't. Any Christian woman can be celibate when she's single, but throw a six-foot-tall, chocolate brown brother with a sharp goatee *and* a good job in the mix . . . hmph, a sister is liable to get all shook up. Yes, Quinn was a wonderful man who loved the Lord, loved me, and treated my eight-year-old son, Eric, like his own. The faith was there, the love was there, the Lord was there. But I won't lie—my flesh was so weak for Quinn I thought I was gonna have to go on eBay and find me a chastity belt.

So when he finally popped the question by calling me out and proposing onstage after the local college's production of *A Raisin in the Sun* (which he directed), I breathed a sigh of relief. Finally, the wait was over.

Don't get me wrong: The single life was good while it lasted. There's nothing like being able to do what you want to do, when you want to do it, how you want to do it. But that gets old after a while—thirty-four years, in my case. I suppose if my best friend, LaShondra, were still single, it wouldn't be so bad. And if Deniessa, my friend and former coworker, hadn't married that good and throwed-off Jamal last year, I would at least have someone to watch *The Best Man* with. Well, now it was my turn to join the ranks of married women and start the next chapter in my life. *Thank you, Lord.*

The first person I called with notice of my nuptials was LaShondra. She and I had been through thick and thin, good and bad, even black and white since she ran off and married a white man. Let me take that back. She didn't "run off," but her husband *is* white, and I was not expecting my girl to cross that line. I ain't hatin', though. Stelson is good people. He took some getting used to, but I'm over it now.

I hooked my cell phone up to the Bluetooth and selected her name from the radio display. "Hey, girl," I squealed when she answered the phone, "we've got a wedding on the way!"

LaShondra screamed, "He finally did it?"

"Yes, girl," I said with a big exhale. "We're looking at the first Saturday in July."

"Congratulations! Ooh—we've got, what, six months to pull this off—in July?" I knew LaShondra was already planning things out in her head. "You told your momma yet? You called the church yet?"

"No, I called you first, girl. You know I have to get your blessing."

"Pulleeze." She laughed. "Quinn is a good man. I've always liked him. He's a Christian, he treats you well, he's good with Eric. What's there to discuss?"

I sighed. "I guess I just had to ask you for the record, so if something goes wrong I can be like 'You da one who tole me to marry him!'"

"Don't even talk like that, Peaches. What God has joined together, let no man—or Peaches—put asunder. This is God's doing and you know it. Who else could match you up with the one man in the world who could get past your mouth and your attitude to find the real you?"

"I do not have an attitude!" I screamed. The woman in the next car gave me a confused look. I ignored her.

"Is this Patricia Miller I'm talking to? Oh, wait, I'm sorry. This must be the new and improved Patricia *Robertson*. My bad."

We both laughed at her enunciation of my soon-to-be last name. We ended the conversation with plans to meet Saturday and discuss the happy, snappy wedding. My second call was to my mother, who almost started speaking in tongues. "Oh, my baby! Finally! The Lord blessed you with a husband and Eric with a father!"

"Momma, Eric has a father," I reminded her. Raphael wouldn't win any Father-of-the-Year awards, but he'd been spending more time with our son and he was finally caught up on child support. I had to give him some kind of credit even though I suspected his fiancée, Cheryl, had shamed him into doing right by his child.

Next, I called Deniessa. I expected her to be ecstatic, but her response was more dramatic than anything. She busted out crying. I mean, boo-hooing. "Oh, Peaches, I just hope your marriage is a million times better than mine. I want the best for you, girl. Somebody gotta be happy, you know?"

Okay, what am I supposed to say to that—better you sad than me? "Girl, what's *really* going on? Why are you trippin'?"

She pulled in a nasty, snot-filled sniff that almost made me disconnect her from my phone. "Go blow your nose!"

"I'm sorry," she apologized. "Marriage is so overrated. People don't understand—I feel like I'm doing hard time here."

I imagine it *is* hard when you're married to a fool. *Lord, don't let me say that.* I was tired of dealing with Deniessa's drama, but I couldn't say so. After all, I was the main one cheering her down the aisle. Matter of fact, I was cheering everybody down the aisle, hoping to keep the line moving so it would be my turn soon.

I searched my mind for one of those good old standby Christian clichés to soothe her pain. All I could come up with was, "Prayer changes things." I said it in an old, deep, soulful tone—like Sofia in *The Color Purple* would say it—for effect.

Deniessa didn't buy it. "Not if the person you're praying for is an absolute idiot."

I was not in the mood to go down that road with her. It always led back around to point A: She married someone she had been living with for three years. The only reason he even asked her to marry him was because she gave him an ultimatum. I can't blame Jamal—he knew which side his bread was buttered on. He had to do *something*, because it gets cold out there on them streets, I hear.

"Girl, I'll be praying for you. How about me, you, and LaShondra get together this weekend and do one of our girls' movie nights?" I offered. I knew it was a long shot—those two had all but kicked girls' nights to the curb since they jumped the broom.

She sniffed again. "I don't know. I have to see. Jamal is using my car right now."

"Is he working a night shift?" I asked.

"No. He still hasn't found anything yet. But he might need the car Saturday night. I just have to ask."

The words flew straight from my brain out of my mouth before I could catch them. "How you gotta ask to use your own car if he ain't got no job?" I could have bopped myself on the head for fueling the hot mess already flaming in their marriage.

"You tell me." She could only laugh at herself.

I shook my head. "I gotta go, girl. Forgive me for adding my two cents to y'all's business. Let me know if you want to come Saturday night. I'll come pick you up if you need me to. I'm sure LaShondra won't mind taking you home."

"Thank you," she said. "I'll let you know."

I ended the call with Deniessa but continued the conversation with myself and my Father. "Lord, if I *ever* let Quinn use me like that, just take me on home to glory."

I talked myself all the way to Raphael's house to pick up Eric. By the time I got there, I had strengthened my resolve not to lose myself in my husband like I had seen so many married women do in my last, say, fifteen years of marrying off friends and relatives. It's like something clicks in their heads and they lose all sense of identity, all sense of independence, sometimes all sense *period.*

I had to give it to my girl LaShondra—she kept moving up in the school district and trying to get where she wanted to be even after she got married. She kept her house; she rents it out. The only thing she didn't keep, which surprised me, was her last name.

"It's not like Smith is a distinctive last name," she had said.

"Neither is Brown! But Smith-Brown—now *that* sounds important."

"Sounds like a law firm," she had said, giggling.

"Like I said—important. LaShondra Smith-Brown. She don't play. She will sue your behind any day." I'd acted it out as though on a low-budget commercial. She had laughed at me in one of those condescending you-wouldn't-understand-because-you're-not-married laughs. I just rolled my eyes at her. Nonetheless, she dropped the Smith and went straight to Brown. Something I sure wasn't about to do, no matter how plain-Jane Miller is for a last name.

Still building my mental list of marital dos and don'ts, I rang Raphael's doorbell and waited patiently for either Raphael or Cheryl to answer the door of their one-story home in one of the older, more crime-ridden areas of Dallas. I had some reservations about letting Eric spend the weekend with his father in this neighborhood, but once somebody got mugged in broad daylight right outside my condo, I said, whatever.

Besides, I figured Eric could use a little "hood" in his life. There's nothing like a good game of baseball in the hood with first base a shoe, second base somebody's car, third base a fire hydrant, and home plate a flattened plastic milk jug to prove that you can be happy with next to nothing.

Raphael opened the door and Eric squeezed past his father's frame to give me a tight hug. "Hey, son," I said as I rubbed my hand across his head. Apparently, Raphael had taken him to get a haircut—without being asked! That was one for the record books.

"Uh." Raphael rudely burped. "Is that a ring on your finger?"

"Yes, it is." I beamed, making note of the mixed expression on Raphael's face. I couldn't tell if he was about to congratulate me or say something sarcastic, so I gave Eric orders to get in the car.

"I'm getting married in July to Quinn. You met him at Eric's school awards ceremony," I reminded him.

Raphael nodded. "Yeah, I remember him. July? Why so soon?" He crossed his arms, looking down from his towering stance. If I could get up on a stool, I might be able to prove he was balding. The hard years of drinking and womanizing had caused him to age quickly. Still, he was good-looking, and I truly hoped that our son would grow up to be as handsome as his father.

"Because we're in love," I replied. "And we're not getting any younger."

Then came his true concern. "You're not planning to take my son away from me, are you?"

I rolled my eyes in disbelief. "You know me better than that."

He let his defenses fall to his side along with his arms. Something in me said, *awww . . . he loves our son.* I almost felt sorry for the poor chap, bless his sorry heart. But it had taken me eight long years, several hours on hold for the attorney general's office, and countless prayers to get Raphael right where I wanted him and Eric needed him. This was *my* victory, not Raphael's.

"Well, congratulations," he muttered.

"Thank you."

And loud silence transpired. I gave Raphael a quick smile before saying, "Good-bye."

His lips said, "Good-bye," but I could tell that he wanted to say something more. Finally, he stepped outside of his house, closed the door behind him, and said softly, "Quinn is a lucky man."

You could have bought me for a quarter.

Raphael turned and went back into the house.

"Thank you?" I whispered after he was long gone.

I drove home halfway listening to my son talk about his weekend and halfway wondering what on earth had gotten into one Mr. Raphael Sadiq Lewis. Well, I suppose I *was* looking extra nice in my form-fitting skinny jeans and my red, stretchy, button-down blouse. And I had just gotten my short do shampooed and flat ironed, not to mention my freshly waxed eyebrows. I wasn't much for makeup, because my skin turned into a pimple factory with most foundations. My deep brown skin tone held its own and fell into a nice glow after five. It was well after five, so I knew I had to be looking good.

Too bad for Raphael. He could have had anything he wanted from me, once upon a time.